DARK CELLS

BOOK TWO
OF
THE SHERMAN BROTHERS SERIES

GREGORY BRAZZIL

LIFE TO LEGACY

Dark Cells:
Book Two of the Sherman Brothers
by Gregory Brazzil Copyright © 2018

ISBN-13: 978-1-947288-35-5
ISBN-10: 1-947288-35-0

Printed in the United States of America

10 9 8 7 6 5 4 3 2 1

Cover design by: Legacy Designs, Inc.
Legacydesigninc@gmail.com

Published by:
Life To Legacy, LLC
P.O. Box 1239
Matteson, IL 60443
877-267-7477
www.Life2Legacy.com

TABLE OF CONTENTS

TABLE OF CONTENTS (continued)

Dark Cells

Book Two of the Sherman Brothers Series

Introduction

The word *revenge* is defined as an action of inflicting harm or hurt on someone for a wrong suffered at their hands. In this case, revenge is served not only in bodily harm, but in murder. The shady character in this story was once a decorated officer with the Chicago Police Department, but the manner in which he enforced the law led to his fall from grace.

Somehow he managed to hold on to his career as a police officer, and appeared to be functioning. However, the word *functioning* can have two sides. Yes, he appeared at morning briefings at the department, and yes, he performed his duties as an officer of the law, but inside him there was a heart beating, and it was the brutal heart of a vengeful murderer.

My story begins two years after this officer has fallen from grace. He knew he'd never have the respect or the power that he once possessed, and just as we all know, misery loves company. His plan was to take down those whom he felt had played a major role in dismantling his career. Back in the good old days, prior to his defrocking, he had a reputation for mingling with the less desirable on the streets of Chicago. Using his past connections, he'd decided to recruit the services of those individuals to help him achieve his goals.

At that point, he had four very special people in the cross-hairs of his sight. These unlucky characters were about to have their worlds turned upside-down. The recipients were Judge Phillip T. Evans, A.D.A. Margaret White, famed attorney Oliver Cartwright, and me, Private Investigator Sherman Brothers.

Relax, and follow along as I tell my story of a new episode in my life that turned out to be another deadly adventure leading me back to my past.

ONE

DOWN TIME FOR SHERMAN

It was another hot and humid day in Chicago. Sitting on the shore of Lake Michigan, I watched sailboats as they caught the wind. My eyes were on the water, but my mind was wrestling with the decision to pack a bag and visit my girlfriend, India. I couldn't believe we'd been seeing each other for nearly two years. Even worse, I'd repeatedly broken my promise to visit her down in Atlanta.

My thoughts got interrupted by the sound of Barney, my Jack Russell Terrier, barking while he chased a squirrel. At least one of us was getting some exercise. Barney has always been a great companion, and even when I'm walking around the house talking to myself, he looks at me like he understands. Since the day I inherited him, we've never been apart, which kind of creates a problem for me. There's no way I could leave him at a pound.

I whistled and he came running.

"Hey, buddy, why don't we go and quench our thirst?"

I got up from the bench, and we began our walk back to the parking lot. Along the way, we came across a teenager walking a pit bull. I immediately picked Barney up and held him in my arms. Not all of those dogs are killers, but you can never tell. At his size, Barney wouldn't be much of a challenge for a pit bull. After we were about thirty yards from the kid, I put Barney back down.

In the parking lot, I opened the car door, and in one big leap, he cleared my seat and landed on the passenger seat, which he'd officially made his. I put the top down to get some sun, and we were off. When we pulled into the City Block Cocktail Bar parking area, Barney knew exactly where we were.

He started jumping around like crazy, because the female staff there spoils the hell out of him. As soon as I opened the door, he jumped over my lap and ran inside, leaving me behind. By the time I got inside, he was comfortably in Mai's arms. She's the only staff member who's not part owner of the bar.

"You lucky dog," I said.

Louie, the only male owner of the group, was tending bar, and he smiled at me. Right about then, Carman, another of the owners, came around the corner with a bowl of water and set it on one of the tables. Mai put Barney down on the table, and he stood on all fours taking a drink. I looked at Carman and asked why does he get served first? Before I got my answer, Angie, the last of the owners, came in and immediately went to Barney.

"Hey cutie, it's good to see you!"

That's when I turned and called out Louie's name.

"Come on over and have a seat, buddy," he said. "You're not going to win! What can I get for you?"

"Let me get a Newcastle."

After catching up on the latest with Louie, I turned my attention back toward the ladies.

"Hey guys, I've got a problem."

Carman picked right up on that. "So what else is new?" she asked.

The other ladies started laughing.

"I need to take a short trip out of town."

"Sure you do!" Carman said. "You're going to see that mystery woman, right?"

"That's none of your business, Carman! I refuse to leave Barney at a pound."

Suddenly in unison, both Mai and Angie volunteered to keep him.

"How are you guys going to keep him and come to work too?"

"Why don't you let us worry about that, and you worry about that mystery woman of yours," Carman said.

"How do you know I'm not going out of town on business?"

"Yeah, monkey business!" she said.

As I went around and around with Carman, I noticed Louie had moved to the far end of the bar. It appeared he was having a private conversation with a good-looking, muscular blond guy. Interesting!

"So Mr. Brothers," Carman said, "when do you plan on taking this mystery trip?"

"I haven't decided yet, but soon."

The whole time, Barney was sitting on the table with a look on his face like he knew what we were talking about.

"I need to make some arrangements. Can I get back to you guys tomorrow?"

Carman just looked at me. Mai and Angie said, "Sure, Sherman." That's when I looked at Barney.

"All right, that's enough of the good life!"

I picked him up and set him down on the floor.

"We've got to get out of here, ladies."

Once again, the ladies all made a big fuss over Barney as we turned to leave. He barked once, and we were out the door.

Later that evening, I had a very satisfying conversation with India. She had just finished another photo shoot. Even though things were going well for her in her modeling career, she was approaching forty and concerned about her future. I encouraged her to check out other areas of the modeling industry. I was sure her experience had to be valuable in some way.

Anyway, I lifted her spirits with the announcement of my visit. It would be my first time visiting the great city of Atlanta. After talking to India, I immediately booked a flight for the next evening, flying out of Midway Airport. In the morning, I'd pack a bag and run over to the pet shop. I needed to leave some goldfish feeders in my aquarium so that Thelma and Louise, my Albino Oscars, would make it through a few days. While I was there, I'd get Barney's favorite meal to leave with the ladies at the Block.

When my day ended, I crawled into bed. I couldn't help but think about Carman's comment about my mystery woman. I hated to admit it, but she was right. The problem was that my history with women around the City Block wasn't good. I'd have loved for everyone to meet India, but I just didn't know. If it was only Louie and Mai, it would have been fine, but with all the years Carman had been trying to get me and Angie together, I didn't think so. It would be a train wreck, not to mention everything Carman knew about my history with Linda and Candee, two female mistakes from my past. It just wouldn't be fair to India. For now I needed to get some rest. Tomorrow was going to be a long day.

Two

DEPARTURE DAY

After running my last few errands, I took Barney over to the ladies. I said my goodbyes and went back home to get a little rest before the airport shuttle would come to pick me up. I like to sit for an hour or two before taking a trip. It gives me time to collect my thoughts. I know the airlines prefer that you arrive early, but there's nothing like relaxing in your own home. I took some time to check the things I'd packed, with the most important item being my cellphone charger. I'd be lost without it. Now that I thought of it, I'd take my laptop along as well.

I stretched out on the sofa and drifted off to sleep. To my surprise, I was awakened by the shuttle company calling me on my cellphone to say they were waiting for me out front.

The airport was your typical cattle call. I checked my bag and carried my laptop in a small shoulder bag. After clearing security, I made my way through the crowd in search of my terminal. I found it and then checked my watch. With an hour and a half before boarding, I decided to have a quick meal and a drink at a bar and grill. As I sat having a beer and waiting for the food, I watched the local news on a TV at the bar. I smiled when I saw my old friend Candee, a local news anchor, reporting. I couldn't hear what she was reporting on, but it looked like she was downtown on Michigan Avenue, near the river. The young bartender walked up and set a burger and fries in front of me. Even though he was serving me, he had one eye on the TV. I told him thanks, and he cheerfully responded.

"Man, she's my favorite!" he said.

"Oh, you like her?"

"Dude, she's a real cutie. I hear she drives a hot little Porsche."

I was amused. I couldn't blame the young man for being impressed by Candee. I was guessing he was around twenty-four years old. Hell, when I was that age, she would've been my dream girl too! She had a great career, a great car, and she could be the centerfold for anyone's magazine. When she finished her report, he took off to serve other customers.

After washing my burger down with a cold beer, I made my way over to my terminal, and before long was buckling my seatbelt. I had the pleasure of sitting between a large woman who made horrible sounds while sleeping and a guy who insisted on giving me the history of politics in America. Never in my life had I tried so hard to fall asleep, but I just couldn't do it. After about two hours in flight, Mr. Red, White, and Blue had talked himself to sleep. Finally I was free, but as they say, all good things come to an end. The next voice I heard was that of the flight attendant.

"Excuse me, sir, do you mind returning your seat back to the upright position? Thank you."

Twenty minutes later we were descending. I'll never understand why people jump up and crowd the aisle after the jet has landed and the final announcement to remain seated has been made. The door isn't open and there's nowhere to go. I remained seated, and was one of five or six people getting off the jet last. India was waiting for me inside the terminal. She was wearing sweatpants, a tee shirt, and a baseball cap. She wore no makeup at all. I'd never seen her like this, but she was still lovely, like the girl next door. She waited for the crowd to clear before running up to me. It was nice to be greeted with a hug and a kiss, kind of like in the movies. Just as quickly as she ran up to me, she let me go and took my hand.

"Come on!" she said. "We've got to go!"

"What's the big hurry?"

"I've got dinner waiting!"

"Dinner? I've got my bag checked."

"That's okay. I planned for that."

After getting my bag, we rushed to the parking lot. The airport was huge, maybe even bigger than O'Hare. When we finally reached the parking area, India led me to a pickup truck. Her theory on owning a truck was that no one would ever guess she's a model. On the way to her place she was shifting gears like a NASCAR veteran, and I was truly impressed. Not only was this woman beautiful, but she was gutsy too.

When we arrived at her place, the first thing she did was kick off her shoes and run to the kitchen. I set my bag down and followed her. I guess I was moving slowly, because when I entered the kitchen, she was already wearing oven mitts and holding a pot roast.

"Wow!" I said. "That looks great!"

"I hope you're hungry."

I didn't respond, and she repeated herself.

"I said I hope you're hungry."

She turned around and gave me a disappointed look.

"Sherman, please tell me you didn't!"

"I didn't."

"Sherman, how could you?"

"Honey, I didn't know. Look, I'll still eat some."

"You know, Sherman, if I didn't love you, I'd punch you!"

"What did you say?"

"I said I love you. It's been two years for God's sake! Why don't you go take a shower?"

"Do you have anything else planned for me?"

"Why don't you hurry with that shower and find out!"

When I finished, I joined her in the kitchen. She'd prepared herself a plate and made a sandwich for me from the pot roast. The table was candlelit, and there was a bottle of wine and two glasses on the table.

"How's this for compromise?" she asked.

"This is perfect! So what's the plan for tomorrow morning?"

"Well, first we're going to make love."

"You know, I've noticed you using that word a lot lately."

"Sherman, do you have somewhere else to stay tonight?"

"No."

"That's what I thought."

"Ha, ha, ha, now that's priceless."

"Stop laughing at me, Mr. Lucky."

"Why are you calling me Mr. Lucky?"

"You are lucky. What would you add to me to make me better?"

"That's a trick question, so I'm not going to say anything."

"Good answer. I like a man who uses his head."

"You're real funny, Miss India. Tell me something. What do you people do down here other than sweat in this God-awful humidity?"

"You should be more concerned about what we do to make us sweat."

"Is that a threat or a promise?" I said.

"It's both, but I think I'll make you wait."

"I guess that means you'll be sleeping on the sofa tonight."

India looked at me and rolled her eyes, and then asked how the pot roast was.

"It's great! Can I have some in the morning with scrambled eggs, potatoes, and fresh fruit?"

"I guess in a sense you're a guest, so I'll consider it. Hey, why don't we go riding in the morning?"

"What kind of riding?"

"Horseback riding, silly."

"You mean those big four-legged smelly creatures?"

"Yes, and I guess that's something else I'm better at than you. Did you pack a bucket in your suitcase?"

"Why would I pack a bucket in my suitcase?"

"You're going to need one to carry your ego in when it falls off your horse!"

"Okay, that does it."

I blew the candle out and grabbed India's hand.

"Let's go, Missy!"

"I was wondering how long you were going to put up with this! I've got a surprise for you."

"That's just great."

To my surprise, India had purchased an intense oil product to add a little fire to our adult playtime.

THREE

DAY ONE IN ATLANTA

When I woke up the next morning, India was sitting up in bed. Apparently she'd been watching me sleep.

"Good morning, Miss India."

"Is it okay?"

"Do you mean that stuff we used last night? It was great!"

"That's not what I'm talking about."

"Is what okay?"

"Is it okay if I love you?"

India had me cornered, and the truth was that I loved her too.

"Let me ask you a question," I said.

"You're avoiding me."

"Is it okay?"

"Is what okay?"

"Is it okay if I love you too?"

India froze, staring at me for a moment before reacting.

"Do you still want that breakfast?"

"Honey, I was just kidding."

"Well, I'm not. Why don't you take a shower, and I'll get breakfast started."

After a great breakfast, we both got dressed and headed for the riding stables. We were paired up with horses based on our riding experience. She was given a horse named Firefly, and oddly enough, my horse's name was Daisy. Of course, India had fun with that. She looked at me and asked if I'd brought my bucket with me. With that she swatted Firefly on the ass and took off. I gave Daisy a kick on both sides, and she took off following Firefly. When we reached the opening to the trails, we slowed down to a slow walk and followed the path. That's when India looked at me and smiled.

"Not bad, Mr. Lucky!"

After spending the morning on the riding trails, we went back to her place to wash off the trail dust. To avoid making my visit completely sexual, we got right back out in public. India wanted to show me some of the city, so we did some sightseeing. It was fun being carefree and not feeling the weight of my pistol on my belt. As much as I loved my job, this was the way life should be.

"Do you want to see a movie?" India asked.

"Some kind of girly flick?"

"As opposed to two guys trying to kill each other over a car?"

"It depends on the car."

"Please tell me you're kidding."

"Okay, I guess a movie is out."

"I've got it!" she said. "Do you remember where we met?"

"Sure I do. You were stalking me in the elevator."

"I swear, Sherman, one of these days I'm going to sock you so hard."

"All right, honey, I'm sorry."

"How would you like to go to the aquarium?"

"That's a great idea!"

The aquarium, the sightseeing and everything were great, but it also wore us out. On our way back to India's place, we stopped off and picked up some groceries to cook a Mexican dinner. We shared the cooking, and it was fun working in the kitchen with her. India even made a pitcher of margaritas.

That night the mood was different when we went to bed. India wrapped her arms around me and looked at me.

"Can you hold me until I fall to sleep, Sherman?"

"Sure, baby. To me, it'll be the perfect ending to a perfect day."

Day Two in Atlanta

The following morning was a lazy one for us. We moved from the bedroom to the living room. We had nothing scheduled, and neither of us cared. It was one of those days when you're glad you have the option of doing nothing. As the day rolled on, we finally got dressed, but we still didn't go out. We talked a lot about our future, the past, and life in general.

I was convinced that India was definitely an asset in my life. We were sitting on the sofa looking at photo albums featuring some of her past photo shoots when my cellphone rang, surprising both of us. I saw that it was my dad.

"It's my dad. I wonder what he wants. Hey, Dad, how are you?"

"I'm fine, son, but Oliver has a problem."

"Mr. Cartwright?"

"Yeah, his home was invaded."

"His home was invaded? Why, and by whom?"

"That's what I'm calling you for."

"Dad, I don't have any jurisdiction down there."

When I said that, India put two and two together, and her face looked like the wind had just been taken from her sails.

"Don't worry about that, son. Oliver can pull some strings if he has to. He said there were some very strange circumstances, and that's why he's requested you. By the way, where are you?"

"I'm in Atlanta."

"Atlanta! Well maybe that's a good thing. Can you get on something moving by tomorrow morning?"

"Sure. Can you tell Mr. Cartwright not to touch anything?"

"He's staying at a hotel until you get there."

"Okay, Dad, I'll call you with my flight information."

CLICK.

I turned and looked at India.

"I know," she said. "I knew it would happen sooner or later."

"I'm sorry, honey, but Mr. Cartwright is a dear friend of my dad's, not to mention that he kept my behind out of prison a while back."

"It's all right, Sherman. Just be careful. Where does this Mr. Cartwright live anyway?"

"He's in Houston."

"At least you have a short flight. Do you have to leave right away?"

"No, first thing in the morning."

"Do you want me to call the airlines for you?"

"That's all right, you just keep being you."

"Why don't I put these photo albums away?"

"Is there somewhere you want to take me while I'm still here?"

India wrapped her arms around me.

"I don't want to share you with anyone. You're all mine until morning comes."

"Why don't I get these phone calls out of the way?"

"Phone calls?"

"I have to contact the people that are keeping Barney for me."

"Why don't you do that, and let me call the airlines for you. Look, I really want to help. It makes me feel like I'm part of your life."

"I guess it would save some time. See what they have around nine a.m."

While India was on the phone, I called the City Block. The phone was answered after three rings.

"This is the City Block, Carman speaking."

"Hey, it's me, Sherman. May I speak with Angie?"

"She's busy right now."

"Can I talk to Mai?"

"She's busy too. It looks like you're stuck with me."

"In that case, I've got a problem!"

"You're telling me."

"Look, I need to stay on the road a few more days."

"That mystery woman must be pretty good."

"The truth is that I'm working on a case for my dad."

"Sure you are. Don't worry about Barney, we actually like him."

"Thank you, Carman. You're an angel!"

"Whatever."

CLICK.

By the time I finished my phone call, India was coming out of her bedroom with a boarding pass she'd printed out on her computer.

"Can I ask you a question, India?"

"Sure."

"Do you think the time we're apart is what keeps us together?"

"I'm sure that's part of it, but I'd like to think there's more. Why do you ask?"

"I just wonder if we'd be this crazy about each other if we were together 24/7."

"Well, I've never lived with a man, but I know that's the risk people take. Are you sure you're all right, Mr. Lucky?"

"Yes, I'm all right, Missy!"

"Look me in the eyes, Sherman. I'm not the kind of woman that hunts a man down, corners him, and nags him until he gives in to marriage. I'm very happy with our situation. Seeing you a little more often wouldn't hurt, but I'm happy. Do we understand each other?"

I looked at her and smiled.

"So what do we do now?" I said.

"Well, you're my man, right?"

"Yes."

"That means I can make love to you anytime I want."

With that she stood and stripped.

FOUR

TEXAS BOUND

The next morning we got up early and had coffee and muffins. It wasn't long before we were in her truck heading for the airport. We parked, and I swear we could've taken a taxi from the parking area to my terminal. Eventually my boarding time came, and we said our goodbyes. As I walked away, it occurred to me that parting was getting easier for us. I hoped it was only a sign of maturing.

This time things were different onboard the jet. The airline gods had smiled on me, and I had two empty seats beside me. At Midway Airport I had purchased a magazine but never read it, and now seemed like a good time. To my surprise, there was a greeting card from India inside. I opened it.

I MISS YOU ALREADY MR. LUCKY!

It was really sweet of India. It's funny how women always think of little things like this. I put the card away and started thumbing through the magazine. As I began to read, my mind kept drifting back to Mr. Cartwright.

Was this a random thing, or was someone from his past sending him a message? One thing about the business we're both in, you never know when your past will come back to haunt you. I knew he lived on a ranch, and if someone wanted him dead, they could do it. I was thinking more and more that this was some kind of warning. With all of the homes in Houston, it seemed strange that someone would go all the way out to a ranch to break in and steal something.

I didn't know anything about Houston, so I was hoping Mr. Cartwright had a lot more for me than my dad did. He must know private investigators in Houston. There had to be a reason he requested me. Well, I guessed I'd find out when I got there.

CHAOS IN THE WINDY CITY

Back home in Chicago, at one of the state-owned buildings, a man wearing a dark suit and shades sat in the lobby. For two weeks now he'd been going there and taking mental notes. He recorded the daily habits of employees, security, and the public in general. One person of special interest to him was the District Attorney's personal driver. He knew that every day between 5 p.m. and 5:15 p.m., the driver came into the building to use the restroom. However, today his routine would be modified.

The mysterious man looked over his shades at his watch. It was 4:55 p.m., time for him to make his move. He got up and went into the restroom. Once inside, he slipped on a pair of gloves, then stepped inside a stall, closed the door, and let the seat cover down on the toilet. He took a loosely rolled length of wire from his pocket and stood on the toilet seat. He looked at his watch again, and it was 4:59 p.m. He waited like a spider waiting for a fly to land on his web. He thought to himself:

IT'S TOO BAD FOR THIS SUCKER! I GUESS THAT'S WHY THEY CALL IT COLLATERAL DAMAGE!

Fifteen seconds later, his mark came in and walked up to the urinal, facing the wall. That's when the mysterious man quickly opened the stall door and sprang out. In a matter of seconds he had the wire wrapped around the driver's throat, and was dragging him into the stall. Inside the stall he wrapped the wire around the man's throat a second time and pulled with all of his might until the body went limp. He then set the body on the toilet seat. He reached into the driver's pocket and removed his car keys. Before stepping out of the stall, he pulled the driver's pants down, and closed the door behind himself. The driver's hat had come off during the struggle. He picked it up, put it on, and made his exit.

Outside now, he stood waiting near the opened rear door of a town car. He smiled to himself because his plan was working.

I'VE WAITED TWO LONG YEARS TO GET BACK AT YOU, BITCH! MY CAREER WAS RUINED, AND YOU GOT PROMOTED TO FUCKING DISTRICT ATTORNEY! I'VE GOT LONG SLOW PLANS FOR YOUR ASS!

At 5:10 p.m. he could see her in the lobby of the building.

WELL IT'S GOOD TO SEE YOU MISS WHITE, OR SHOULD I SAY MADAM DISTRICT ATTORNEY?

He watched as she approached carrying her purse, a briefcase, and a cellphone to her ear. In a hurry, she totally disregarded him. As she bent her head down to get into the backseat, he stuck her in the backside with a tranquilizer dart. In a matter of moments she was out cold. He closed the door, got into the driver's seat, and slowly drove away.

ARRIVAL IN HOUSTON

It was a little before noon and I was standing in front of the baggage carousel, alongside Mr. Cartwright. The air conditioning felt great, but I knew that once we were outside, the humidity was going to be deadly. However, there was a ray of light, because Mr. Cartwright had a town car waiting outside. Once we were in the car, he spoke.

"Son, I wanna thank y'all fo' comin' down here."

"That's all right sir. If you hadn't kept my butt out of jail, I might not be here."

"Yeah, those were some good times! I wonder whatever became of that ol lieutenant fella."

"I don't know and I don't give a damn! All I know is that he hasn't been slapping me around! As far as I'm concerned, he's dead!"

"I reckon there ain't no love lost between you two boys. Well, why don't y'all just relax a spell? We got us a little ol ride ahead of us."

After twisting through the airport maze, we finally made it to the ramp for the interstate. From what I could see, Houston was a typical big city with people and cars moving in every direction. As we rode along, I could see the city fading into what I thought was suburban living. That went on for quite some time.

Eventually we turned off the highway into a more wooded area. Cattle and horse ranches came into view. It was beautiful countryside. I now knew the crime wasn't the work of some group of punks. Most crack heads don't have cars. The most popular vehicle out here is the pickup truck. I didn't know how smart these guys were, but they did do their homework well enough to get in and out without being noticed.

We continued on a country road that snaked through trees and more cattle ranches. Finally Mr. Cartwright pointed at a small ranch house about a block down the road. When we pulled off the road, the driver stopped the car, with Mr. Cartwright's window right near a keypad mounted on a post. He punched in a code and the big gates opened, giving us access to the main road leading to the house.

The house was a wreck on the inside. The major thing that stood out was a message spray painted on the wall.

PAYBACK IS A BITCH!

I read the message and looked at Mr. Cartwright.

"Na the insurance adjuster done been here already. Ya daddy told me y'all wanted me to leave things like this."

"So what's missing?"

"That's what's kinda funny. Them ol boys did take some valuables, but they done left a whole mess of stuff. They didn't know what they was lookin' fo', or theys just plain stupid!"

"Mr. Cartwright, I think these guys were hired to send you a message, and stealing was just something they did on their own."

"Well, son, them ol boys done did me a mighty big favor."

"How's that?"

"Hell, I had this stuff insured fo' a hundred times what it's worth!"

"You're always thinking, Mr. Cartwright!"

"Na son, did y'all bring that lil ol computer wit ya?"

"Yes sir, I did."

Mr. Cartwright pointed at a shelf.

"Let me show y'all somethin'. See this ol wooden horse standin' up on his hind legs?"

"What about it?"

"It ain't worth much, but see that lil ol spot on the pony's belly? That's a camera."

"I'll be damned!"

"That ain't all, son. I got a picture of Roy Rogers hangin' on my bedroom wall, and hell, one of his eyes is made outta glass too!"

"Are you saying what I think you are?"

"Ya cotton pickin' right, son! Hell, I got about five of these lil ol cameras all over the damn place! Na I got a lil ol room hidden out in the barn that's the nerve center fo' all these ol toys of mine."

"Mr. Cartwright, you never cease to amaze me! I'll tell you what. Why don't I help you clean this mess up, and then we'll go out to the barn and see what kind of fish you caught."

"Y'all know what? Them ol boys did leave us a couple of beers in the box. Y'all want one?"

"That sounds good to me."

It took the two of us around three hours to restore his place to reasonable living condition. Aside from the missing items, most of the damage was broken stuff that had to be picked up by hand. Once we piled the big stuff up, we were able to use the vacuum. Mr. Cartwright focused on his bedroom, and I focused on the living and family rooms. These guys had left behind everything that could've been sold in a matter of moments on the street.

There were a state-of-the-art stereo system and a flat-screen TV still there. I couldn't believe how stupid they were.

PAYBACK IS A BITCH!

Did that mean it was over or just beginning? Maybe when we looked at the video we'd be able to see what they touched with their hands. A good set of prints might save us some time. I went to Mr. Cartwright's bedroom.

"Do you know anyone that can dust for prints? If prints were left, I can take them home and trace them."

"Well, I did know one ol boy. Let me see if I can track em down."

"That'll be great! I think I have a plan."

"What's on ya mind, son?"

"I figured we can save your guy some time by looking at the video to see just where these punks put their hands down."

"That's good thinkin! Remind me of ya daddy."

"Mr. Cartwright, did you notice anything odd missing?"

"It's funny y'all should mention that. I had a lil ol newspaper clippin' with a picture of me comin' down the steps of that ol court buildin' at the trial in Chicago, but it done disappeared."

I agreed that was strange. What I didn't say was that this thing wasn't over yet. They took that picture so Mr. Cartwright could be identified later.

"Na what in Sam hell would they want wit that?"

Now I was beginning to get worried about his safety.

"Mr. Cartwright, where were you when your place was being invaded?"

"I was at a dinner party."

"Did anyone other than the host know you wouldn't be at home?"

"No one but my driver, and hell, I done known that ol boy for a coon's age!"

Now I knew he was being watched, and by more than one person. I had to believe the worst. That picture was taken to make sure they had the right person when the time came. If Mr. Cartwright was anything like my dad, he had a shitload of pride. The two of them are among the smartest men I know. What they didn't know was that these young fools on the street don't value life, not even their own. They'll gun you down in broad daylight, right in front of the police station if they have to. Going to jail is just a family reunion with their boys from the hood. It would be difficult to talk Mr. Cartwright into hiring a couple of bodyguards. Maybe I could suggest another trip to Chicago, where I could keep an eye on him.

It had been dark out for well over an hour, and we were just heading out to the barn. Just inside, he flipped a switch and lit up the entire barn. Over in one corner was an old flatbed wagon with a couple of bales of hay on it. In front of it was a wheelbarrow with a saddle in it. To the side were several yard tools leaning against the wagon.

"Y'all give me a hand wit this, son."

After moving everything out of the way, we rolled the wagon to the side, revealing an old American flag. It was dirty and beat-up, but hanging on the wall. At least that's what I thought. Mr. Cartwright pulled it down, and behind it was a door. He took a key from his pocket and unlocked the door. When he opened it, I was blown away. I swear it was like a scene from a James Bond movie. I felt like I'd stepped into a different dimension. For starters, it was a beautiful office, small, but nice. On an L-shaped desk in the corner were five twelve-inch flat-screen monitors. Each of them was dedicated to one of the cameras in the house. On a long table against the wall were two computers connected to the monitors. Also on the table was a photograph of a beautiful young woman. I assumed she was his deceased wife. What I didn't see at first was monitor number six, mounted overhead on the wall. It showed an exterior view of the house. I couldn't help but tell Mr. Cartwright how impressed I was.

"What's next, son?"

"I want to download all of your footage to my computer, but for now, let's just take a look at what we've got."

The first scene we viewed was in the living room. The room was empty, but then the front door opened.

"Wow, did you see that?" I asked.

"Did I see what?"

"They just walked right in! Somehow they knew your alarm code."

"So these ol boys had some help," Mr. Cartwright said.

"That's right, because we both know they're too stupid to figure it out on their own!"

There were two of them, and judging by their skin color, I'd say they were Hispanic. They wore bandannas. However, you could see the area from their nose up. Not only did they have tattoos on their arms and neck, but I saw something that scared the hell out of me. They also had tats on their faces, below the eyelids. This was major freaking trouble! We watched as they went through the house randomly destroying a little here and a little there. One of them then removed a can from his back pocket and began spraying the message on the wall. I started taking note of every piece of furniture and item that they touched.

"All right, Mr. Cartwright, I've seen enough. Let me get my laptop and start downloading some of this stuff. You need to try and track down your buddy and see if he can get out here first thing in the morning."

"All righty son, let's get this buggy rollin'!"

We both went back inside the house. He got on his phone, and I grabbed my laptop and headed back out to the barn. I loaded as much footage as I needed from each of the rooms and closed everything down, making sure I kept the cameras ready for operation. Mr. Cartwright soon came out, and we redecorated the barn just the way it was when we first came out.

After that I stood and shook my head.

Are ya hungry, son?" Mr. Cartwright asked.

"I could go for a bite."

"Well, let's see what I've got in the icebox. Will a turkey sandwich and a little potato salad work fo' ya?"

"That sounds good."

"Well, let's get a move on."

"What do you make of those guys knowing your alarm code?"

"Well, there's one thang fo' sho'. I done been in this here business long enough to know that every man has a price. If you can afford em, he's fo' sale."

"Sure, but there has to be someone else with the brains leading these clowns around. This person has money, connections, or maybe both. Can you excuse me a minute? I need to make some phone calls."

"You go right ahead, son."

I went to the family room and called my dad. After giving him the details, he stressed his concern for Mr. Cartwright's safety. Dad agreed that he wasn't the type who would run with his tail between his legs. I told him I'd feel better if Mr. Cartwright were in Chicago, where I could keep an eye on him for the time being.

"I agree with you," my dad said. "But it won't be easy."

"Why don't you suggest a little getaway to get his mind off of things? Maybe give the insurance company time to do their thing and get his house back in order."

"I'll give it a shot."

"Hey, Dad, do you know anyone in security down here?"

"No, I don't, but I can make some phone calls. Why do you ask?"

"I have an idea. Call me back and let me know how it goes."

CLICK.

Mr. Cartwright grabbed our sandwiches and another beer and came into the family room.

"Do you mind if I turn on your TV?" I asked.

"Go fo' it, son."

"I like to keep up with what's going on back home."

"I see. Well haw y'all gonna do that?"

"One of the stations back home also broadcasts on cable."

I turned to the program guide and started searching. It took a while, but I finally got it. The newscast was on, and a young Asian woman was reporting live. Behind her were paramedics rolling a gurney with a body bag on it. That's when I turned up the volume to hear what she was saying.

"The body of the man was found in the restroom of this Illinois State building. The authorities haven't identified him yet, nor have they determined what the cause of death was. All we know right now is that the cleaning crew found him in the wee hours of the morning."

When she finished her report, the broadcast switched to the weather. That's when I turned the volume back down and Mr. Cartwright spoke up.

"Ya know, son, there's some downright evil folks in this ol world of ours!"

"They're also very bold. That building holds the office of the District Attorney."

"Is y'all tellin' me that's where A.D.A. White holes up?"

"As far as I know."

"Man, talk about right under ya nose!"

While I was eating, my cellphone vibrated. It was Dad, and I excused myself.

"Hey, son, if I can talk Oliver into it, I've got a man who can shadow him on the train. If he agrees, I want you on the first thing flying. I need you to be at Union Station before he is. There's one other thing. I'd feel better if you wore your vest when you go to meet him."

CLICK.

FIVE

REACHING OUT TO REPORTER CANDEE HARRIS

When I returned to the family room, Mr. Cartwright had something on his mind.

"Son, I was doin' some thinkin' while you was on the horn. Why would some fella leave a dead body in a place like that?"

"I don't know. Maybe it's where the murder took place. I think I'll give an old friend a call and snoop around a bit."

I took my cellphone out and pressed a couple of buttons. "Hello there," I said.

"This can't be who I think it is," Candee said. "Don't tell me it took you two years to see things my way!"

"You'd love that," I said.

"So would you. What's up, Mr. P.I.?"

"I'm just fishing. It's not important. What do you have on the guy who was found in the restroom?"

"Sherman, that story just broke, and I didn't cover it."

"Come on, Candee, you know you can't win 'em all."

"Well, it hasn't been aired yet. He was a personal driver for a limo service."

"That seems kind of strange."

"It is, and get this: the D.A. didn't report to her office this morning, and she can't be reached."

"I thought the D.A. was a man."

"Jesus, Sherman, have you been living under a rock or something?"

"What's her name?"

"It's White, your old buddy."

"You're kidding me."

"You know, if you gave a girl a break sometime, you'd know these things."

"How did you find out about her not showing up to work?"

"I can't tell you that, not unless you want to trade."

"I remember the last time I made a deal with you. Hey, Candee, thanks!"

"You're welcome, and don't be a stranger."

CLICK.

MR. CARTWRIGHT IS PISSED!

I hung up to find Mr. Cartwright on his phone as well. It wasn't long before he hung up too.

"Mr. Cartwright, you're never going to believe the conversation I just had."

"Well, y'all ain't gonna believe the conversation I done had! That was yo' daddy on the horn. He wants me to pack a bedroll and saddle up. He come givin' me some song and dance 'bout clearin' my mind. Hell, it ain't nothin' wrong wit my mind. He talkin' 'bout lettin' them ol insurance folks do their job and such. Boy, I love yo' daddy, but sometime he ain't nothin' but an ol mother hen!"

As hard as I tried, I couldn't keep a straight face. I started laughing, and to my surprise, so did Mr. Cartwright.

"So tell me 'bout yo' call, son."

"Do you remember the TV reporter that helped us out in Chicago?"

"That pretty lil ol thing? She's kinda hard fo' a fella to forget."

"Well, she told me that dead guy was a personal driver for a limo service."

"Ain't that somethin'!"

"Now you have to hold on to your hat for the next part. Do you remember your girlfriend, A.D.A. White?"

"Na there's another one that's hard to forget. She's a horse of an entirely different color."

"She's now the D.A."

"Hush yo' mouth! Well, I'll be dipped in hog slop! Boy, y'all's political arena is somethin' else."

"That's not all, Mr. Cartwright."

"What, there's mo'?"

"She's been missing, but the media hasn't released it to the public yet."

"I'll be damned, and they call my act a circus! Well, I'd bet a dollar to a cow chip that ol boy in the restroom was her driver!"

"I was thinking the same thing."

"Well, y'all better stay on top of that one, because I got a feelin' it's gonna get right ugly! Maybe yo daddy's idea ain't so bad after all. One thang fo' sure, it ain't gonna be borin' in that fine city of y'all's."

"If you don't mind, I'd just assume fly back."

"That's fine wit me, son."

SIX

HEADED HOME

Ibooked my return trip before I went to bed. The plan for the morning was for Mr. Cartwright's driver to take him to the train station first. I'd ride along, and he'd drop me off at the airport. When we arrived at the train station, I was surprised at its size: roughly the size of two garages combined. It was staffed by only two people. The funny part was that the platform was nearly a block long. Mr. Cartwright described his accommodations as a sleeper. Apparently it was a small, private berth with a convertible sofa. I hoped dad's guy would be on the ball, because that berth could be a double-edged sword.

We said our goodbyes, and just as I turned to walk away, this guy carrying a small carry-on bag purposely bumped into me. With a certain look in his eyes, he said, "Excuse me." He was dad's guy letting me know he'd made it. It was a relief, at least for the moment.

As I was passing through the train station headed back to the town car, I saw a black SUV racing into the train station's parking area and make a sudden stop. I froze for a moment, but then I saw a guy jump out of the passenger door with a carry-on bag and a baby's car seat. I assumed he was running late for the train. I continued on and got in the car.

During the ride to the airport, I had a creepy feeling, but every time I looked behind us, there were big trucks blocking the view of smaller vehicles. When the driver dropped me off at the departure entrance, I panned the entire area and saw nothing. While I was standing in line to check my bag, there was a teenaged girl in front of me applying eyeliner with the aid of a small makeup mirror. After giving her a big, bright smile and saying hello, I asked to borrow her makeup mirror for a moment.

"Sure, Mister," she said.

I held it up to get the view behind me. Sure as hell, there they were. Only this time with a big zoom lens pointed right at me. Now that was just getting weird. Why the hell would the Feds be watching us? When I got to my terminal, I took a seat and sent Dad a text message. He sent me one right back.

OBVIOUSLY THIS THING IS BIGGER THAN WE THOUGHT. LET'S KEEP IT BETWEEN US FOR NOW SON.

I responded right away.

BUY THREE BURNER CELLPHONES. I'LL EXPLAIN LATER.

The flight home was both nerve-wracking and a relief. It was nerve-wracking because of everything that was going on, and a relief because I was on the plane, a relatively safe place. At Chicago's Midway Airport I waited for the next available shuttle to take me home. I thought about my next move and how I was going to keep Mr. Cartwright alive, as well as myself. Maybe having the Feds watch our every move was a good thing. I decided to give the City Block a call while I was waiting.

"You've reached the City Block. This is Louie speaking."

"Don't say my name."

"What's up?"

"I'm at the airport, but I have a problem to tackle before I can pick up Barney."

"Don't worry, he's fine."

"How's everything going?"

"Everything here is fine. No, wait. There's been a guy coming in for the last three days. He orders a beer but doesn't drink it. He sits for an hour, pays, and then leaves."

"What does he look like?"

"He's white, and about six feet tall, medium build and wears a cheap suit. If you ask me, he's a cop nosing around for something."

"If he comes in tomorrow, give me a call."

"Will do."

CLICK.

Jesus, this whole world was coming unglued! What the hell did this guy want? One thing was for sure, he was no Fed. My shuttle arrived and I jumped in. The driver must've had quite a schedule, because he put the pedal to the metal, which was fine with me.

When we reached my place, I gave him a tip and ran inside. The first thing I did was go to my closet. I pulled out my arsenal and started strapping it on. In my ankle holster was a 380 automatic. The holster on my belt held my 9mm. Perhaps I was overdoing it, but better safe than sorry. I pulled off my shirt and strapped on my vest and slipped on an oversized football jersey. Aside from being slightly out of my mind, I was ready. I called Dad and suggested we get together and have a more informative conversation about what I'd discovered so far.

"I'm making some security arrangements here at my house right now," he said. "Why don't you let me call you back?"

"All right. We've got plenty of time before Mr. Cartwright arrives," I said.

CLICK.

TIME TO KILL

It was almost noon, so I turned on the TV to catch the noonday news report. I turned to WLOK and waited for the broadcast to begin. At twelve sharp they aired, and there stood Candee in front of what looked like a wooded area of some kind. Behind her was a tow truck pulling a car out of some water. She started her report.

"Hi, I'm Candee Harris with the WLOK News Crew. We're coming to you live from south suburban Blue Island, where a car is being pulled out of the canal. This morning a couple of joggers saw the rear bumper of this vehicle sticking up out of the water. They called the police immediately. Both the police and fire rescue arrived within minutes. Since then, the divers have been brought in. The good thing is that no bodies were found inside the car. We got the chance to talk to Inspector Calvin Tyler, and this is what he had to say."

At this time an earlier recording was played.

"Thank you, Inspector. Can you tell us about your findings this morning?"

"Early this morning around seven a.m., joggers discovered this vehicle and contacted us right away. It appears the vehicle is owned by a local limo service and was reported stolen two days ago."

"Do you have anything on the driver?"

"Not at this time."

"Is there any chance that he or she may be in the canal?"

"No, there isn't. The doors and windows were closed before the vehicle went into the canal. That's all that I have right now."

"Do you suspect foul play?"

"That's all that I have right now. Thank you."

"Well there you have it, folks, a second mystery in just two days. I'm Candee Harris with the WLOK News Crew. Now back to the studio."

I didn't know how Candee kept a straight face while doing her report. A better question was who had the power to make the police drag their ass on this investigation? It all came down to the disappearance of D.A. White. You'd think every law enforcement agency in the state would be working on this thing. I was kind of glad that Dad was busy. It gave me time to calm down and relax. I make better decisions when I'm in a mellow mood.

Dad did call me back and asked that I meet him at his place. He wanted me to meet the security staff and help to arrange them in and around his property.

It took me thirty minutes to get to his place. I arrived before the staff did, which was a good thing. It gave Dad and me time to verify weak points of entry on his property. My first question was rather or not the staff would be armed. I was glad to hear that they would be.

"Now, Dad, there's something I want to tell you that I didn't let on to Mr. Cartwright."

"What is that, son?"

"The guys that broke into his place weren't typical punks. I recognized the tattoos they were wearing. They're an extremely ruthless gang. They're a gang that originated out of El Salvador. These days they're spreading across the states in huge numbers. Dad, these guys control the drug trade, prostitution, gun running, contract hits, and they're also connected to the Mexican Cartel. These guys are a cop's worst nightmare, and I'm sure they're under contract with someone."

"Why do you think that?"

"They didn't even have to break in. Someone with connections got to the alarm company employee. All they had to do was punch in Mr. Cartwright's alarm code."

"Thank God he wasn't there!"

"They would've killed him just for the sport of it."

"These guys sound real nasty, son."

"You have no idea. Let me put it this way, in some places, it's obvious they have the police in their pockets."

"Jesus Christ! But why Oliver? There have to be more people involved than him. In all of my years in law, I've never seen anything like this. We've got gangbangers, dirty cops, and federal agents. It has all the signs of World War III. I just can't place Oliver's role in this thing. It's not that I don't trust him, but hell, he doesn't know what's going on either."

"Let me ask you something, Dad. Have you been following the local news lately?"

"A little bit, not much."

"Did you hear about the personal driver that was found dead in the restroom at that state building?"

"No, I didn't."

"This morning a car was pulled out of the canal out in Blue Island. The police won't say it's connected to the driver, but they do say it's owned by a limo service."

"You know, my mind's been on Oliver."

"Dad, that's not all. The media hasn't released the story yet, but the D.A. is missing."

"How long has he been missing?"

"It's not a he."

"You're kidding me!"

"It's the one and only Miss White!"

"Why aren't the cops allowing the media to release the story?"

"I don't know, but does anything seem strange to you?"

"Yeah, but we've got to be wrong."

"What are we wrong about?"

"I can't believe the D.A.'s and Oliver's issues are related."

"Well, I just wanted to hear you say it. Look at it this way. The Feds have been tracking me and Mr. Cartwright. Who do you think has the power to make the cops keep quiet about a D.A. that's been missing for two days?"

"It wouldn't be the first time the Feds took over a police investigation, especially when there's a high profile involved. The problem is, son, who would want to do harm to the both of them?"

"Are you kidding me? A lot of people would. It's just a thought that I wanted to run by you."

SEVEN

OLIVER ARRIVES

After meeting with the security staff, we walked around the property so they could familiarize themselves with it. The head guy divided them into two teams and gave them assignments.

We still had time to kill before Mr. Cartwright's train arrived. Dad took the time to send his guy on the train a text message to see how things were going. His response was A.O.K. He then sent a second message to Dad:

WE'RE TWO HUNDRED MILES OUT. I WILL TEXT AGAIN WHEN WE'RE ONE HUNDRED MILES OUT.

Time passed, and the local news stations were recapping the information that we already knew, with one exception. The police revealed that they had a connection between the man found in the restroom and the car pulled out of the canal. When asked by reporters, they wouldn't say who the driver had been hired to drive for. By tomorrow morning it would be seventy-two hours that D.A. White had been missing. They'd have to say something.

It wasn't long before Dad's guy sent another text message. They were less than one hundred miles away. We figured it would take them an hour and a half or so, and we could get to Union Station in less than half that time. Personally, I wanted to get there early anyway. It would give me time to scope out the lobby.

Dad requested that one of the guys from the security detail ride shotgun with him. We explained to him what our plan was, and thirty minutes later we headed out for Union Station. When we arrived, I was able to park at a meter right outside. I saw that Dad had parked across the street, about a half block down. Once inside the station, I had to go down two floors. The trains actually entered the station through tunnels that ran parallel with the river. I tried to look like everyone else who was waiting for a loved one.

In a place this big, in a city like Chicago, it's hard to tell who's out of place. As I looked around the lobby, it occurred to me that I was the only person who looked like he was up to something. I worked my way over to a wall with monitors on it, showing arrivals and departures. It really didn't say what time Mr. Cartwright's train would arrive, just that it was on schedule. That was fine, because some trains were delayed. I moved around for another twenty minutes. Finally an announcement was made. Train number 23 from San Antonio, Texas, was now arriving on track number 16.

I thought it would've been coming in from Houston, but I figured Mr. Cartwright must have had to make some kind of transfer. It was at least fifteen minutes before people actually started coming down the platform toward the lobby. I could see Mr. Cartwright walking in a crowd of about thirty people. About twenty yards behind him was Dad's guy. I gave him the eye to let him know I had things from there. Mr. Cartwright and I didn't waste time. We went straight to the elevator.

It had been dark out for two or three hours now, so we'd have to depend on the phones that Dad picked up for us. I'd memorized Dad's headlights and grille right away. On the way back to his place, I could see that he was staying six or seven car lengths behind me. A couple of times he had to blow a traffic light to keep up with me. After a while, Mr. Cartwright started asking questions.

"Son, I was wondering. Have there been any new developments on that ol boy that was found in the restroom?"

"Well, the police pulled a vehicle out of the drink this morning and tied the two together."

"Ain't that somethin'!"

In my sideview mirror, I saw a set of headlights turn the corner and come about two car lengths behind Dad. I reached into my pocket and took out the new phone. I hit speed dial.

"Hey, Dad, did you catch that?"

"I did, son. Just stick to the plan."

As we continued on, I could see that the vehicle behind Dad was another black SUV. Mr. Cartwright also realized that something was up.

"What in Sam hell is going on?"

"This morning you and I were tailed by the Feds."

"What the hell!"

"After we dropped you off, they followed me to the airport."

"Holy shit, son!"

"Dad and an armed guard are about six car lengths behind us."

"Did yo' daddy put a boy on that train?"

"Yes, sir, he did."

"Damn it, I knew it!"

"I hate to tell you, but the Feds just came up behind Dad a little ways back, and they're still there now."

"So what's the plan?"

"We're going to act like we don't see them, and wait for them to make a move."

When we reached Dad's neighborhood, the Feds dropped back. When we pulled up to his place, we were momentarily greeted by the business end of a shotgun at both our windows. The guards then lowered their weapons and waved us in. Mr. Cartwright was furious. Personally I thought it was money well spent.

"Yo' daddy done turned this place into Fort Knox!"

"There's a lot you don't know. Dad will fill you in. Mr. Cartwright, this thing is far bigger than your house being broken into."

"Hell, you tellin' me!"

MY NEW ACQUAINTANCE

Once we were safely in the house, Dad told me to take off, be careful, and stay in touch. The drive home was quiet, and no one was tailing me. When I got home, the first thing I did was take off my pistols and vest. I was about to sit down and have a well-deserved beer when my personal phone rang. It was Louie at the City Block.

"Hey, he's here."

CLICK.

I put my 9mm back on my belt and took off immediately. As soon as I walked into the Block, Louie motioned toward the guy. I didn't feel much like beating around the bush, so I took a seat right next to the guy. I ordered a beer and drank about half of it. This guy didn't say a word, so I decided to take a different approach. I got up and headed for the parking lot. As soon as I cleared the door, I stepped to the side and leaned against the wall. Two minutes later he came out. In one quick move I grabbed him, bent him over the hood of a car, and stuck the barrel of my 9mm in his ear.

"Who the hell are you and what are you doing hanging around here?"

"Sherman, don't do it! I'm a cop!"

"How the hell do you know my name?"

"In my pocket you'll find my badge and I.D. I'm telling you I'm a cop!"

"Well, I'm telling you if you so much as blink an eye, I'm going to paint the hood of this car red!"

Keeping my pistol in his ear, I took my left hand from his back and reached into his pocket. He had a badge and an I.D. that said he was Detective Maxwell Little of the Chicago Police Department. I dropped the wallet on the car and took my pistol out of his ear.

"Jesus, you could've killed me with that thing!"

"For a cop it was pretty stupid to follow me out here. You still didn't answer my question."

"Sherman, I know a lot about you. Why don't we go back inside and talk?"

I took a chance and went back inside, ordering a couple of beers for us after letting Louie know that everything was okay.

"So what exactly do you know about me?"

"I know that you've had a pain in your ass for a long time now."

"Tell me more."

He reached into his pocket and pulled out a photograph.

"Do you know this guy?" he asked.

"That's Lt. Ricardo Lopez."

"Not anymore he's not. He's been busted down to uniform."

"Good for him. So that's why you've been hanging around here, Detective Little?"

"Please, call me Max."

"Well, Max, what does that have to do with me?"

"Let's just say there's no love lost between Lopez and me either. Years ago I used to ride with Lopez. He's the nastiest bastard I've ever seen, and I hate dirty cops. They make us all look bad. I put in for a transfer, and for a long time he made my life a living hell."

"I can see that, but why are you suddenly looking for me?"

"Well, Lopez got demoted right after the Lipstick Murder trial, and it was mostly because of his ties to you."

"I still don't get it."

"I've been keeping him under surveillance when I can, and he's up to something."

"I'm listening."

"Something is going on in this city, something big and ugly."

Max didn't know it, but the hairs on the back of my neck were standing.

"To be frank with you, certain names were bounced around following the trial, and Lopez drew the short straw," Max said.

"You mentioned something big going down."

"Have you been watching the news lately?"

"I have from time to time."

"Well you're a smart guy. Look, I've got to go. Here's my card."

As he walked away, I called out, "Hey, Max, have you seen any strangers in town lately?"

"Like flies on shit! I just can't find the pile. Watch yourself, Sherman."

EIGHT

THE AWAKENING

With a major headache and blurry vision, District Attorney White was waking up. In a daze, she felt cool, damp air. She realized her clothes had been removed and that she was lying on a cold concrete slab. Not only that, she was handcuffed to bars. She tried to break free, but couldn't. In frustration she screamed out. From behind her she heard a voice she knew. It was Officer Ricardo Lopez.

"It's no use, bitch! You're not going anywhere!"

"Lopez, what the hell are you doing? Where am I? Let me out of here!"

"Get comfortable, honey! This is your new home. How do you like it? I bet you never thought you'd be the one in jail!"

"Why are you doing this to me?"

"You've got a bad memory, Miss D.A. Two years ago you took my career away from me, and now I'm taking yours."

"You're out of your mind, Lopez. You'll never get away with this!"

"Sure I will. Dead bitches don't talk! I'd love to stay and chat, but I've got things to do."

Lopez turned off the lights and walked away, leaving her to scream into darkness.

"You can't leave me here!"

With her wrist swollen and in pain, she broke down and cried. It was dark and cold, and she started shaking from the chilly air. Suddenly she started feeling something nibbling at her toe. She screamed and kicked it away. She heard the sound of a squealing rat, and she cursed Lopez.

It had been hours since Lopez left. D.A. White was staring into darkness and fighting to stay awake. As hard as it was, she started accepting the fact that she might never escape. Thoughts of her career, life, and family passed through her mind. Wondering how she ever got there, she thought back. She remembered leaving her office and being on her cellphone while crossing the lobby. She was getting into the town car, and that was it.

As the hours went by, her arms and shoulders began to ache. She tried to think of where in the city there could be an abandoned police station. Assuming that she was in one, no one would ever think of looking for her there. She had no idea how long she'd been in captivity. For all she knew, Lopez could've taken her out to the old prison in Joliet. Slowly losing her will, she hung her head and drifted off to sleep.

Day Two at Dad's House

Morning came and I went to the kitchen to start a pot of coffee. With phone in hand, I turned on the small TV on the counter. I speed dialed dad on my phone.

"Good morning, son."

"Good morning Dad. How did it go last night?"

"It was pretty quiet."

"Well, you're not going to believe what happened to *me* last night."

"Jesus, are you all right?"

"Don't worry, I'm fine."

"What the hell happened?"

"Lately there's been some guy hanging around the City Block, giving everyone the creeps. Last night I went in to see for myself. It turns out he was looking for me, and he's a cop."

"What the hell did he want with you?"

I ended up giving my dad the whole spiel on my encounter with Detective Maxwell Little, including the part about keeping surveillance on Lopez, as well as him warning me to watch my back.

"That's not good, son. I can just imagine who the other people involved are."

While Dad was talking, I could see a ticker-tape running across the bottom of my TV screen. Breaking news was about to interrupt what was on.

"Hold on, Dad. Turn on your TV. The chief of police is about to hold a press conference."

On the TV screen was the chief, the mayor, the A.D.A., and some other guy. They all gathered around a podium that had at least seven microphones on it. You couldn't see the media, but there were dozens of camera flashes going off.

"All right," my dad said. "I've got it, and Oliver's sitting right here beside me."

The chief was first to speak.

"Good morning. Thank you for coming. Three days ago District Attorney Margret White was reported missing. Since then the police department has stepped up all available manpower and resources to find her and apprehend the people responsible for her disappearance. Our investigation will be aggressive. We intend to turn over every stone and look behind every door."

After wiping his forehead, he began to speak again.

"What we know now is that the night before her disappearance, her driver was found dead in the restroom of her office building. The following day, his car was found in a canal out in Blue Island. What we don't know is whether or not his death is related to the disappearance of D.A. White. At this point in the investigation, there are still a lot of questions to be answered, and any accusations would be pure speculation. The police department has now teamed up with the FBI to get to the bottom of this. At this point I'm going to turn the podium over to Special Agent Calvin."

The special agent was direct and to the point, and he kept it brief.

"Thank you. As the chief said, we'll be combining our resources. At this point our people are canvassing the entire state, as well as the neighboring states. We will find D.A. White."

Next up was the mayor, but I wasn't much interested in what he had to say, so I turned the volume down.

"Well, Dad, what do you think of that?"

"I hate to say it, but if this guy is willing to kill the D.A.'s driver just to get to her, there's no telling what he's capable of."

"Dad, we need to come up with some kind of plan, but how can we plan for something we don't know anything about?"

"Look, son, you and I both know that Lopez is behind this thing. He's in control, pulling all the strings."

"For crying out loud, Dad, that guy is out there in a squad car patrolling the street like any other cop."

"Look, we already know he has these gangbangers on his side, and we're outnumbered. Let him bring the battle to us. We'll be ready."

After talking to Dad, I took out Max's card and placed it on the table in front of me. As I drank my coffee, I debated about whether or not to call him. Not even ten minutes went by before I made my decision. I went to my personal phone in the bedroom and dialed his number. He answered on the third ring.

"This is Detective Little, may I help you?"

"Hey, Max, this is Sherman."

"I didn't expect to hear from you."

"And I didn't expect to call you."

"So what's up?"

"Did you see the press conference?"

"I was there, and guess what? So was your boy!"

"No kidding! Did you talk to him?"

"No. He just looked at me with a big shit-eating grin. I got the impression he was enjoying the whole thing."

"What's your next move, Max?"

"I'm going to stay on his ass! What about you?"

"I don't know."

"Do you own a vest?"

"I do."

"I suggest you wear it."

"Max, do you think he has her?"

"It's damn possible. I've been tailing him over to the Pullman area. Each time, he disappears into thin air."

"What's in the Pullman area?"

"Nothing. That's the point. You know as well as I do that it's a forgotten, run-down part of the city. There's not even any place to shop for the people who live there."

"It definitely sounds like Lopez is up to something. Now that I think of it, that area is a good place to hide a body."

"I sure hope you're wrong, Sherman. Look, I've got to go. And I'll say it again: Watch your back."

After talking to Max, I realized that for sure there would be strength in numbers. I packed an overnight bag and headed for my dad's place. When I got there, he was glad to see me. Things were really quiet, but I still felt like my hands were tied.

Nighttime came, and I decided to take a walk around the grounds. There had been a shift change with the security detail, so there was a different group of guys than that morning. After checking in with each of them, I went back inside the house. As the night dragged on, none of us could sleep, so we gathered in the family room, facing the rear of the property.

WORLD WAR III

In the garden area, a security guard stood in the shadows. Things were so quiet that he decided to have a smoke. He rested his automatic weapon against the fence, reached in his shirt pocket and took a pack of smokes. After lighting one, he took a long slow drag and blew the smoke out. Without any warning a large hand wrapped around his face, and his throat was cut from one side to the other. Dropping to the ground, he bled out almost immediately.

❈❈❈

Mr. Cartwright and I sat at a card table, while Dad stretched out on the sofa. A guard sat on one side of the room. Suddenly he jumped to his feet, raised his shotgun and started pumping rounds through the glass doors to the patio. I jumped up and tried to shield Mr. Cartwright. By then automatic rounds were flying through the house. Just as I screamed for Dad, I took two rounds in my side that flipped me completely over. The next thing I knew, two guards were dragging Dad into another room.

I could hear rounds being fired all over the property. Windows and things in every room were being shattered by bullets. The grounds had turned into the O.K. Corral! It was all-out war between our guards and the intruders. The next sound I heard was that of a helicopter overhead. With one hand I managed to raise myself enough to get a quick look outside. After several attempts, I managed to see a caravan of black SUVs with flashing red and blue lights in the grille. They had crashed the front gates and were all over the place. The gunfire continued for at least another minute. Holding my side, I rolled over and leaned against the wall. That's when federal agents in dark suits came from every room and hallway leading to us. They were all armed and yelling out, FEDERAL AGENTS! At the same time they were scattering like ants.

IS EVERYONE ALL RIGHT? IS ANYONE HURT?

That's when Mr. Cartwright screamed, "Yes! Over here, this boy's been shot!"

One of the agents ran over to me and fell down on his knees. He then ripped my shirt open and saw that I was wearing a vest.

"You're one lucky son of a bitch!"

He touched my side, and the pain was so horrible that my entire body jerked. It was nothing less than torture. My vest had stopped the bullets, but at the cost of a couple of broken ribs and swelling that was growing by the second.

"Help is on the way, buddy. You'll be fine."

In the background I could hear the ambulance sirens as they arrived. As a precaution, the paramedics gave me an IV drip and oxygen. After the very painful experience of being placed on a gurney, I was wheeled outside. Every exterior light that wasn't broken was on. Even the headlights of all the SUVs were on. The grounds were lit up like a football field on Friday night. There were over a dozen guys lying face down with their hands cuffed behind their backs. At least five bodies were on the ground and covered with plastic tarps. Agents were all over the place, and the helicopter was still in the air, flying in circles. Paramedics were tending to both the guards and the intruders.

During the excitement, I hadn't noticed, but Dad was being loaded into an ambulance as well. Later I would learn that he had shattered glass embedded in the side of his face. My ride to the hospital included two black SUVs full of agents as an escort. Arriving at the hospital brought back memories of when I busted my ribs the first time after falling over a kid's bike. I don't know what it was, but the pain reliever I was given was great! I was then X-rayed and wrapped. For the moment life was good, but I knew from past experience that the days ahead of me would be incredibly painful. That was the perfect example of putting a bandage on a bullet wound.

That night I shared a room with a federal agent. When I asked about my dad's condition, I was told he was fine and I'd get to see him in the morning. As for Mr. Cartwright, he was under the trustworthy care of the Feds. I couldn't help but think that the Feds had been watching before all of this shit went down. At the speed they reached us, they had to be.

NINE

DAY ONE IN THE HOSPITAL

When I woke the next morning, two things occurred to me immediately. The pain reliever had worn off, and Max was standing over me.

"Hey, buddy, I see you took my advice."

It hurt like hell to talk, but I asked, "What advice?"

He reached over and picked up my vest off of a chair.

"So what's it like being in World War III?" he asked.

"Honestly, I missed most of it. It all happened so quickly, and there was so much confusion and rounds being fired, I felt like a kid that was running for his life in a desert village that was being attacked from the air and on the ground. It was a nightmare, but there's one thing I can say: those MS-13 boys don't mess around!"

Max gave me a very strange look as I tried to recover from the pain of trying to talk and breathe at the same time.

"What makes you think those guys were involved?"

"I'll show you when I get out of here."

During our little talk, Max had been holding a paper bag under his arm.

"Hey, I've got something for you," he said.

He opened the bag and took out both of my firearms.

"How did you get them?"

"I pulled some strings."

"Max, what would you say if I told you these guys were fulfilling a contract hit?"

"Knowing their reputation, I wouldn't question it, but I get the feeling you believe they were hired by our friend Lopez."

"That's definitely what I believe!"

"When we were partners, he was pretty tight with street scum, and I wouldn't put it past him."

"I have a question for you, Max."

"Shoot!"

"Ha, ha, that's real funny! Why do you think the Feds just fell out of the sky last night?"

"I was wondering the same thing, my friend."

"For a while they were tailing us."

"You're kidding me!"

"I first spotted them in Texas a few days ago and then again the day I met you."

"But why would they tail you?"

"I think it's because of my association with Oliver Cartwright."

"Why would the Feds be watching him?"

"After what happened last night, I don't think they were."

"Wait a minute. You think they were on to this MS-13 bunch?"

"Why else would they just drop out of the sky like they did?"

"If that's true, they've got their hands full."

"And there's still the matter of the D.A."

"You'd better hurry and heal, my friend. I get the feeling we're going to need each other before this mess is over."

I reached over and pressed the call button. Max reacted right away.

"Are you all right, man?"

"I'm fine. I just want to see if the nurse will let you wheel me down to my dad's room."

The nurse immediately came in and started checking my vital signs.

"How do you feel this morning, Mr. Brothers?"

I took a deep, painful breath and said that it hurt a lot. The nurse lifted the sheets and touched my ribs, and of course I jumped. It hurt like hell.

"Let me see what I can do about that pain," the nurse said.

"Excuse me, Nurse, but I was wondering if the detective here could wheel me to my dad's room?"

"I don't know about that, Mr. Brothers. Are you sure you want to try and get out of this bed?"

"I'm sure. I really want to see my dad."

"Okay, I'll make a deal with you. First let me see you get out of this bed."

I pressed the button on the side of the bed that made it rise. I then attempted to turn my legs to the side of the bed. The pain was incredible.

"There's your answer, Mr. Brothers," the nurse said.

Max was smiling at my efforts the whole time.

"Well, Nurse, maybe you can see about getting him in here."

As Max and the nurse turned to leave, Max still had a smile on his face. I put the bag he brought me in the nightstand drawer. I was in bed in pain for at least an hour before the nurse returned. While she was adding a pain reliever to my IV drip, a federal agent wheeled my dad into the room. He had a butterfly bandage over his left eye and two large patches over the left side of his face and neck. His left hand was also wrapped in a bandage.

"Hey, Dad, you look like you lost!"

"It's good to see that under all of that pain, you still have a sense of humor. How are you feeling, son? I hear you took a couple of rounds in your side."

"I feel like I got hit by a bus, twice. How is Mr. Cartwright?"

"The Feds have him at a safe house."

That's when the agent who wheeled dad in spoke up.

"Don't worry, Mr. Brothers. No one can get to him."

"Excuse me, but what is your name, sir?"

"I'm sorry. I'm Special Agent Calvin."

"Can you tell me something?"

"It depends on what you want to know."

"How is it that you guys just happened to be around last night?"

Special Agent Calvin asked the nurse if she didn't mind giving us a little privacy. She excused herself and left.

"Here's the situation. For nearly a year we've had this bunch under surveillance. They have new chapters developing all across the country. Their latest claim to fame is handling contract hits. We followed them to Texas. We know they ransacked Cartwright's place, but we chose not to move in on them. We were hoping they would lead us to the person that put the contract out. We've arrested the alarm company employee that sold the alarm code to them, but he has the fear of God in him, and he won't talk."

"So, it was you guys who were taking pictures of me at the airport?"

"That was one of our guys. You two gentlemen are lucky to be alive. These punks rarely leave witnesses behind. We have a complete background on both of you, and we know what you're capable of, but it's my job to tell you to back off of this investigation."

That's when I got pissed.

"No offense, Agent Calvin, but they brought this shit to us, we didn't go to them! We hired security to protect us in our own home. What else could we do?"

"I just want to warn you, gentlemen, these guys multiply like cockroaches. I'm going to leave you two alone for now. There will be an agent right outside your door."

Dad shook his head after Agent Calvin left the room.

"Well, I certainly can see why the cops and the Feds don't get along. The cops are forced to deal with matters at hand, while the Feds have the luxury to spend a whole year on an investigation."

"Hey, Dad, they're likely to release you before they do me. Why don't you camp out at my place until we can get your place back in order?"

"That's not a bad idea."

There was a knock at the door, and the nurse walked in.

"I'm sorry, Mr. Remington, but it's time for you to go. Mr. Brothers needs his rest."

"I'll see you later, Dad."

MY CITY BLOCK FAMILY

I figured I'd better break the news to the guys at the Block. I picked up the phone and dialed nine to get out. Louie answered.

"Hey, it's Sherman."

"Jesus Christ, where in the hell are you? We've been worried sick about you!"

"I'm fine, but I've been shot."

"You've been shot!"

Carman must've heard Louie and snatched the phone out of his hand. The rest of the gang gathered around as Louie put the phone on speaker and Carman went off.

"Sherman, what the hell did you get yourself into? It looked like a damn battle zone at your dad's place!"

Then she started crying.

"You'd better not get yourself killed! Where are you, and how many times did you get shot?"

"I was shot twice, and the Feds won't let me say where I'm at."

Barney must've heard my voice, because he started barking.

"Look, I was wearing a bulletproof vest. I have a couple of broken ribs and a lump on my side the size of a grapefruit. Listen, guys. I don't know when I'm going to see you. The Feds have taken over this whole thing. Don't be surprised if Candee Harris shows up nosing around. I've got to go now."

That's when Mai spoke up.

"We love you, Sherman!"

CLICK.

India's Turn

I hung up and took a deep breath, which hurt. It was time for me to make the toughest call yet. I dialed India's number, and a soft, sweet voice said hello. Trying not to sound like I was in pain, I said, "Hi, it's me."

"Oh my God, you were involved in that mess! Oh God, no! Please no!"

"Honey, honey, please calm down. I'm fine."

"I'm coming there. Where are you? I knew I was going to lose you!"

"Calm down. You're not going to lose me."

"Sherman, I'm scared! I saw that mess on CNN this morning."

"Look, honey, first of all, I'm being protected by the FBI. I'm surrounded by them 24/7. No one can get near me."

"Well, what about me?"

"I'm sorry, honey, but if you're not a cop, you can't get within a mile of me. I'm sorry."

"I guess there's no use in asking where you are."

"They won't allow it, but that doesn't mean we can't stay in touch."

"Can I stay at your place until you're free?"

"That wouldn't be safe, plus my dad is staying there."

"I know it's not your fault, Sherman, but this hurts. I feel like I'm part of the team, but I'm forced to sit on the bench. I want the world to know I have your back."

"You've got my back just by loving me, and by being there when I get out."

"Well, I guess I should say goodbye for now."

"India, I'll talk to you again tonight. I love you."

CLICK.

D.A. WHITE'S NEW WORLD

When I hung up, I realized that India was there for the long haul. In another part of town, D.A. White was waking up to the realization of where she was. It wasn't just a bad dream. Although she was still in darkness, she could hear the voices of men arguing in Spanish. She couldn't understand what they were saying, but she knew one of them was Lopez, and he was pissed off about something. From his tirade, she could also tell that he was the boss of whatever was going on. Suddenly, he lost his cool and switched to English.

"You and your boys fucked up the hit! All you had to do was kill one old man! Now he's in the hands of the Feds, my friend! Just forget about Cartwright. I'll take care of him myself. You and your boys have one more chance. Don't fuck it up!"

Lopez handed a small Styrofoam box to one of the guys.

"Take this and go feed that bitch! I've got to go and try to clean up your mess!"

When D.A. White heard Lopez give the order to feed her, she closed her eyes and pretended to be asleep. Even with her eyes closed, she could see through her eyelids the glow of the light that had been turned on. She could also hear footsteps coming toward her. The next thing she heard was a key in the cell door lock, but she still kept her eyes closed.

There were two men talking in Spanish and laughing. One of them grabbed her chin and lifted her head. In English he said, "Wake up, bitch!" She opened her eyes and spit in his face. That's when he gave her a swift backhand that nearly ripped her head off her shoulders. His buddy smiled and grabbed his hand before he could do it again. He then told his friend to be gentle, as he softly caressed one of her breasts. She tried to turn away.

"Be nice, bitch," said the punk that slapped her. "I've brought you something to eat."

He opened the container, revealing rice and beans. His buddy took a key from his pocket and unlocked a cuff on one of her wrists so she could eat. For the moment she felt relief, but it was too little too late considering the slap that she'd taken. One of the guys lifted her head again and looked her in the eyes.

"Behave or else, bitch!"

Thinking that she'd be killed anyway, she told him to go to hell, and then kicked the food container out of his buddy's hand. That's when he lost his smile.

"You shouldn't have done that, baby."

He slowly unbuckled his belt and started pulling his pants down. His buddy told D.A. White to relax and enjoy it.

By the time they were finished with her, her will to fight or to live had been broken. Before leaving, they cuffed her hand back to the bar. Her lip was busted, her nose was bleeding, and one side of her face was swollen to the point that her eye was closed. The area between her thighs was bruised, and she had unimaginable vaginal damage. The men locked the cell door and walked away. With the energy that she had left, she mouthed the words, YOU BASTARDS! Through her one good eye she could see that two rats had come out of the shadows and were eating the wasted food. This was truly hell for her, and she screamed out loud.

GOD, TAKE ME AWAY! I WANT TO DIE.

TEN

MAX CONFRONTS LOPEZ

It had been a week since the attempt on Mr. Cartwright's life, and nearly ten days since the disappearance of D.A. White. Max was sitting in on a briefing in the squad room. The captain was talking about the details of the case that had been gathered so far. Max noticed Lopez leaning against the wall drinking coffee. He got up from his seat and approached him.

"Well, well, if it's not my old partner, Maxwell Little."

"I see you haven't changed, Lopez!"

"How about you, Max, have you grown any balls yet?"

"That's real cute, Lopez! Have you been keeping any special company lately?"

That pissed Lopez off.

"Don't fuck with me, Max! You're out of your league!"

"What's the matter, your little game not going as planned?"

"Mind your own business! Why don't you go over there and play nice with the Feds?"

That's when the captain yelled across the room.

"Would you two like to join us?"

Max returned to his seat, and Lopez just stood there smirking. Max was thinking that Lopez had just admitted his guilt. As far as he was concerned, it was game on. The briefing ended, and the day went on.

Still under the protection of the Feds, I lay in bed watching the midday news. Of course Candee was on the air representing WLOK. She was reporting live from outside my dad's place. She was standing across the street, and in the background I could see that the property was still taped off. There were three or four agents milling around the grounds.

"Hi, I'm Candee Harris with the WLOK News Crew. We're coming to you live from outside the scene of last week's home invasion and shootout."

The TV screen flashed scenes from that night.

"The police haven't released any information on what the intruders' motive was. We do know that the home was heavily guarded by private security before the invasion took place. Our sources tell us that this case is now in the hands of the FBI. The owner of this residence is none other than high-profile lawyer Carlton Remington. We've been unable to reach him for comment. At this time, any comments about his involvement would be purely speculation. We've also found out that Mr. Remington was a silent partner working with famed lawyer Oliver Cartwright. To refresh your memory, Mr. Cartwright successfully cleared the defendant in the Lipstick Murders case two years ago."

The TV screen was now showing old footage of Mr. Cartwright walking down the steps of the court building.

"Ladies and gentlemen, there's never a dull moment in this city! We'll keep in touch with you as this story continues to develop. I'm Candee Harris with the WLOK News Crew."

I turned off the TV and yelled out: "Damn it, Candee, sometimes you talk too freaking much!"

I had known the fact that my dad was the homeowner would soon have come out, but Candee didn't have to publicly tie him to Oliver and the Lipstick Murders case. All that I could do now was just lie there and be pissed off. I wanted out now more than ever. I needed to hook up with Max and nail Lopez, and put an end to this madness.

GOOD NEWS

There was one good thing, though. I'd been getting some physical therapy, and now I was able to stand up and move around a little. As I lay there in bed thinking, I got a surprise. There was a knock at my door, and in walked Special Agent Calvin pushing a wheelchair.

"What is this?" I asked.

"How about we get you out of here? There's one condition, though. You stay put and don't make a move. I'm going out on a limb here, and you need to know that shit flows downhill! Don't screw this up!"

"Well, in that case, can I ask you a favor?"

"What's that?"

"Can we make a stop along the way?"

"Jesus, Sherman, you don't ask for much! My balls are already on the chopping block!"

"It would mean a great deal to me, and to some people in my life."

"Sherman, this is not protocol by any means. Where do you want to stop off at?"

"It's a place called the City Block. I can show you how to get there."

"We already know where it is."

"I guess you do."

"Look, if we do this, we do it my way! Do you understand?"

"I understand."

"You get exactly five minutes, not a second longer!"

I grabbed the bag from the nightstand and my vest from the chair next to the bed. Agent Calvin helped me into the wheelchair, and then he got on his cellphone. When he was done, we left the room.

When we got to the Hyde Park area, each corner of the street where the City Block was located was blocked off by a black SUV. Before we went inside the bar, two agents entered from each of the doors, at the same time.

Louie immediately yelled out, "What the hell is going on?"

One of the agents then flashed his badge.

"FBI, sir. Get your customers out immediately!"

"What!"

"Just do it, sir!"

The other agent drew his sidearm and headed toward the rear rooms of the bar. Moments later he came back and yelled, CLEAR!

"All right! I want everyone out right now," Louie said. That's when Angie, Mai, and Carman gathered and hugged each other closely. One of the agents then made a phone call. Moments later two additional agents entered from the side door with their weapons drawn. Behind them I was wheeled in by Agent Calvin. Both doors were immediately closed and locked.

That's when Barney came running, jumped in my lap, and started licking my face. Everyone was stunned but relieved to see me. I turned and looked at Agent Calvin.

"This is Barney."

For the first time, the agent actually had half of a smile on his face. He then looked at his watch.

"You now have exactly four minutes!"

He stepped back, and everyone surrounded me. There were hugs, kisses, and tears. Agent Calvin was overwhelmed by the affection. After I'd been bombarded with questions that I couldn't answer, Agent Calvin said it was time to go. I looked at the gang with disappointment on my face.

"I don't know where I'm being taken to, but I love you guys."

"That's it, it's time to go," Agent Calvin said. Another agent said that it was clear outside. The ladies huddled again and watched as I was wheeled out the door. Back inside the SUV, I thanked Agent Calvin.

"You have no idea of how much that meant to both those guys and me. Thank you."

"They seem like real nice people," he said. "Even that gay guy."

"What gay guy?"

"Oh, that's all right."

"So, I guess you can't tell me where you're taking me."

"Just sit back and relax."

Along the way I started to recognize the route we were taking. I thought no, it can't be. When we turned onto my street, I said, "Calvin, you're amazing!" I then pointed at a black SUV parked across the street from my place.

"I see your guys are already here."

"No, that's just a video surveillance vehicle. My guys are around the corner sitting in a Public Works vehicle watching everything."

Just about then two agents stepped out of the lobby of my building to greet me. Agent Calvin then gave me a funny look.

"What's up?"

"You've got to do those stairs, buddy! Let me take your vest and that bag of guns!"

"How did you know? Oh, forget it!"

Standing in the front lobby now, I took a deep breath and said, "Let's do this!" When it was over, I'd never been happier to see my apartment door in my life, and the best part was being greeted by my dad. Special Agent Calvin gave us strict instructions before leaving. As it turned out, during my absence my neighbor across the hall had moved out. How convenient! One of the agents had set up shop in the apartment and would be checking in with us by phone from time to time. I'd always enjoyed one-on-one time with my dad, but not like this.

"How are you doing, son?"

"It's good to be home, but what I'd really like is some food that I can actually taste."

"Well, I've been digging around some in your kitchen, and there's plenty that tastes better than hospital food."

"Tell me, Dad, have you been in touch with Mr. Cartwright?"

"We've spoken by phone. He's still pretty upset, and of course he has issues with not being in control."

"What about you?"

"Control issues, I've put them aside for now. I do my best work in the courtroom and leave the gun slinging to the pros. So, did you catch your loudmouth friend on the midday news?"

Before I could answer, my personal cellphone rang.

"Who the hell could this be?" I said. I pressed the button and listened, without saying anything.

"Sherman, it's me, Max Little. I'm at the hospital, and we need to get together."

Knowing that it was Max, I spoke up.

"It's out of my hands now, Max. You need to get in touch with Special Agent Calvin."

"I'll do that. See you soon!"

CLICK.

THE ROOKIE

"What was that all about?" Dad asked.

"Remember I told you about the cop I met at the City Block? We've been keeping in touch. His life goal is to nail Lopez."

"So what does that have to do with us?"

"He's very well informed, and he can be a major asset to us. Anyway, he's on his way here right now. He has clearance with the Feds."

Just like that, there was a knock at the door. I took my 9mm from the bag and pointed it at the door, and then Dad opened it and stepped to the side. On the other side of the door was an agent holding up his badge. I lowered my weapon.

"You gentlemen have a visitor on his way up. I have to stay here until he arrives."

"Sorry, come on in," I said.

The agent stepped in, looking at my pistol.

"Are you guys sure you need me?"

I said no, but Dad said yes.

"Have a seat, Agent," Dad said. "Can I get you something to drink?"

"No, thank you. I'm fine."

"So, what do you guys have planned for us next week?" I asked.

"I don't know, sir. I guess it depends on what happens out there on the street."

"Can I ask you a question, Agent?" I said.

"Ask me anything you want."

Dad and I looked at each other, because we both knew what that meant.

"What's going on with the investigation of the missing D.A.?" I asked.

"What missing D.A.?"

"So you're a true-blue company man!"

"Sorry, sir."

"Then tell me this. How long have you been with the bureau?"

"It's been a little over a year, sir."

"Great, they hooked us up with a rookie!"

For the first time, I was disappointed with Agent Calvin. There was another knock at my door, and both the agent and I drew our weapons. Once again, Dad opened the door and stepped aside, this time to let Max in. We lowered our weapons. The agent went back across the hall to the apartment, and I shook my head. That's when Max gave me a funny look.

"Must be a rookie. He didn't ask to see my badge. I guess good help is hard to find."

"Hey, Max, this is my dad, Carlton Remington. Dad, this is Detective Maxwell Little."

"I'm sorry we have to meet under these circumstances, sir," Max said.

"I know what you mean," Dad said.

"Sherman," Max said, "at the hospital you said you had something to show me."

"Let me grab my laptop."

"I'll get it," Dad said.

I didn't bother to tell Max about the setup that Mr. Cartwright had in his barn. I knew he would've gotten a kick out of it, but at this time it didn't matter. Moments later I booted up my laptop and brought up the footage from Mr. Cartwright's house. The three of us then sat and watched.

"Wait, wait!" Max said.

"Oh, you caught that?" I said.

"Caught what?" Dad asked.

"You mean to tell me they didn't even have to break in?" Max asked.

"You've got it! The Feds have already picked up the alarm company employee."

"Let me guess. He's not talking."

"You're right again! Agent Calvin says the guy has the fear of God in him. Now I'm going to freeze this next frame. Tell me if you notice anything."

Max studied the frame for a few moments.

"MS-13. Okay, that's enough! I've seen those tattoos before. This is ugly!"

"So Max, I got the impression you were on a mission to get together," I said.

"This morning I attended a briefing in the squad room."

"That's normal, isn't it?"

"It's normal, but Lopez was there, and we had a little chat. I couldn't help but get in his face. After asking him about the company he's been keeping, he warned me to mind my own business. From my point of view, it was an admission of guilt. It was either that, or a challenge."

"So what do we do now?" I asked.

"We stay on his ass!"

"What about the other cases you're working on?"

"I'll do my best, but this is priority."

"So where do we start?" I asked.

"I'm stuck on this Pullman thing."

"I haven't heard that place mentioned in years," Dad said.

"I've been tailing Lopez over there for weeks now," Max said. "Every time he sets foot in that community, he disappears into thin air."

That's when I told Dad what we were up to.

"The truth is that before all of this other stuff happened, Max and I discussed the Pullman area in detail. The police haven't found a body yet, and there's a possibility that D.A. White may still be alive. That means Lopez needs a place to keep her and still go out on patrol."

"On at least two occasions I was on 111th Street, and that's where I lost him," Max said.

"So what streets border the Pullman area?" I asked.

"Just taking a guess, I'd say somewhere between Cottage Grove and Michigan Avenue," Max said.

Dad interrupted by saying that we were doing this all the wrong way.

"Son, you have your computer sitting right here. Check out the classifieds. All you guys have to do is look at what's available, and then determine what would suit Lopez's needs."

"That's a great idea," I said. "And it'll save us some time."

"Look, Sherman, I've got to get back out on the streets. Give me a buzz if anything catches your eye," Max said.

Dad and I spent the rest of the day picking each other's minds, and enjoying a potluck dinner. After dinner, Dad enjoyed scotch on the rocks, and I enjoyed his company. Due to the medication that I was taking, booze was off limits. After chewing the fat for a while, we both dozed off. It was after eleven that night when Agent Calvin called to check in with us. I told him that everything was quiet.

"Have you heard from your friend, Detective Little?"

"We talked earlier today. Why do you ask?"

"Did you watch the ten o'clock news?"

I looked at my watch and said no.

"There should be a recap at midnight. You may want to check it out. I'll talk to you gentlemen in the morning."

CLICK.

LOPEZ STRIKES AGAIN

Dad walked in and noticed the strange look on my face as I hung up.

"Is everything all right, son?"

"I don't know. Agent Calvin suggested that I catch the recap of the ten o'clock news at midnight."

"Jesus, what's happened now?"

"I guess we'll see at midnight."

"What else did he say?"

"He asked me if I'd talked to Max. In fact, I think I'll give Max a call right now."

Max's phone rang six times and then went to voice mail.

"Hey, it's me Sherman. Give me a call. Okay, Dad, now I'm worried. He did say that Lopez had warned him."

"Let's not jump to conclusions," Dad said. "Remember that he's a cop, and he can be anywhere, doing anything."

The minutes dragged by slow as hell, and it seemed like midnight would never arrive. Finally, following a commercial, an announcer said to stay tuned for the rebroadcast of the ten o'clock news. Listening to stories that didn't mean anything to me was killing me. There had to be something that Agent Calvin thought I should see.

Finally something did catch my eye. It was the scene of a broken fire hydrant that had water shooting fifty feet into the air, and behind it was a car that had been driven into a vacant storefront. A reporter then stepped into the picture frame.

"Earlier this evening a Police Department squad car in pursuit clipped another car in cross traffic and caused it to leave the road, go onto the sidewalk, and just before it landed in the storefront across the street, it took out a fire hydrant. The ironic thing is that the car that was hit was an unmarked squad car itself. Witnesses say that the squad car in pursuit, driven by Officer Ricardo Lopez, didn't have the siren on. However, some witnesses tell a different story. The unmarked squad car was being driven by Detective Maxwell Little, who was treated at the scene and released. In any case, the two vehicles collided at the intersection of 103rd Street and Michigan Avenue."

I turned off the TV.

"Now come on, Dad. That wasn't an accident!"

"Under normal circumstances I'd disagree with you, but after what the detective told us earlier, I have to believe it was deliberate."

"He was trying to kill Max because he knows what he's up to!"

"There has to be a way to expose this rogue cop, son."

"How is it that we're the only ones who can see this?" I said.

"I don't know, but if your detective friend doesn't bring this out in the open, Lopez is going to keep on killing. Even if he's caught and arrested, he'll never tell where he has D.A. White hidden."

"That's true, but for all we know, she may be dead already."

"Well, there's nothing we can do tonight, so we may as well get some sleep."

While lying in bed, I knew I had to get more involved. First, I had to get out of this jail cell I called home. I hated myself for thinking it, but Dad wasn't going to support me on this, so I was going to have to outsmart him as well. He'd be pissed off, but hopefully he'd forgive me later. I needed Max to help me pull this off, and it was going to take some planning.

ELEVEN

THE PULLMAN AREA

The next day was all business. The best part was Max showing up. He had his left arm in a sling and a bandage on his forehead. Other than that, he looked all right. Dad had set up office in the kitchen and was trying to organize a cleaning crew to go out to his house. At the same time, he was interviewing contractors. There were windows and doors to be replaced, as well as drywall repairs.

While Dad kept busy in the kitchen, Max and I put our heads together in the living room. We agreed that Lopez was definitely holed up in the Pullman area, and not only that, but now he knew that Max was aware of it.

"Why don't we just do this the old-fashioned way?" I asked Max.

"What do you mean?"

"Yesterday I pulled up a listing of commercial real estate available in that area. I think we should physically check out each and every one of them."

"Are you out of your mind?" he said. "That could take weeks!"

"I've thought about that. What if we divide them into two categories? We've got buildings that sit alone on dead-end streets. But there are also the ones that are right out in the open. My guess is the ones out in the open would be our best bet. Let's face it. Lopez is a bold son of a bitch!"

"Well, we have two things to consider," Max said. "First, it has to be a place he can get in and out of without being seen. Second, it has to be insulated well enough that a person could scream but not be heard."

"That narrows it down, but not enough," I said.

"Why don't we eliminate all storefronts?" Max said.

"That's good!" I said. "And we can eliminate buildings that don't have loading docks or garage doors. After all, he has to hide a squad car when he's out doing his dirty work."

"Now we're getting somewhere! You know, Sherman, what we really need is manpower. The problem is that I'd never get the department to believe my theory, and if they did, Lopez would find out about it and lie low."

"This might sound crazy, but the city has Feds up the ass. Why not use them?" I said.

"You're kidding, right? On TV they say they'll work with us, but the truth is that they'll work around us."

"That's even better," I said.

"How do you figure?"

"It's a damn good way to keep Lopez out of the loop."

"You're right about that, but I just don't know. Sherman, why don't we put that on the back burner and let it simmer for a while?"

"I can live with that."

"So what else do we have?"

"This may be a stretch, but what about landmarks and major changes made over the years?"

"In that community you're talking decades! We'd have to go to the archives, and the police department wouldn't have records on any place unless a crime was committed there."

"What about the main library? If anyone has the records, they'd have them. I might even have an easier way."

"What's that?"

"Have you ever heard of a woman name Candee Harris?"

"You mean that hot little motor mouth that does the news?"

"Maybe I can call in a favor or two from her."

"You mean she's a friend of yours? Now I know you're losing your mind! How in the hell could she possibly help us?"

"Max, if this woman thought for a second that she could get the lead story, she'd rip the archives to pieces."

"Yeah, but at what cost?"

"Let's just say it wouldn't cost you anything."

"And what would it cost you?"

I looked at Max and lowered my head in shame.

"No, don't even tell me. Why would a woman that sexy have to stoop so low?"

"Wait a minute! What am I, chopped liver?"

"I didn't mean that, Sherman. But dude, you really get into your work. Candee Harris… how the hell did you meet her?"

"I was driving my Vette down Lake Shore Drive one day, and she nearly ran me off the road in a hot little Porsche."

"You're kidding me."

"Not at all. That's when the craziness all started. The rest is history."

"I have to tell you, Sherman, there's a shitload of men in this city that would love to have your problems."

"Why don't we get back to the problem at hand? Perhaps we can put her on the back burner too?"

While Max and I were talking, there was a knock at my door. He drew his sidearm and I took a look through the peephole. It was the Fed from across the hall. When I opened the door, he handed me a note.

"Excuse me, Detective Little, but an officer just left this on your windshield."

I gave the note to Max and he read it out loud.

THE NEXT TIME I WON'T MISS!

"What a bold son of a bitch!" I said.

"Sherman, this is great news. That asshole just drove another nail into his coffin!"

"I take it Lopez doesn't know the Feds just filmed him leaving that note on your windshield."

"And he also doesn't know that this proves our little incident was attempted murder."

"You're right."

"What we're going to do now is just sit on this. It'll be the ace up our sleeve."

"I love a smart-ass. Give 'em enough rope, and they'll hang themselves every time."

Shortly after the note arrived, Max took off to go on routine patrol. Things were quiet the next couple of days. Max and I communicated by phone. My ribs were starting to feel better, but there was still the matter of coming up with a plan to sneak out of my place. It wasn't going to be easy, so I set the idea aside for a while.

GREETINGS FROM INDIA

One afternoon while just sitting around, I got a small surprise. It was a package from India. After opening it, I had to laugh, because it was a video cam for my computer. Along with it was a note that said USE ME RIGHT NOW. Following the operating manual, I hooked it up to my laptop. I started typing and bang, there was my baby sitting at her desk, saying hi, honey, with a big beautiful smile and waving.

"Hey, honey, how you doing? This was a great idea!" I said.

"Do you like it?"

"I love it!"

"You're not going to get tired of me, are you?"

"No, I'll never get tired of you."

"Stand up and let me see your ribs."

"Hold on. How's that?"

"Oh, honey, I'm so sorry!"

I sat back down.

"Okay, I showed you mine, now show me yours."

"Don't be nasty! That's not why I did this. Plus I don't trust these computers. Someone could be stealing our images, and my career could be finished."

"I'm sorry, honey, I was just kidding around."

"How is your case going?"

"It's moving slow, but there's never a dull moment. I love seeing you, but I really need to get back to work."

"Okay, I love you. Bye!"

Just like that, my monitor went blank.

The Governor's Ball

Downtown at one of the luxury hotels, a large banquet hall was being decorated, and a portable stage and dance floor were being assembled. Chandeliers were being dusted and tables were being arranged. In a big stainless steel professional kitchen, a chef was meeting with his cooks and serving staff. In the banquet hall, dozens of floral arrangements were being delivered. The hall was buzzing with all kinds of staff, including a security detail.

Once the stage was completed, the orchestra started rehearsing. Huge banners promoted the Governor's Annual Charity Ball. Each year a ball is thrown to raise funds for a different charity. This year it was for Breast Cancer Research. At a cost of fifteen hundred dollars a plate, the menu included lobster, prime rib, roast duck, and all the trimmings.

Dozens of cases of wine were wheeled into the kitchen. The governor's guests included a who's who of the celebrity world, as well as Chicago's own movers and shakers. There would be local politicians and a couple of senators as well. One of the top ten bashes thrown in the city every year, this event promised to have limos parked bumper to bumper for at least three blocks. With the ball scheduled to be held tomorrow night, the staff had the rest of today and tomorrow morning to complete the finishing touches.

Out on the Kennedy Expressway, Governor Phillip T. Evans was sitting in the back seat of his town car with his bodyguard. He had just left O'Hare International Airport and was heading for his hotel downtown. Traffic was light, and his driver was making good time. As they passed through an unincorporated area near north suburban Park Ridge, the driver looked into his rear view mirror.

"Excuse me, sir," he said to the governor. "I think we have a problem."

The bodyguard turned and looked behind them.

"It's a cop, sir," he said. "I wonder what he wants."

Behind them a squad car with flashing lights on was coming up behind quickly. As the town car slowed down, all other traffic zipped past them, except for a van that pulled over to the shoulder behind them. The squad car stopped on the driver's side of the town car. The door to the squad car opened, and surprisingly, Officer Ricardo Lopez stepped out. The governor recognized him right away. The driver let the windows down on his side of the car, and the governor yelled out.

"Lopez, what's the meaning of this?"

Behind the town car, two men wearing bandannas had jumped out of the van brandishing pistols. They split up, and one of them joined Lopez and immediately fired a bullet into the head of the governor's driver. The second gunman stepped up to the rear window and fired a shot into the head of the governor's bodyguard. It happened so fast that neither man ever had a chance. The governor was then dragged from the back seat into the waiting van. His face was covered at once with a chloroformed cloth. The squad car and the van then took off. The whole procedure took roughly fifteen seconds. As a precaution, the governor was injected with the same animal tranquilizer that had been used on D.A. White.

Twelve

THE NEW D.A. WHITE

D.A. White had lost all sense of time. As much as she wanted to die, her human spirit was fighting with every breath. Over the past week she'd adjusted her attitude and accepted the food she was offered. Deep down inside, she knew that the dark cell would be her final resting place. She'd already made her peace with God, and she was now waiting for the Angel of Death to pay her a visit. The rapes and beatings had stopped, and for that she was grateful. She also noticed that she was no longer being left alone. It seemed that whenever she was awake, she heard the voices of men speaking in Spanish. Once again the lights came on. That normally meant someone was approaching. Moments later her visitor appeared.

"How are you, bitch? I've brought you more grub."

He unlocked and opened the cell door. After setting the food on the cold concrete slab, he removed a cuff from one of her wrists. She'd learned not to smart off anymore. He patted her on her head.

"That's a good girl! Hey, guess what? You're gonna have company." He laughed harshly. "I'll bet you can't wait!"

DISTURBING NEWS

Trying to keep up with what was happening on the streets, Dad and I were sitting in the living room watching the evening news. There was a report on the upcoming Governor's Ball, and the reporter was interviewing the chef in his kitchen. He was displaying each of his entrées and a variety of French desserts.

"Look at that food!" I said.

"It sure does look good."

"I could go for one of those lobsters right now!"

"Well, son, maybe after all of this mess is over, I'll treat you to one."

Next they showed a wide-angle view of the ballroom. That's when my cellphone rang and the screen said Candee Harris, so I answered it.

"Sherman here."

"Are you sitting down?"

"What's up?"

"Some really bad news just came over on my police scanner."

"Damn, now what?"

My *damn* got Dad's attention.

"They just found the governor's car out on the Kennedy. The driver and his bodyguard are dead. They both took a slug in the head, point blank."

"Jesus Christ! What about the governor?"

"He's missing. I'm en route to the scene right now. Turn on your TV!"

"Candee, wait! Call me back tonight. We need to talk!"

"Okay."

CLICK.

I hung up, picked up the remote and changed the channel to WLOK.

"What's going on?" Dad asked.

"He has the governor!"

"I don't believe it!"

"Lopez is going to kill them both! In his sick mind he believes that Mr. Cartwright, D.A. White, and Governor Evans are responsible for him being busted down to uniform. The worst part is that he's already had all these people killed that didn't have a damn thing to do with it!"

"Why do you want that Candee Harris woman to call you back?"

"Believe it or not, Dad, she may be able to help us."

"For the life of me, son, I don't know why you screw around with that woman!"

"Look, I want to schedule a meeting here tomorrow."

"Who do you want to meet with?"

"I want to get together with Agent Calvin, Max, and the two of us. I think we have the pieces to this puzzle, need to get together and figure this thing out. I get the feeling we're at the doorstep but don't know it. There's something over there in the Pullman area. It's right in front of our face, but we can't see it."

"Son, I really don't believe the Feds are going to be willing to work with us."

"Normally I'd agree with you, but they've got bodies piling up, and they're not getting anywhere. Not only that, they've got the manpower. We can't go to the police, because Lopez will find out."

"I still don't see how this Candee woman can be any help."

"That network she works for has archives on every major item or event that's ever taken place in this city. That includes commercial buildings, buildings that are vacant that would make the ideal place for Lopez to do his dirt."

"So why would she be willing to help?"

"She'd do anything to get the lead story."

"I should've known! Son, I realize that this is a huge mess, but if it's all the same to you, I'd rather be in my own home while you guys track this nut down. Why don't you contact Agent Calvin and see what you can work out?"

"Okay, but we may have to wait a while. I'd imagine he's out at the scene investigating the governor's disappearance."

While Dad and I were talking, I was keeping my eyes on the TV, and I noticed that Candee had appeared on the scene.

"Hold on, Dad, there she is."

Candee was on the side of the expressway, standing next to the WLOK news van. On the other side of the road was the governor's car surrounded by Feds, as well as the local cops. It appeared that both sides of the expressway were blocked off, and every news station in town was broadcasting live. Candee cut through the usual introductions and got straight to business.

"We're coming to you live from north suburban Park Ridge. Earlier today Governor Phillip Evans was abducted here on this lonely stretch of the Kennedy Expressway. We're sad to report that the bodies of his driver and bodyguard were found inside the car. At this time, a major investigation is taking place by both the Illinois State Police and the FBI. Our sources say the governor had just left O'Hare and was on his way to his hotel in the Loop. He's in town to host his annual fund-raising charity ball. This is the second abduction of a high-profile person in as many weeks. Who's behind these abductions? No one knows. What we do know is that everyone's nerves are on edge. Stay tuned. I'm Candee Harris with the WLOK News Crew."

Even though Candee was always professional on the air, it was clear she'd been shaken by this latest abduction and the murders. For the first time since I'd met her, she showed a vulnerable side. I was proud of her.

"I was thinking, son. That Agent Calvin may not be able to meet with you tomorrow."

"I was thinking the same thing. There's a good chance Max may not be able to make it either. Nevertheless, I'm going to leave them both a message. I don't think Agent Calvin has any idea that Lopez is behind this mess. His whole reason for being here is those gang-bangers. Maybe my knowledge of Lopez will get his attention."

"Good luck with that!"

Later that night Candee did return my call. I was right about her feelings. She didn't sound like her old self. I told her about the conversation that I'd had with Max and pitched my idea to her. She agreed without putting up a fight or asking for anything in return. I thanked her and said good night.

Thirteen

THE CELLMATE

By the time I woke up in the morning, the city of Chicago had become a media nightmare. Any place even remotely related to the governor—from the airport to the police station to his hotel—was crawling with reporters.

I finally heard back from Max, who was furious. He wanted to choke Lopez to death with his bare hands. I told him I had Candee working on the archives. I also told him about my idea for a meeting at my place, and at that point he was up for anything. As he put it, it beat the hell out of being yelled at by his captain. All he needed was a time, and I told him I'd get back to him after I heard from Agent Calvin.

❖❖❖

As Governor Evans was slowly coming to, he felt a strange chill in the air. His first instinct was to jump up in anger, but he was handcuffed to bars. The pain in his wrists immediately brought him back to the cold concrete slab on which he lay. He moaned and yelled out. In the darkness he couldn't see a thing, but he heard a woman's voice.

"There's no use."

"Who's there?" he asked.

"It's no use. We'll never get out of here alive."

"Where are we?" he asked.

"In a jail cell."

"In a jail cell! What in God's name is going on here? I demand to be released!"

"If I were you, I'd just settle down."

"Who are you, anyway?" he asked.

"Not that it matters, but I'm D.A. Margret White."

"Oh my Lord, the entire nation is looking for you!"

"Well, soon they'll be looking for you too, whoever you are."

The governor could tell that her spirit had been completely broken.

"I'm Governor Evans."

"Judge, is that you?"

"Yes, it's me. Who the hell is behind this?"

Right about then the lights came on, and there stood Lopez.

"I am, sir!"

The governor looked up.

"Officer Lopez! Are you crazy? Release us at once!"

"I can't do that, Governor. This isn't your courtroom, and you ain't running shit! Now shut up!"

That's when the governor realized that the chill he was feeling was due to the fact that he wasn't wearing anything. He could also see that D.A. White too was naked and had been beaten.

"What have you done to this poor woman? Can't you see she needs medical attention?"

"I didn't do anything to her. Hey, isn't this a nice reunion? Three old buddies back together again!" Lopez said.

"What's the meaning of this?" the governor asked.

"You know, Judge, you should be more like your cellmate and keep your mouth shut. By the way, she's also a lot smarter than you. Tell him why we're here, honey."

"Officer Lopez blames us for his demotion."

"Demotion?" the governor said.

"It looks like you have a piss-poor memory, Judge! You do remember the Lipstick Murders, don't you?" Lopez said.

"My God, that was over two years ago!" the governor said. "D.A. White had nothing to do with that. Let her go!"

"That's awful gallant of you, Judge, but if I were you, I wouldn't be doing a whole lot of bragging right now."

"What do you plan on doing to us?" the governor asked.

"You're the big man. What do you think?"

"Is it money you want?"

"Judge, every time you open your mouth, you insult me more."

"You'll never get away with this, Lopez!"

"Okay, have it your way!"

Lopez stepped away for a few minutes and returned with a rag and a roll of duct tape. He unlocked the cell door, and the governor again tried to free himself without success. His wrists were bleeding from the handcuffs. Lopez grabbed his head and jerked it around. The governor pulled his head back, so Lopez sucker punched him in the stomach, and he folded in pain. On Lopez's second attempt, the governor kept still while Lopez stuffed his mouth with the rag and wrapped the tape around his head.

When Lopez turned to walk away, the governor struggled to moan something, which earned him a swift backhand. When his face flew back, it made immediate contact with Lopez's fist. There was now blood soaking the duct tape, and the governor's nose was broken as well.

During the beating, D.A. White couldn't help but scream. That's when Lopez yelled out, "Be quiet, or you'll be next!"

Lopez closed and locked the cell door. Shortly after that, the lights went off.

With the exception of Oliver Cartwright, he had completed his plan.

As Lopez stood looking in the mirror in the restroom, he straightened his tie and thought about how he'd kill the two of them. Maybe he should just let them starve and let the rats finish them off? He checked one more time to make sure his uniform met department standards before going back on patrol.

He drove through town like he owned it, but he knew that sooner or later, he'd be asked to join some task force. He'd be forced to participate in the search for the D.A. and the governor. It might be fun, but mostly it would be a waste of his time. He didn't want to be away from his "guests" for too long, because he didn't quite trust his gangbanger buddies. After all, they had screwed up the hit on Cartwright. He didn't mind them having a little fun with D.A. White, but still they weren't the brightest bunch. They knew he now had what he wanted, and it was just a matter of time before they wanted to move on to other things.

❖❖❖

Just about midmorning, I got a call from Candee.

"Hi, I didn't think I'd hear from you so soon."

"Well, after what I saw yesterday, I decided to take a day off. I can access the studio's archives from my home computer."

"How convenient."

"For starters, I see a bank building. It used to be the Pullman Bank."

"I wonder if it has a basement."

"I don't know. It doesn't give me that kind of information. I also see the old Hotel Florence."

"That would be a great place too, but it's a landmark if I'm not mistaken, and there would be too much traffic. What else do you see?"

"I see a couple of supermarkets, but mostly vacant apartment buildings. There are some new places, but they're all occupied."

"Well, it was worth a try. Thanks, Candee."

"Hey, don't give up so easy! I'm going to keep on looking, and I'll call you back if anything catches my eye. You see, Sherman, I can be nice without asking for anything in return."

"You're right, and I'm sorry for thinking anything else. Bye, Candee."

CLICK.

I was thinking that this thing must really have Candee shaken up. As I was putting my phone down, it rang again. This time it was Special Agent Calvin.

"This is Sherman."

"What's this about a meeting?"

"I'd like to get together with you and Detective Little."

"I'm kind of pressed for time. This thing with the governor is out of control."

"The information that the detective and I have is directly tied to the governor. I know how busy you are, but I think it will be worth your time."

"Okay, when?"

"We're ready when you are."

"Let's say an hour from now."

"Great, I'll see you then."

CLICK.

My Crazy Plan

I immediately called Max and told him that Agent Calvin was in. While waiting for the guys to arrive, I sat dwelling on all that had happened since I met Lopez. When I thought back, he always did have the capacity to do something like this. I guess it was just a matter of time before he went over the edge. I tried to look at all of the possibilities we had regarding him. I was afraid if he found out the Feds were on to him, as well as Max, he might force our hand, and if that happened, we might never find D.A. White and the governor. That was assuming they were still alive.

I went to the kitchen to tell my dad the guys were coming over.

"That's good. Maybe it's a step in the right direction. When the meeting's over, do you think one of them can drop me off?"

"I'm sure one of them will, but first we still need to clear it with Agent Calvin."

"You're not going to believe this, son, but while you were on the phone I had the TV on, and guess what? They're still going to have that ball tonight. The Lt. Governor is going to host it. He says it's what the governor would've wanted."

"That actually gives me an idea!"

"Come on, I know you're not thinking about crashing that ball."

"Why not? Can you imagine how Lopez would react if he saw Angie and me there?"

"I imagine he'd be pretty pissed off."

"I've got a tux in the closet that's been waiting for an evening just like this!"

"Well, son, from my point of view you've got problems."

"Like what?"

"For starters, there are Angie and Agent Calvin."

"I'm going to call Angie now, before Calvin gets here."

I speed dialed the City Block.

"City Block, Carman speaking."

"Carman, it's me."

"Sherman, how are you?"

"I'm good, honey, but I'm kind of in a hurry! Can I speak with Angie?"

"Angie? Well it's about damned time!"

"Carman, please, just put her on the phone."

I could her Carman yelling in the background.

"The phone is for you, Angie. It's lover boy!"

A few moments passed before Angie got on the phone.

"Angie speaking. Who is this?"

I could picture Carman looking right down Angie's throat, the same way that Barney looked at me.

"Angie, it's Sherman. I know you're not going to understand this, but do you have a formal evening gown?"

"I think I do, but why are you asking?"

"It's a long story, but I need a date for tonight."

"Tonight? Where are you going?"

"I may be going to the Governor's Ball."

"You're kidding, right?"

"It would mean a lot to me, Angie."

"Sherman, I don't know."

"Just think about it, okay? I'll call you back in an hour and a half. And tell Carman she can get back to work now!"

"Okay."

CLICK.

A few minutes later there was a knock at my door. I looked through the peephole and saw that Max and Agent Calvin had arrived at the same time. We all took a seat in my living room, and Agent Calvin got the ball rolling.

"So, what is this information you two have been sitting on?"

I looked at Max and then spoke up.

"To the best of my knowledge, you guys came to town tailing MS-13, and that's when all hell broke loose. I think we all can agree that things have only gotten worse. I'm going to take you back to where it all started with me."

While I was talking, I opened my laptop and started a slide show of front-page stories covering the Lipstick Murders.

"For starters, there's a police officer name Ricardo Lopez. He and I go back a few years. Once upon a time I was his favorite whipping post. He slapped me around whenever he felt like it. Now, let's move up to a couple of years ago. Lopez is now a decorated lieutenant, and still kicking my ass, I might add. One day we crossed paths while working on the Lipstick Murders."

"Wait a minute," Agent Calvin said. "You were working that case? Sherman Brothers, you're the guy who was in that Corvette!"

"That was me. All of the charges against me were dropped."

"Why were they dropped?" the agent asked.

"They were dropped because of film footage showing him and me collaborating over the case. There was also additional footage of him beating the hell out of me. My attorney, Oliver Cartwright, blew his testimony out of the water. The result was the A.D.A.'s case going down like a lead balloon. Lopez embarrassed the entire legal system. Following the trial, he was demoted down to uniform. Since then he's gone completely off the edge. The guy from the alarm company down in Texas, it was Lopez who got to him. Not only that, he put the contract out."

"What contract?" Agent Calvin asked.

"The contract put out on the three major players in the Lipstick Murders trial. Those people are Cartwright, D.A. White, and the governor."

"You're saying these are revenge hits?"

"Think about it. First the D.A. disappears, and then there was the attempt on Cartwright's life at my dad's place."

"So what does the governor have to do with this?"

"At the time, he was the judge presiding over the trial."

"I've heard enough!" the agent said. "I believe you."

"But there's more," Max said. "Lopez used to be my partner when we were rookie cops. He was the nastiest son of a bitch you'd ever want to meet! He was so out of control I put in for a transfer. He didn't like that and made my life a living hell. To bring you up to date, I've kept him under surveillance for years. For the last three weeks I've been tailing him down to the South Side, to an area called Pullman."

"As in George Pullman?"

"You know about that?"

"Not the area itself, but I'm kind of a railroad buff. He created the Pullman Car."

"Well, each time I tail him over there, he disappears into thin air. We believe there's an abandoned building where he's keeping the D.A. and Governor Evans."

"Why do you guys think that?" Agent Calvin asked.

"For one thing, it's not his turf, and the other day he tried to kill me after we had words at a briefing. He ran me off the road, sent me flying into a storefront."

"I saw that on the news," the agent said. "But let me make sure I'm hearing this right. This guy is responsible for multiple deaths, attempted murders, and the kidnapping of two high-profile people?"

"You've got it." Max said.

"Well, let's take this bastard down!"

"I like the way you think, but there's a problem," Max said. "If we take him out now, we run the risk of never finding the D.A. and the governor."

"So what do we do now?"

"We know MS-13 has his back. We also know we can't go to the department, because Lopez will know we're on to him. Calvin, you have the manpower. Let's start grabbing these bangers and squeeze them."

"Do you have any other ideas?"

That's when I interrupted Max and looked at Agent Calvin.

"It's a long shot, but we can start flipping every abandoned building in the Pullman area. We've already narrowed it down to the type of building Lopez would need. Oh, there's something we forgot. The day after Lopez ran Max off the road, Max was here and parked right outside. One of your men brought us a note that Lopez left on the windshield of Max's squad."

"So what did the note say?"

"THE NEXT TIME I WON'T MISS!" Max said.

"Didn't that bastard know the cameras were rolling?"

"I guess not."

"That's as good as an admission of guilt to me," the agent said.

"Yes, sir, it is," Max agreed.

It was now time for me to throw my curveball at Max and Agent Calvin.

"You guys know that the Governor's Ball is still going to go on tonight."

Max nodded.

"I'm pretty sure Lopez will be part of the security detail," I said.

"The nerve of that bastard!" Agent Calvin said.

"Well, we never said he doesn't have balls. Anyway, I have an idea. Max, I know you won't like it, and Calvin, you're going to think I've lost my mind. Now, before you guys freak out, just listen to what I have to say. I want to go to the ball tonight."

Max was the first to speak up.

"So far you're right about losing your mind!"

"I also have a very special date in mind," I said.

"Don't stop now," Agent Calvin said.

"It's the woman Lopez tried to put behind bars for the Lipstick Murders."

Max looked at Agent Calvin.

"Do you want to ask him, or should I do it?"

"You can do it," Calvin said.

"Are you crazy?"

"Look guys," I said, "once he sees the two of us there, he'll completely say or do something really stupid! Calvin, your guys will be right there to grab him. He may even go running to his little hole in Pullman."

"I can see where you're going with this," Max said. "But it doesn't mean he'll lead us to the governor. You'll also be risking this woman's life."

"The place is going to be crawling with cops," I said.

Agent Calvin spoke up.

"If something happens to this woman, both the detective's and my career will be finished. What's your plan for getting into the ball?"

"I was kind of hoping you could work something out," I said.

"Why of course you were," Agent Calvin said. "I have to tell you, Sherman, I don't think much is going to come from this."

The two men took deep breaths and threw up their hands in surrender. It was killing him, but Max said he was in. Agent Calvin shook his head, but then he also agreed.

"Great! Do you guys want to see my tux?" I asked.

"Don't push it, Sherman," Max said.

"Agent Calvin, there's one more thing," I said.

"Of course there is."

"My dad would really like to go home."

"That's the most reasonable thing you've said since I got here. Tell him let's go."

Max couldn't help but start laughing.

Fourteen

PARTY TIME

After the guys left, I called Angie back. She was still a little apprehensive, but she wanted to go to the ball. I had to admit, I was a little excited myself. Ordinarily something like that wouldn't move me much. I'd never been one to hobnob with big money, but as long as I was going to be there, I might as well make the most of it. It was now six p.m., and the ball was scheduled to start at eight p.m. I started to get dressed. I didn't want to blend in with the other guests. It was important that Lopez see us.

I checked and double-checked myself from head to toe. Aside from a little pain in the ribs, I looked really good, but I also knew Angie would be the one turning heads. I didn't want to make her look bad, but once I felt confident, I strapped my 380 to my ankle. It was too bad India wasn't there to see me. It was nearly seven p.m. when Agent Calvin showed up at my door. He was shocked to see the transformation I'd gone through.

"You sure don't look like you're going to work."

I gave Angie a call and told her I was on my way. When we got to her place, she was standing in the lobby of her building. When I opened the door she stepped out, and for a moment I was completely taken back. She looked incredibly lovely. She was wearing an outrageous long black gown with a slit up to her thigh. She wore black high heels and the whole nine. From her ears dangled white gold bars with five diamonds running the length. Around her neck was a thin white gold chain with an oval-shaped diamond resting above her cleavage. Around her right wrist were four white gold bands. Her lips were bathed in red, and her hair was in a bun. Even with her glasses on, she was a complete knockout.

I extended my elbow, and she took my arm. When we got to the government-issued black SUV, Agent Calvin was standing with the back door open. It was then that he and I both noticed that the gown Angie was wearing was backless. For first time ever, I was thinking that maybe Carman was on to something. Calvin closed the door behind us, jumped in, and we were off.

"Good evening Miss Cruz. I'm Special Agent Calvin."

Angie was looking at me, but responding to Calvin.

"Hi, it's a pleasure to meet you."

I hadn't exactly been clear to her about what was going on tonight. That's why I got the strange look from her. As we rode along, Agent Calvin reached in his pocket and took out two small items.

"Here, take these. The American flag is a microphone. Pin it to your lapel. Take the little cone-shaped piece and stick it in your ear as far as it will go."

I did as he instructed.

"Okay, I got it."

"Detective Little and I will be outfitted with the same equipment. Oh, there's one more thing. This little venture is putting quite a dent in my expense account!"

I smiled at him in the rearview mirror, and he smiled back. Angie was the only one not smiling. In fact, she gave me a little elbow in my side. The bad part was that she didn't know it really hurt. I guess my tux made her think I was as good as new. During the rest of our ride I informed her of what was going on. She couldn't wait to see the look on Lopez's face. However, she was imagining a completely different picture than I was.

When we pulled into the downtown area, one out of every three or four cars was a limo. As we got closer to the hotel, we could see three rotating lights pointing up into the sky, like a car dealership advertising a huge sale. As we rode up, I saw Lopez standing on the sidewalk, talking to another cop.

"Hey, Calvin, there's our boy at two o'clock."

"I see him. Why don't you roll down your window and I'll creep along."

As I rolled down the window, Lopez was watching, and he noticed the government-issued vehicle. He looked me straight in the eyes, but I don't think he recognized me. Maybe it was too hard for him to believe. Agent Calvin stopped the vehicle right in front of the hotel entrance.

"Hey, Calvin, I need a favor."

I reached down and removed my 380 from the holster.

"Can you take this in for me?"

"Sherman, you're killing me, man!"

"Come on, they've got to have some kind of metal detector at the door."

"Okay, I'll meet you in the john later. By the way, your name is on the guest list."

Agent Calvin then got out and came around to our door and opened it. While I was helping Angie out of the car, I could see Lopez on the sidewalk trying to focus on us. Again I extended my elbow, and Angie took my arm. In my ear I could hear Agent Calvin telling me to scratch the back of my head if I could hear him. I did as requested.

"Great, good luck in there," the agent said.

After a series of smiles and being overly polite, we made our way through the hotel lobby. The strangest thing happened when we passed a small table by an armchair. On the table were several magazines, and one of them had India on the cover. For a moment I was stung. Angie stopped walking and looked at me.

"Are you okay, Sherman? You look like you've seen a ghost."

"Oh, I'm fine."

We were greeted by hotel staff at the entrance to the ballroom. Before we stepped in, I turned to Angie.

"I want to thank you for coming."

"I'm glad I came."

"I also want to say you look absolutely lovely!"

"Sherman, you're embarrassing me!"

"I'm going to be the envy of every man in this place!"

"Please stop!"

"Okay, are you ready?"

"I guess so."

A staff member escorted us to our table, where he pulled out the chair for Angie. Tonight I'd be doing my best to be a gentleman and make Angie feel like a queen. Almost immediately, one of our servers was pouring champagne into crystal flutes for us. In my ear I could hear Max talking to Agent Calvin.

"Does that gorgeous woman know she's with Sherman?"

I smiled, and Angie asked me what I was smiling at. I told her I was just having a good time. When the guests had all arrived, the orchestra stopped playing, and the lieutenant governor stepped up to the microphone on the stage.

"Good evening, everyone. Welcome to the Governor's Annual Fundraising Ball. Before we get started, I'd like to ask everyone to bow their heads for a moment of silence as we ask for the safe return of Governor Evans and D.A. White."

After a few moments, he began to speak again.

"A lot of people have been asking why I'm going ahead with the governor's plan to have this ball. The answer is quite simple. This is the way he would've wanted it."

There was a round of cheers.

"This year we're lending a hand to breast cancer research."

The cheers came again.

"Please, everyone, eat, drink, and be merry!"

That's when the orchestra broke into their rendition of the classic "Moonlight Serenade," and I extended my hand to Angie.

"Oh, Sherman, you don't have to do this!"

"Are you kidding? It's a privilege!"

I stood up, and she joined me as I led her to the dance floor. She was very light on her feet and smelled like heaven. Maybe it was my imagination, but it seemed like when I held her tighter, she held me tighter also. I had to remind myself of why I was there. In her ear I asked her if she was having a good time.

"Yes, I am, even though you are on the job."

"Well, don't think of it like that."

"So, I'm supposed to think that after all of these years, you picked tonight to kill two birds with one stone?"

"Can we just enjoy ourselves without the deep conversation?"

"I'm sorry. I didn't mean to corner you like that."

"Why don't we call it even?"

"Do you know any of these people, Sherman?"

"Not really."

"Well, they're looking at us like they know you."

"You still don't believe me, do you?"

"Will you stop it?"

"Okay. Look around the dance floor and see how many men smile at you."

Angie turned her head slightly.

"Okay."

"Now look around and see how many women don't."

"But they don't know me!"

"If I were on the floor with another woman, I'd be looking over her shoulder at you, even if I were madly in love with her."

"Sherman, that's the sweetest thing any man has ever said to me! Can I ask you something?"

"Sure."

"Why do you think it never happened for us?"

"Remember, Angie, no deep conversation. Look, I'll say this and then no more. It's not because of you. In my book, you're as perfect as they come."

Angie pulled back and gave me a strange look.

"Is that printed in some kind of stupid male manual?"

I just laughed and kissed her on the cheek. Oops, where the hell did that come from? In my mind I was thinking *Quick, Sherman, do something!* So I released her and spun her around. Just as she returned to my arms, the music came to an end. Thank God!

While we were heading back to our table, a photographer stepped in front of us.

"Would you folks like an everlasting memory of this wonderful evening?"

Angie turned to me.

"Carman will kill me if we don't!"

"In that case, let's make it look good!" I said.

I stepped close and wrapped my arms around her waist. We smiled, and the flash went off.

"Thank you, Sherman. She's going to love this."

"I bet she is!"

"Why do you guys treat each other like that?"

"It's just the way we say I love you."

"Well, I think you two are silly."

Shortly after we sat back down, our waiter arrived to take our order. Angie ordered the lobster, and I had the roast duck. I wanted the lobster, but I reserved it for a meal out with my dad.

After the waiter walked away, Angie asked, "What was that you did on the dance floor?"

"What was what?" I asked innocently. Thankfully, right then I heard Agent Calvin in my ear.

"Why don't you meet me in the john and get this thing?"

I lowered my head and said softly, "Okay, Good timing!"

"Angie, Agent Calvin would like to meet me in the restroom."

"I know why too!"

"You're not going to run off with another man, are you?" I teased.

She rolled her eyes at me as more champagne was being poured. I excused myself from the table and took off. In the restroom, we made the exchange quickly, and I put my 380 back in the holster. When I stepped back out I saw Lopez had made his way into the ballroom, and he was headed toward our table. I spoke into my lapel pin.

"Max, do you see what's happening?"

"Yeah, I'm all over it!"

Lopez reached the table before Max did and was verbally attacking Angie.

"Are you going to poison your boyfriend, bitch?"

That's when Angie stood up and threw her champagne in his face. Just when he was about to lose it, Max stepped into the picture.

"Is there a problem here?"

"There's no freaking problem, Detective!" Lopez snarled.

"Well, don't you have something to do outside?"

"Yeah, sure I do!" Lopez said. When he turned around to leave, he walked right into me.

"Can't you beat cops afford a tux?"

"Fuck you, punk!" he said, spittle hitting my face.

"Where's your date?" I asked.

"I've got a date all right! She's at home tied up and waiting for big daddy!"

I stepped out of his path, and he stormed out of the ballroom. I looked at Max and smiled.

"Do you think that will do it?"

"I'd bet the farm on it," Max said.

"Good! Mission accomplished!"

I looked at Angie.

"Please forgive my rudeness, Angie. This is Detective Maxwell Little of the Chicago Police Department, and this is my lovely date, Miss Angie Cruz."

"It's a pleasure to meet you, Detective, and I must say you look far nicer tonight than you did when you were hanging around the City Block."

"I'm sorry for giving you guys the creeps. Right now I'd better get outside and make sure our boy isn't out there stealing hubcaps! It was nice to meet you, Miss Cruz."

After Max walked away, we sat down and enjoyed our dinner. A glass of chardonnay was poured for Angie and a glass of cabernet for me. With a strange expression on her face, Angie stopped eating for a moment.

"Can I ask you something, Sherman?"

"It's not anything deep, is it?"

"No, and you can stop worrying! Did you guys come here tonight just to piss that man off?"

"Yes, we did. He's up to something no good and we were trying to make him lose his cool and screw up, but that's all I can say. Just for the record I'd like to say there's no reason why we shouldn't enjoy a night out."

"Well, that man gives me the creeps!"

"He gives everyone the creeps!"

"You know, Sherman, despite everything, I feel good tonight."

"Seeing that Uncle Sam is picking up the tab, I feel good too!"

FIFTEEN

DANGEROUS TRAFFIC

The rest of the night couldn't have gone better. After eating, Angie and I danced and laughed the night away. I can't remember the last time the two of us had been able to sit down and talk. I was amazed that there was no man in her life. I swear that if it weren't for India, I'd have reconsidered my options.

After the crowd started thinning out, Max joined us at our table. The photo we took came out great. We actually looked like a couple that belonged together. It was inside a decorative cardboard frame that had "The Governor's Ball" printed on it. I took one good look at it and gave it to Angie to keep.

In my ear, I heard Agent Calvin asking if we were ready to roll.

"Well, Angie, it looks like our carriage is about to turn into a pumpkin!"

"Oh, is it time to go?"

I could hear the disappointment in her voice.

"I'm afraid so."

During the ride home, I noticed that every three or four blocks, a black SUV would cross the intersection, either in front of us or behind us. Agent Calvin was still on the job. He had his men working a grid as they tailed us home. When we got about halfway between Hyde Park and the near downtown area, Calvin looked at me in the rearview mirror. He had a strange look in his eyes. I looked behind us and saw what he'd seen. It was a low rider tailing us. That's when he raised his hand and spoke into his sleeve.

"Okay, everyone, here we go!"

The low rider was speeding up quickly, and Angie asked me what was going on. I reached down and pulled out my 380, and pulled Angie's head down to my lap. The low rider then pulled up beside us and its windows went down. At the same time, two AK-47 assault rifles were stuck out the windows, and that's when Agent Calvin slammed on the brakes. The low rider flew past us and went straight into the intersection, where it was T-boned by a city bus. The car flipped over from right to left twice.

Coming around the side of the bus was a black SUV. Agent Calvin yelled into his microphone, "Don't shoot! Don't shoot, we need them alive!"

I told Angie to stay down as we got out of the car. The low rider had landed on its smashed-in rooftop. The driver was dead, and the other two passengers were racked up, stuck inside the vehicle. In a matter of minutes, there were all kinds of emergency vehicles at the scene. By now Angie had decided to get out of the SUV. I ran to her and took her in my arms.

"Are you okay?"

"I'm fine," she said.

"Are you sure?"

"Yes, yes!"

"I'm sorry, Angie, I really am!"

"What are you talking about?" she said. "To me it looks like you saved my life again!"

My emotions were running high, and for a few moments, I just stared at her. The Fire Department arrived and had to cut the gangbangers out of the wrecked vehicle. They were definitely Lopez's boys, all right. There was even a program from the Governor's Ball inside the vehicle. As we stood taking it all in, Angie got my attention.

"Sherman, I don't feel comfortable going home knowing that man is still out here on the streets."

"I don't blame you." At that point, I knew what was coming.

"Can I stay at your place tonight, and tomorrow I'll work something out?"

Before I could answer her, Calvin broke in and said, "That's not a bad idea."

That's when Max showed up.

"Hey, guys, listen up! Lopez didn't check out, and he's not answering his radio! It's only a matter of time before my captain starts asking questions!"

"About how long do you think that will take," I asked.

"I'd say if he doesn't pop up by tomorrow with a damned good excuse, his ass is toast! That little show he put on at the Governor's Ball somehow got back to my captain."

"Okay, that's it! Angie, you're staying at my place."

Agent Calvin felt he had to take over.

"Look, Detective Little, I know you don't want to, but I think it's time we bring your captain in on our little game. If he puts a bulletin out on Lopez, he's going to run, and I really believe those two people are still alive. The way he's been killing people, I'm sure we would've found their bodies by now. I'll tell you what. Why don't you let me talk to your captain? That way he can't nail you for not speaking up. I'll tell him I asked you for your cooperation. For now let's all try to get some rest tonight, and tomorrow we'll work something out."

Angie and I climbed back into the SUV, and Agent Calvin took us to my place. Before we got out of the vehicle, I told him I guessed that this wasn't such a good idea after all. Right away I could see he was a bit disappointed with my attitude.

"Don't start blaming yourself now. I still need you. We're going to get this bastard, Sherman! I've been here a hundred times. These guys always screw up. Get some sleep. I still have one of my guys across the hall in the apartment if you need anything. Good night."

Inside my place, I told Angie to make herself at home.

"You've got a nice place. I've never been here before."

"I thought all of you guys had been here at one time or another."

While we were talking, I went to the hall closet to get some fresh linen for the sofa. Feeling kind of nervous, I continued rambling. When I returned to the living room, Angie had taken off her heels, stretched out on the sofa, and had fallen asleep. She looked like Sleeping Beauty. I sat down on the edge of the sofa and gently rubbed the back of my hand across her cheek. She half woke up, and I placed a pillow under her head. I removed her glasses and was startled to discover how some features on her face reminded me of myself. It was really strange.

I gently placed a blanket over her and headed to my bedroom. As I walked away, I heard her softly say, "Thank you, Sherman." I got in bed and let out a long breath. I'd been expecting a tense, uncomfortable situation between the two of us at my place. Maybe it was my imagination, but for a moment at the ball, I thought Angie had feelings for me. I now lay there wondering where she was going to stay tomorrow. God forbid that India would pay me another surprise visit. Maybe tomorrow Angie could stay with Carman, and if Lopez showed up, Carman could nag him to death!

Tossing and turning, I couldn't fall asleep. A couple of times I even got up to check on Angie. To my surprise, she was sleeping, but roughly. She was also mumbling in her sleep. I could hardly make out what she was saying, but it sounded like something about a brother, and she kept repeating Carman's name. It was weird.

I felt guilty, like I was listening in on a private conversation. The investigator in me made it hard to walk away. I went back to my room and sat on the side of my bed. It was then that I noticed the light blinking on my phone. I checked it and found I had five messages from Carman and one from Louie. I decided to listen to the one from Louie.

SHERMAN, PLEASE GIVE CARMAN A CALL! SHE'S DRIVING ME NUTS ABOUT YOU AND ANGIE!

I laughed to myself and erased the messages. I never got any real sleep, and by five a.m. I gave up. I got up and went to take a shower. Finally I got dressed in the bathroom and then went to the kitchen to make a pot of coffee. On my way to the kitchen, I was stunned to see that Angie was no longer on the sofa. My heart started racing, and I went into tactical mode. Running to my bedroom to get my pistol, I froze. While I was in the bathroom, Angie had gotten up from the sofa and climbed into my bed. Now that was not a good thing.

I grabbed my phone and went back into the kitchen. I had to get this woman off of my mind. I knew Dad was an early riser, so I gave him a call. I wanted to tell him about last night's events, but he immediately started talking about the repairs at his place. Finally I got the chance to tell all that had happened.

For some reason, he was overly concerned about Angie's safety. I thought that was strange, since he'd never shown any particular feelings toward her. Anyway, I went on talking and told him that Agent Calvin and I agreed that it was best that Angie stay at my place.

"Well, how is that going, son?" he asked.

"I guess it's going okay."

"I know you, and something's bugging you. What's up?"

"Well, Dad, last night I got up and went to the living room to check on her. I feel horrible! She was talking in her sleep and saying something about a brother."

I must have touched a nerve with my dad, because he didn't say anything.

"I know I shouldn't have listened," I said, feeling guilty.

I waited for his comment, but he remained silent until I said his name.

"Dad, are you still there?"

"Sorry, I got distracted. Son, I wouldn't pay too much attention to that. It sounds like she was just babbling. If I were you, I'd just forget about it."

DAD FLASHED BACK

The last thing I need is for Sherman to go nosing around in my past. I feel like I did my fatherly duty when I saved Angie's life a couple of years ago, and I was really starting to feel good about myself. I need to shorten this conversation by telling Sherman that I need to get my day started.

"Keep in touch, son, and take care of yourself."

"Okay, Dad."

CLICK.

MISS SUNSHINE, A.K.A. CARMAN

I poured myself a mug of coffee and turned on the small TV on the kitchen counter. With all that had happened I really wasn't paying too much attention to the TV. I was thinking about what to do with Angie when my cellphone rang. This early in the morning, I knew it could only be one person.

"Good morning, Carman."

In the background I could hear Barney barking. I really missed the little guy.

"Well, it's about damned time! Did you guys elope or something? Where is she?"

"Calm down! She's in bed. I mean…"

"You mean what? Please tell me you didn't take advantage of her!"

"Have you taken a good look at your friend?"

"You're a pig!"

"I didn't do anything to her!"

That's when I felt a hand on my shoulder. A few hairs had fallen out of place and were covering one of Angie's eyes. My God, this woman was sexy even when she'd just woken up. She knew it had to be Carman on the phone.

"Let me speak to her, Sherman."

"Please do."

"Hey, girl, I'm fine. It was great! I had a wonderful time. He was an absolute gentleman. No, he really was. Yes, I did. I tried to sleep on the sofa, but I couldn't get comfortable. Besides, he wasn't with me. I don't know. He had left the room when I got there. Well, I didn't think he'd mind. I don't, girl, but I've got to get out of this dress."

I could tell that Carman was interrogating Angie, and I had a picture in my mind that I didn't want to see.

"He'll give me something. I can't just walk around in my underwear."

Now she was just playing with my head. I got up and left Angie talking on the phone. In my bedroom I took out some sweatpants, a tee shirt, and a pair of flipflops that I'd never worn. I laid them all out on the bed for Angie. Moments later she walked in.

"Here's your phone. I'm sorry if I ran you out of your bed last night."

"That's okay. I wasn't sleeping very well anyway."

"Look, I know I'm making you feel uncomfortable. If you want, I'll find some place safe to go to."

"You're fine."

I then motioned toward the things on the bed.

"These things are for you. I hope they'll be all right."

"Sherman, we've got to get past this. We're not kids, and we only have two choices. We can take the high road and do the right thing, or we can throw caution to the wind. I know you've always seen me as being quiet and cautious, but I'm also a human being. Now we can do this and keep it a secret, and ruin years of a wonderful friendship, or we can leave our lives intact, the way they are. It's up to you."

"What do you want to do?"

"You know what I want to do. You don't think I felt something last night on that dance floor when you held me in your arms? And what was that kiss on my cheek all about? This isn't easy for me either! Over the years I've watched women walk in and out of your life like it was an open door. I know you didn't have to take me to that ball, but you did."

Now tears were running down Angie's cheeks.

"I wake up in your bed, and now I stand here looking like a fool! If you're going to make love to me, you'd better be sure of what you're doing. The clock is running."

Once again I was looking down the barrel of my life. This time I was responsible for two lives. A picture of every woman I'd ever known was passing through my mind. I remembered Rebecca's letter telling me about her dream that I'd find the right woman. Well, that woman was India. I took both of Angie's hands, held them in mine, and looked her in the eyes.

"You're one of the most incredible women I've ever met, but I also think our friendship is incredible as well. Let's keep being strong for each other."

Angie drew in a big breath of air and then let it out.

"Thank you, Sherman, and just for the record, I do love you!"

"And I love you too."

"Can we keep this between us?" she asked.

"I wouldn't have it any other way. Why don't you take a shower and get dressed?"

"Maybe I'll take a nice cold one."

We both laughed as she headed for the bathroom.

Sixteen

THE HOSPITAL VISIT

Man, I was glad that was out of the way. While Angie was taking a shower, I received a call from Max.

"Hey, buddy, did you sleep all right? You should have. I wish I had to take a beautiful, scared woman home with me."

"It's not like that. She's just a friend."

"Right. Anyway, Agent Calvin and I are headed over to the hospital to interview the two punks that survived last night. Do you want to join us?"

"I wouldn't miss it for the world. Let me arrange to have a family member come and stay with Angie."

"That's so sweet of you."

"I know. Let me call Agent Calvin and arrange it."

I called Calvin and dropped another bomb on him. Since he had an agent across the hall, he went along with it. Forty minutes later, he and Carman were at my door. She brought Barney with her, and he jumped straight into my arms.

"Hey, buddy, how you doing? I miss you, pal!"

Calvin said, "Come on, time's flying!"

When I turned to leave, Carman punched my arm.

"What was that for?" I asked.

"That's in case the two of you are lying to me."

Angie just laughed as we walked out the door. As soon as we got into the hallway, I started asking Calvin questions.

"Have you heard anything from the hospital?"

"It doesn't look like these guys are going to make it."

"Then maybe they'll talk."

"I don't know, Sherman. Normally these guys aren't afraid of dying. It's not like they're going to turn to Jesus and confess."

"What if we make them believe they're going to live and do life in prison while Lopez lives large?"

"That may work, but I wouldn't bet the farm on it. Hey, Sherman, off the record, that family member of yours, she's a real firecracker."

"She's a live wire all right. She's a good girl, just a little bold. Her bark is worse than her bite. Maybe when this thing is over, you can drop by the City Block and have a cocktail. You know she's part owner."

"Well, I may just drop in."

Max met us in the lobby of the hospital. They had both of our boys in the same room with a curtain between them. They each had a variety of tubes going into their bodies. One of them had a tube in his mouth, running down his throat. Interviewing him would be out of the question. The other guy was in better shape, but not much. Max and I looked at him and gave each other a strange look. Agent Calvin noticed and asked what was going on. I told him that we knew this guy.

"You guys know this punk?"

"Not exactly, but he's one of the guys that turned over Cartwright's place down in Texas."

To my surprise, Max slapped the guy in the face.

"I'm going to give you one chance to tell us where Lopez is holed up at! If you screw it up, I'm going to unplug this machine that's keeping your ass alive."

"No, you won't, gringo! You're a freaking cop!"

I pushed Max out of the way.

"I'm not a cop, home boy!"

Agent Calvin had been standing on the other side of the curtain, but now he joined us.

"Your buddy over there just brought it! Do you know what that means? I'll tell you what it means. It means six counts of attempted murder and over a dozen counts of premeditated murder. I don't know what they call it where you come from, but in my world that's life in prison!"

That's when I told Calvin he'd forgotten something, and I looked at the guy.

"While you're being treated for the AIDS you'll catch in prison, Lopez will be drinking piña coladas in Cancun."

Finally the punk got the picture, and he spoke up.

"Even if I knew, I'd still do time!"

"That's true," I said.

"Maybe you'll only do time as an accessory, and get out of prison before you need a walker. What are you going to do, amigo?"

Max jumped in again.

"Let's just pull the plug on this jerk! No one will know but us."

Max must've really touched a nerve.

"All right, all right!" the punk said. "I don't know where he's holed up at. Some other guys handle that. I just wait for him to call me. I get instructions and that's it. I don't even know those dudes. They ain't from my 'hood. I was told to do that old man in Texas, but he wasn't home."

"What are you doing in Chicago?" Max asked.

"I was told to come here and wait to be contacted."

"What is Lopez to you?"

"Nobody. I don't even know him. He's just a paying customer."

"Do you know his next move?" Max asked.

"No one does! That guy is loco!"

The three of us stepped out into the hallway, and Agent Calvin asked our opinion of the gangbanger. Max hated to, but he believed what the banger had told us.

"Well, Max, I think it's time," Calvin said.

"You're talking about my captain?"

"I'm sorry, buddy!"

"Why don't you go and do that while Sherman and I go and turn over Lopez's house?"

"Won't you need a warrant?"

"Yeah, but Sherman doesn't!"

Agent Calvin smiled and told us to be careful. He got on his cellphone, and the two of us got on the elevator.

PARTY AT MY PLACE

In the meantime, back at my apartment, Angie had given Carman every detail of the Governor's Ball, including showing her the photograph we took. Carman pushed Angie hard trying to find out if anything special happened between us during the night. Finally she gave up and said she was thirsty.

"What's Sherman got in his kitchen to drink?"

"Girl, I don't know. You're something else!"

Carman took her hand.

"Come on, let's go and see what he has."

The first thing Carman found was a bottle of merlot.

"Help me find a corkscrew."

Just as they sat down to make a toast, Carman's cellphone rang. It was Mai.

"Hey, where are you guys at?"

"We're at Sherman's place, having fun at his expense," Carman said.

"I wanna come!"

"There's a cop outside that's going to stop you. Just tell him you're family."

"I'm on my way."

CLICK.

Carman raised her glass to make a toast.

"Come on Angie, let's toast. Here's to hot guys and small thighs!"

They both giggled and took their first swallow. While the girls were having a good time, Barney was sleeping on my bed. They were halfway through the bottle of merlot when there was a knock at the door. Carman looked through the peephole and saw the agent from across the hall. She opened the door to find Mai standing behind him. He stood with arms folded, a serious look on his face.

"This woman says she's a family member."

A little tipsy now, Carman said, "Yeah, she's my sister."

"What, you want me to believe she's your sister?"

Angie let a giggle slip out.

"I don't know what you ladies are up to, but I don't want any funny business!"

Mai stepped around him and went inside. The agent then closed the door and went back across the hall. Using a deep male voice, Carman stuck her chest out, striking a pose.

"I don't want any funny business!"

The three of them started laughing as Mai reached into her oversized bag.

"I didn't know what to do, so I brought this from the bar."

She had a bottle of white zinfandel and one of chardonnay.

"Put them in the refrigerator, girl!" Carman said. Mai kicked off her shoes and headed for the kitchen. When she returned, she had a glass in her hand. It didn't take long for her to catch up to the others. She suggested some music and started pushing buttons on the stereo until she got some sound. Angie asked her how Louie was doing by himself.

"He's all right. It was kind of slow."

It wasn't long before their little get-together was in full swing. The ladies were feeling good, and the music was sounding good. To Carman it seemed like the right time to put Mai on trial.

"Mai, Angie and I were talking before you got here, and we were wondering."

"No, girl," Angie said. "Carman was wondering."

"You never talk about your love life," Carman said.

"What love life?"

"Girl, you're young and lovely!"

"The truth is that guys my age just want to jump in the sack, and the older guys are full of themselves."

They each held their glasses up, and Carman said, "I'll drink to that." They continued drinking and laughing the time away.

Seventeen

THE LOPEZ SHRINE

In the Uptown area of Chicago, Max and I were cruising the neighborhood where Lopez lived. We were looking for either his personal car or a department squad. Not finding either, we decided to go to his house. He lived in a small brick house, what looked like a two-bedroom. Max released the safety on his weapon as we approached the front door. I reached in my pocket and took out a small coin purse that held a variety of small, odd-shaped tools. I took one out and jiggled the doorknob. When I touched it, it opened slightly. I stepped back, and Max entered with his gun drawn. I pulled mine from its ankle holster and followed him inside.

The living and dining rooms were empty. We went through each room in the house. In one bedroom the drawers had been pulled out and items removed. On the bed was a box that once held 9mm rounds. We went back to the dining room and were shocked at what we had missed when we first entered the house. Max took out his cellphone and immediately called Agent Calvin.

"Hey, it's Max. Where are you?"

"I'm sitting in your captain's office."

"You and the captain better get over here right away! You're not going to believe this shit!"

CLICK.

It appeared that Lopez was what the Feds call a Functioning Murderer, meaning he holds down a job, has a normal social life, but also has the heart of a coldblooded serial killer. On the dining room wall was a total dedication to me that instantly gave me the chills. There were photos of my old girlfriend Maria and me having dinner. There was another photo of Nurse Linda, another mistake in my life, with me at the zoo. There was even one of Candee and me on my dad's boat at the harbor. Each one had a bullseye drawn over my face with a red marker. Off to the side of those photos was one of me and Angie in my car on the day we were arrested two years ago.

The most disturbing of them all was one of Rebecca and me at the lakefront. If Lopez were standing here now, I'd put a bullet between his eyes for that one alone! On the opposite wall were front-page clippings from every single Lipstick Murders case. There were also photos of Mr. Cartwright and D.A. White walking down the steps of the court building. Above all those clippings were four photos of Mr. Cartwright, D.A. White, Governor Evans, and me, all with bullseyes over our faces.

The photos of D.A. White and Governor Evans also had big red X's over their faces, as if Lopez were keeping count of his victims. Max went to his squad and came back with a camera. While he was taking pictures, he stopped and looked at me.

"Sherman, this guy isn't angry, he's sick. That changes everything, my friend!"

It wasn't long before we heard a car come to a sudden stop out front. Moments later, Max's captain and Agent Calvin came running into the house. Neither one of us said a word. We just led them to the dining room. The captain was so pissed off, he threw his handheld radio against the wall, busting it into pieces. He and Calvin stood in one spot rotating, totally amazed at what they were seeing. The captain stopped looking at the wall and turned toward me.

"What's your name, son?"

"I'm Sherman Brothers."

"That's just freaking great. Little!"

"Yes, sir."

"You and Mr. Brothers get the hell out of here! Agent Calvin and I need to talk," the captain said. "There's one more thing, Detective. Good work!"

"Thank you, Captain."

As we drove away, neither of us had much to say. I guess we both were still a little stunned. Finally Max broke the silence.

"Now where do we go?"

"I guess we can go to my place. I've got half a bottle of scotch and a couple beers."

"That does sound good right about now."

"You know the way, buddy."

SURPRISE

When we parked in front of my place, the agent from across the hall greeted us.

"I'm glad you're here. I'm sorry, but I couldn't stop them."

Max immediately drew his sidearm.

"That won't be necessary," the agent said. "Come with me, sir."

He led us to my apartment and swung the door open. We were shocked to see Mai, Angie, and Carman dancing in my living room. The stereo was jamming, and there were three empty wine bottles on my cocktail table. They were all smashed! I couldn't believe it. They didn't even know we'd walked in until I turned the music off. That's when the whole world stopped, and Max looked at me.

"Brother, you sure do know how to live!"

Mai finally saw us and yelled out my name. Angie covered her mouth in embarrassment, and Carman's crazy ass kept on wiggling. That's when I lost it.

"What the hell are you guys doing? Are you trying to get me evicted or something?"

"Sherman, we're just having a little fun," Carman said.

"I don't want to hear it, Carman!" I picked up the three bottles. "A little fun, my ass!"

"Okay, a lot of fun," Carman said.

Believe it or not, the three of them started laughing in my face.

"I'm going to get you all for this!"

"Does that mean we can turn the music back up?" Carman asked.

"I should turn your butt up and spank it. Come on Max, let's go to the kitchen."

I grabbed a couple of glasses and the bottle of scotch.

"Have a seat, buddy."

"Man, Sherman, this scotch is just what I needed. You know, that's quite the Rainbow Coalition you've got out there."

"They all work at the City Block."

"I recognize Angie, but the other two don't ring a bell.

"Well, they all know you from hanging around the bar."

"I feel bad about that."

"Forget about it. In ten seconds Carman's going to come nosing around in here."

I counted off the seconds in my head, and when I reached one, she popped in.

"So, who's your friend, Sherman?"

Max and I smiled at each other.

"What's so funny?" she asked.

"Nothing. This is Detective Maxwell Little with the Chicago Police Department, and this is Carman with the Chicago Nut Squad!"

"I love you too, Sherman!"

"It's a pleasure to meet you," Max said. "I'm sorry for giving you guys the creeps over at the bar."

"So, you're a cop?"

"I'm afraid so."

"Are you married?"

That's when I stepped in.

"Jesus, Carman, talk about giving someone the creeps."

"Sherman," she said, "why don't you go to the living room and take care of your woman?"

"Max, don't pay any attention to her. She's a sick puppy. By the way, where's Barney?"

"He's lying on your bed. Why don't you go check on him?"

"Why don't we all just join the others?" Max said.

The hours rolled on, and it started getting dark outside. There was a lot of laughter, music, and storytelling. Everyone was really taking to Max. The tension between Angie and me was gone, and things were back to normal. After a while, though, we all started running out of gas. One by one, my guests found a spot and crashed out. It was a perfect ending to a less-than-perfect day.

Eighteen

THE BEAT GOES ON

The next couple of days were quiet in the city. I spent most of my time talking to India over the web cam, which she loved. Barney and I hung out a little over at the lakefront. Even Dad was making progress with his house. Life as I knew it was almost normal. The discovery we had made at Lopez's place was kept strictly between the four of us. Even when we did discuss it, it wasn't over the radio. We worried about someone like Candee getting hold of it and going public.

Lopez still hadn't reported in. It had become obvious he'd committed himself to this horrible task. Captain Leonard didn't want to go public with our discovery, because he was hoping Lopez would still lead us to D.A. White and Governor Evans. At that point we believed Lopez was holed up at the same place he was keeping his captives.

The entire Pullman area was under surveillance. There were cops and Feds posing as trash collectors, taxi drivers, you name it. As the days went by, the department was getting more creative with their undercover tactics. It was an attempt to keep the community looking as normal as possible. A lot of federal agents were posing as homeless people. They slept in doorways, alleys, and even picked through trash dumpsters. This was the biggest joint task between the cops and the Feds in the last ten years. There was no way Lopez could slip through the cracks.

In the meantime, Captain Leonard had been leaking information to the press, which they'd taken and run with. The idea was to make Lopez think we still didn't have a clue. So far it appeared to be working. At the same time, we couldn't ignore the fact that we'd found an empty bullet box and signs that he'd packed a bag. If nothing else, he was prepared for an emergency exit.

Back in the cold dark world of D.A. White, her health was deteriorating, and she was hanging on by a thread. Any mention of medical care by her cellmate resulted in him taking a beating. Like D.A. White, Governor Evans was also starting to lose his will to live. When left alone in the darkness, the two tried to console each other. They agreed they were in an abandoned police station. The fact that they were drugged made it impossible for them to know how long they'd been there. Even if they knew where they were, it wouldn't have mattered. In the beginning, they noticed that Lopez would be in uniform when he entered the cell, and they believed they were within city limits.

There were times when they had a false sense of hope, because they'd hear Lopez arguing with the other men. It was starting to make them believe that Lopez's plan might be falling apart. They'd been captives for weeks now, and maybe Lopez's buddies were getting tired of the whole mess.

❖❖❖

I'd been keeping in touch with Candee, who was still suggesting possible buildings of interest, none of which had produced any positive results. One day while patrolling with Max, we were southbound on Cottage Grove, just zigzagging through the area when we noticed a squad car following about two blocks behind us. We wondered if it was Lopez but decided not to make a move. It was better that he thought we didn't see him.

❖❖❖

Restless Animals

On 111th Street, a few blocks west of Cottage Grove, a young Hispanic woman was working behind the counter of a neighborhood liquor store. In walked two hard-looking Hispanic men she'd never seen before. She got nervous when one of them immediately started hitting on her. In Spanish she said thanks, but I'm married. Insulted, the guy reached over the counter and grabbed her by the throat. She screamed and pressed the panic button. The second assailant attacked and pistol whipped the store owner as he ran in from the back room.

Due to the young woman pushing the panic button, the robbery had been broadcast over the police radio, and Max stepped on the gas. We were only two blocks away.

In the meantime, one of the robbers jumped over the counter and emptied out the cash register. When we arrived, the two guys came running out of the store with their pistols pointed straight out. Max slammed on the brakes, and both our doors flew open. Those punks saw us, froze, and pointed at us. That's when Max and I fired two rounds each at them, and they both went down. Max ran to them and went down on his knees, trying to get information out of them, but they could hardly speak. By the time the EMTs arrived, both of the assailants had bled out. It didn't feel good, but we had no choice. It was either us or them.

It was sad that two lives had been taken for what amounted to nothing, not to mention that we got no information regarding Lopez. The tattoos on their faces revealed that they were definitely members of his hired help. As horrible as it sounded, at least Lopez's army was getting smaller. The young woman was treated and released. The store owner wasn't so lucky. He was taken to a local hospital, where he'd be spending weeks in recovery. The total take from the cash register was one hundred twenty-seven dollars.

When other officers arrived on the scene, Max gave his account of what had happened, and following standard procedure, we both had to temporarily surrender our weapons. I sat in Max's squad while he talked to the other officers. A few minutes later, he got in the squad and we took off. While I was waiting for him, something had crossed my mind.

"Max, let me ask you something. Just as we were rolling up on the scene, did you notice anything behind us?"

"Do you mean that squad car that suddenly made a U-turn and went the other way?"

"So you did see him!"

"It was him all right!"

"That son of a bitch is watching us!"

"It seems that way, and now we go home. Tomorrow is another day!"

There was silence in the squad as we rode along, but the wheels in my head were turning.

"Nothing personal, Max, but I don't know how you do it. I mean, you just go home, and that's it?"

"You don't understand, Sherman. I'm sure that in your investigations you rarely have a mess like this. For cops it's almost daily. Every time I arrive on a scene, and my actions result in death, I feel a little bit less like a human being. Do you know how many people I've shot?"

"No, I don't."

"Well, guess what, neither do I! Now you know why I'm going home."

"I'm sorry, man!"

"Don't be sorry. You feel and think the way a human should. Like I said, tomorrow is another day, and I'll get over it."

Again there was silence in the squad, but this time the wheels in Max's head were turning.

"Sherman, as long as we're being open, what's the real scoop on you and Angie?"

"Honestly, the whole time I've known her, there's been something truly magnetic between us, but at the same time there's been a power stronger than both of us that keeps us apart. I can't figure it out, so I've moved on."

"Do you mean there's someone else?"

"That's not the power I'm talking about, but yes, there is someone else."

"She must be one hell of a lady!"

"You may have seen her before. She's a model."

"Really? I thought models went after celebrity types!"

"Maybe, but my only claim to fame is being arrested by Lopez on TV, following a high-speed chase!"

"Does she know about that?"

"That's the funny part. In the beginning she didn't, and when she finally put two and two together, she freaked out. She actually thought I was a bad man who was taking her away to do harm to her. I'm telling you, man, it was hilarious, and she got pissed off because I laughed at her! In the end it all worked out, and now we're doing the long-distance thing. She lives down in Atlanta."

"So how's that working out?"

"Actually, I like it! She's a busy woman, and me, I'm not very dependable for being home in time for dinner."

"Then tell me this. Why did you take Angie to that ball?"

"Dude, on a moment's notice, who would you want to take?"

"Good point! So you agree that she's lovely?"

"Without a doubt."

"All I can say is that you live quite a life."

"You know, Max, you may want to think about trading in that badge one day. With the connections you already have, you'd make a great P.I. It's more money and fewer rules. If you want to work today, you do, and if you don't want to work today, you don't."

"If the job comes with a supermodel, I'm in!"

"Seriously, I rarely deal with scum like Lopez, but the job does keep me on my toes. Most of the time, the work is far less dangerous. Do you remember a couple of years ago when two Asian punks were found by the cops, taped to a light post?"

"Was that near Chinatown?"

"That was it."

"That was you?"

"Yours truly, and it was fun!"

"I'll be damned! How did you get wrapped up in that mess?"

"Those two punks carjacked Mai, and she was hysterical! I had to do something."

Max was pulling over in front of my place.

"Sherman, I know you're on top of your game, but Lopez isn't the guy I used to know. You should seriously watch your back!"

"You do the same, Max."

Nineteen

GUESS WHO'S COMING TO TOWN

The following day I got a call from Dad, a.k.a. the Silver Fox.

"Hey, Dad, how are you doing?"

"I'm doing better than ever, son! I've finally got my house back to normal."

"That's good news."

"I do have one problem, though. It's Oliver. He's sick of that safe house, and he wants out."

"I don't think he should go back home yet. Yesterday Max and I had an altercation with a couple of Lopez's punks at a liquor store robbery that ended badly. They're going crazy, Dad!"

"Well, how about him coming here to stay? I've got a whole army of Feds here! I need you to talk to that Agent Calvin. I'd really like to make Oliver feel like he has a family here. Why don't we get everyone together and have a barbecue? We haven't had the family together in years."

"I know what you mean, but the timing worries me. I'm nervous, but I'll give it a try."

"Thanks."

"I'll talk to you later, Dad."

"Hey, why don't you try to get that big friend of yours to man the grill for us?"

"You mean Tiny? I'll give it a shot."

"Thanks again, son."

CLICK.

I loved my dad, but this was crazy. Agent Calvin was going to think we'd lost our minds. I figured I'd run it past Max first. I might as well let him be the first to laugh in my face. I had my cellphone in hand about to call him when it rang. It was India.

"Hey, honey," I said, "it's good to hear your voice!"

"I've got some good news!"

"I sure could use some!"

"I'm doing a photo shoot for a travel agency."

"That's great!"

"Wait, I'm not finished yet."

I listened for a bit. "No, you're kidding me!"

"I'll be there in two days. The shoot is going to be at Union Station."

"You're not going to believe this, but my dad has been pushing me to get everyone together for a family barbecue at his place."

"That's great, honey!"

"This isn't the time or the way I wanted you to meet everyone."

"Sherman, honey, have you been hiding us?"

"Not exactly."

"Do we need to talk? Are you ashamed of me?"

"India, please stop!"

"Well, what am I supposed to think?"

"I love you, and when you get here, I'll tell the world!"

"Sherman, I really believe you're the one, but I have to tell you that you're scaring me. That's all I have to say right now. I'll see you when I get there."

CLICK.

Great, that was just what I needed. I fell back in my easy chair and called Max.

"You're up kind of early. What can I do for you?"

"Well, now that my dad's house is back in order, he wants to have family and close friends over for a barbecue."

"So what's wrong with that? As I recall, his place is crawling with Feds."

"Don't you think this is a bit much, a bit too soon?"

"Kind of, but I think the focus is off his place for right now."

"There's more to it. My dad's friend Mr. Cartwright wants out of the safe house. He's been there for weeks now, and it's making him crazy! My dad thinks he'd be more comfortable at his place. At least he'd be around family."

"That may not be out of the question, but it's up to Calvin, and my captain too, now that he's in on the game."

"Well, I just wanted to run it by you first, and of course you're invited, but trust me, buddy, some things are going to happen that you would pay to see! Yesterday I told you about my long-distance thing. As it turns out, she's coming to town for a photo shoot."

"That's great, isn't it?"

"Well!"

"Let me guess? You've been hiding this woman from your family and friends, and she picked up on it and isn't taking it very well?"

"She's trying to be strong, but I can tell she's hurt. I didn't really mean to do this. It just kind of happened."

"So tell me, Sherman. Just how many of these fabulous women do you think are going to walk into your life?"

"I get your point, and if Calvin doesn't approve of the barbecue, she'll never believe it."

"Buddy, I suggest you have a backup plan. Look, I've got to run."

CLICK.

I now needed to call Tiny to make sure he'd be available, but first I figured I'd better call India back and show more interest in her visit. I caught her as she was stepping out of her place to get into a taxi. She answered, but only listened.

"I'm sorry, and you were right," I said. "I understand now how you must feel. I'll be sending a shuttle to the airport to pick you up. Can you text me your flight information?"

"Sure I can."

CLICK.

If India was trying to make a point, she did it well. Next I called Tiny and gave him the whole spiel about the barbecue. Fortunately, he said he'd be available. We chatted a minute to catch up on old times, and touched base on what had been going on with my dad. Before we hung up, I told him the Feds would be present if we got the green light for the barbecue. He was good with it.

Now for the hard part! I had to make one more call. One ring, two rings.

"Special Agent Calvin here."

"Good morning, this is Sherman."

"There haven't been any new developments, if that's why you're calling."

"Well, that's good news."

"I get the feeling that's not why you're calling."

I took a deep breath, then exhaled.

"You know, Sherman. I'm starting to recognize that deep breath you take before dropping a bomb on me. Just spit it out!"

"It's Mr. Cartwright. He's had enough of the safe house, and he wants to camp out at my dad's place."

"Yes, I know. He's been voicing his opinion quite a bit lately. I guess it will be okay. It looks like Lopez has shifted his concerns to his captives."

"Thanks. He'll be very happy, but then there's my dad. He wants to invite family over for a barbecue."

For a few moments there was silence on Calvin's end.

"Sherman, please tell me you're kidding! We've got people dropping like flies, most of them in his front yard! I'd imagine the word family includes your friends at the bar?"

This time there was silence on my end.

"I'm going to allow this, but your dad needs to understand there's a thin line between being fearless and being careless! I need you to text me the names of the people that I haven't cleared yet."

"Thanks, Calvin."

CLICK.

India's Arrival

Well, that had gone a hell of a lot better than I thought it would! I called my dad and told him we had the green light on Mr. Cartwright, as well as the barbecue. Next I extended the invitation to the gang at the City Block, and of course Carman gave me hell about my mystery woman. With time on my hands, I started straightening up things around my apartment so I'd be ready for India's arrival.

❖❖❖

In the meantime, further south in the Pullman area, a federal agent had gone deep undercover. He was posing as a homeless man and had recently made some new friends. The last couple of days he'd been hanging out with two other homeless men. He believed it was as close as he could get to being a fly on the wall. Not only did he look like those guys, but he was now starting to smell like them. They'd taken him under their wing and taught him how to panhandle. In the evenings they'd combine their bounties to buy cheap food. They spent their nights drinking cheap wine and whiskey. They slept in alleys, sometimes between dumpsters. To say that agent was dedicated would be an understatement.

❖❖❖

I stretched out on the sofa to take a nap, and it wasn't long before my cellphone rang. It was India.

"I'm in the shuttle."

CLICK.

Still a little frosty. I could see now this was going to be one interesting day. Hopefully we could fix this problem before we got around the guys. Time suddenly began to fly, because an hour later I got a call from the agent across the hall from me.

"Mr. Brothers, you have a female guest that's been cleared. She'll be here soon."

Barney's ears perked up before India could even knock on my door. He jumped out of my easy chair and stood at attention in front of the door. Through the peephole I could see India standing beside the agent. I opened the door, took her bag, and thanked the agent. To my surprise, she gave me a quick hug, and then went straight to Barney.

"Hi, honey. Did your daddy tell you he's in trouble?"

Just like always, he barked like he understood her.

"Can we talk, India?" I asked.

"Sure, but can I freshen up first?"

"Please, go ahead."

With nothing else to do, I stretched out on my bed and waited. It seemed like it was taking India forever to freshen up, and I must've dozed off, because when I woke up it was nearly two in the afternoon, and India was lying beside me, just staring at me.

"I guess you couldn't wait! Did you sleep well?"

"I get the point, okay?"

TWENTY

ONE OF OUR PLANES IS MISSING

After an evening of drinking and spitting out some serious rotgut whiskey, the homeless federal agent leaned back against a building wall with his buddies. It was going to be another long, restless night sleeping in the alley. An hour had passed, and his buddies had fallen asleep. That was the norm for them. While tossing and turning against the wall, trying to find his spot, something caught his side vision.

Among the dumpsters and utility poles, he saw the rear end of a blue and white Chicago squad car turn into what had to be a building, and disappear. It was across the alley, about a half block down. He slowly got up and made his way down the alley. Finally he came to a building that had several garage doors along the alley. Being undercover, he wasn't carrying a radio, so he'd have to investigate on his own. What really got his attention were wet tire tracks turning right into one of the big doors.

To the side of one of the garage doors was a regular entry door. He put his ear to the door and heard voices speaking in Spanish. Suddenly the door opened and he damned near fell inside. Lopez immediately took direct aim and shot him with his stun gun. As the electrical current passed through the agent's body, he trembled and fell to the floor. After that, two of Lopez's gorillas beat him beyond recognition. Lopez then ordered them to put him in the trunk of their car, take him a few blocks away, and throw him into a dumpster. Like trained dogs, they were happy to do it.

They picked up the agent and threw him in the trunk of an old sedan. Inside the trunk, the agent was fading quickly, and he knew he might not make it.

Using his own blood, he wrote the letters PS on his forearm. He rocked and rolled as the sedan was driven down the alley until it came to a stop. When they opened the trunk, one of the punks noticed he was still alive. He pulled his pistol from his belt and slammed the butt against the agent's head. The blow was so hard it crushed his skull, killing him instantly. The two punks lifted him and dropped him into a dumpster. They laughed as they drove away.

❖❖❖

India and I had slept most of the morning. I had to get the ball rolling for the gathering at my dad's place. We stepped out of my place, and the agent across the hall popped out and offered to run us around. I gave him directions to Tiny's place, and we were off. I told India that our first stop would be the Daily Café.

"What's there?" she asked.

"It's not what. It's someone I want you to meet. A while back I told him that someday I'd introduce you to him."

"Oh, honey, you did tell someone about us!"

"I guess I did, didn't I? You're going to love him too! He's going to be manning the grill at my dad's place."

"Is he really?"

"Yeah, and he's already crazy about you! He used to watch you go by every day on the side of a bus."

"This isn't going to be creepy, is it?"

"Not at all. He's a normal guy."

When we arrived at the café, the agent went in first. He looked to his left and then to his right, then motioned for us to come inside. As soon as we walked in, I saw Tiny's big, bright smile behind the grill. He came over, and he and I did the man hug thing. He used one of his huge mitts to lightly move me out of his way, then gently lifted India's hand and kissed it.

"Why have you been hiding this lovely creature, Sherman?"

Laughing, I said, "Tiny, this is India, and India this is Tiny." After some more laughing and talking a bit, I told him we had the green light and he could put together a menu, and that I'd contact him when it was time to take off. In the meantime, India and I headed back to my place.

Back at home, I had to go to the john. Along the way I dropped my cellphone on the cocktail table. When I came back, India was sitting on the sofa.

"Who is Candee Harris?

"What?"

She looked down at my phone, which was sitting right in front of her.

"She left a message for you, see!"

"She's a TV news reporter. Do you mind if I check it?"

"Please do!"

"Why don't you turn on the TV? You might catch her doing the noonday broadcast."

India grabbed the remote, and I played back Candee's message.

HI SHERMAN, THIS MAY NOT MEAN ANYTHING, BUT BACK IN THE SEVENTIES A NEW POLICE STATION WAS BUILT ON 111TH STREET, BETWEEN COTTAGE GROVE AND THE EXPRESSWAY.

I already knew about the new police station, but things were too busy for Lopez's needs.

TWENTY-ONE

WHO'S WHO?

We had a little time to kill before the barbecue started, so we sat around talking. Finally, the one thing I'd been waiting for since India arrived happened. She started grilling me about the women who were going to be at my dad's place.

"So, what friends of yours other than Tiny are going to be at the barbecue?"

"The guys from the City Block will be there."

"Is that the jazz bar that you won't, I mean that you haven't, taken me to?"

"It is. And Detective Little will be there too."

"Tell me about your friends."

"Well, there's Angie. She's tall and attractive, but quiet. There's also Carman. She's short and attractive, but nosy! There's also Mai. She's young and attractive, and is building a new life. Finally, there's Louie. He's a tall, handsome Italian guy."

"Are all of the women you know attractive?"

"Yes, but I'm only in love with you."

"What about your family?"

"What about them?"

"Who's going to be there?"

"My brother Carlton and his wife Abigale will be there, and yes, she's attractive also. The only other people I can think of are Mr. Cartwright and Rex. Rex is a lawyer at my dad's firm, and he's like family. That's all I know, your honor. Please don't throw the book at me!"

"Oh, that's real funny!"

"So, are you ready for everyone?"

"Why wouldn't I be?"

"I love them all, but I have to warn you that there's one of every kind! Just Mr. Cartwright alone will keep you on your toes! He's visiting from Texas, and he's quite the charmer. To be honest, they're a great group of people, and you're going to like them all. I know they're going to love you."

It was now close to showtime, and we were getting our things. India picked up Barney, and just as we were ready to leave, I got a call from Max.

"Damn, this isn't good!" I said.

"What's the matter, honey?

"This is Max, and he shouldn't be calling me right now. Hey, Max, what's going on?"

"Agent Calvin has an agent who hasn't reported in."

"Where was he working?"

"He was undercover as a homeless man in the Pullman area."

"Do you think they might've caught on to him?"

"It's too soon to say. I guess I'll see you at the barbecue."

"Okay, Max."

CLICK.

"What did he have to say?" India asked.

"It looks like we've got a federal agent missing."

"Oh, Sherman, I'm really sorry to hear that!"

"It could be that he just can't communicate at the moment. You know, honey, I'm really uncomfortable with my dad having this thing right now."

"It's too late to turn back now. Let's just go and try to have fun."

BARBECUE TIME

We climbed into the black SUV and headed back to the Daily Café. Considering the recent developments regarding the missing agent, I thought it would be better to have Tiny follow us. He already had his van loaded and was ready to go. He followed us through town, and twenty minutes later we were pulling into my dad's community. After a few twists and curves, we were met at his driveway by armed federal agents. The side and rear doors of Tiny's van were opened, and the inside was inspected. India was blown away by the presence of the agents.

"What is this place, Fort Knox?"

"Almost, honey, but you'll forget about those guys after a while."

After Tiny had parked, one of the agents took him and showed him where to set up, and India and I went inside the house. We were greeted by Dad and Mr. Cartwright, and before I could say a word, Mr. Cartwright was on India like flies on you know what! While he was hugging her, she looked over his shoulder at me, and I gave her that I told you so look, and smiled.

"Where y'all been hidin' this lovely creature? No wonder y'all done had my hide hogtied in that godforsaken place! Honey blossom, let me sho' y'all around this ol ranch. Carlton's a good ol boy, he don't mind none!"

Mr. Cartwright took India's hand and led her out on the grounds. While this was going on, Max had showed up. We immediately started talking about the investigation. According to Max, the missing agent still hadn't checked in. I asked if we'd be seeing Agent Calvin here at the barbecue.

"Due to the latest developments, I'd doubt it."

While we were talking, we could see my brother Carlton's BMW pulling into the driveway.

"Who's that?" Max asked.

"That's my brother and his wife, and don't stare at her, Max!"

"You're kidding me!"

"It is what it is."

"Is there a farm or something where you guys grow these women? Man, I've been a cop way too long."

The two of them finally made it inside.

"This is my brother, Carlton, and his wife, Abigale. Guys, this is Detective Maxwell Little."

"It's a pleasure to meet you both, and please, call me Max."

"Hi, Max. We're a strange bunch, but harmless," Carlton said. "Have you tasted Tiny's cooking before?"

"No, I can't say that I have," Max said.

"Well, you're in for a treat! Do you know if Rex has showed up yet?"

"I'm afraid I haven't met Rex before," Max said.

Abigale told Max that he was lucky, and he got a strange look on his face.

"We're going to head out back," Carlton said. "Maybe we can track down Dad and Mr. Cartwright."

Max decided to check out the grounds himself, and his nose led him straight to Tiny. It was also where he found India. He looked at Tiny and smiled.

"Judging by your size and the smell in the air, you must be Tiny!"

"That's right, my man!"

"I've been hearing good things about you. You look like a stand-up guy, Tiny. Tell me something. Where do all of these beautiful women come from? Sherman won't tell me!"

"Brother, I've been trying to crack that code since I first met Sherman!"

I made it out and over to Tiny's grill to find the three of them laughing.

"Sherman, you never did tell me how you two met," Max said.

India instantly gave me the eye and balled up her fist.

"Say it, I dare you!"

Max stepped back and started laughing.

"We met at an aquarium in New Orleans," I said.

"Why do I feel like there's more to the story?" Max said.

"There is more, but India is ready to punch me in the mouth if I say another word!"

"You guys are a mess," India said before walking away.

Across the lawn we could see that Angie and Carman had arrived and were heading our way. Along the way, they crossed paths with India and introduced themselves, as well as bringing her back with them.

Before they got to us, Max commented, "Hey Tiny, watch this! Sherman has a train wreck coming right at him!"

"Will you two stop it?" I said.

When the ladies reached us, Carman went straight up to Tiny and tried to wrap her short arms around his huge mass.

"How are you, my big sweet man?"

"Oh, sweetie, I'm wonderful now that you're here!"

With that Carman turned around and punched me in the stomach!

"So this is the mystery woman! Why have you been hiding her from us?"

I looked at India, and she just stood with her hands on her hips. Max was in heaven watching it all unfold. Trying to change the tone, I asked if Rex had shown up yet. From behind me came his voice.

"I'm right here!"

I immediately said, "This is India." She then gave me another one of her looks, and I quickly added, "My girlfriend."

"Hi, Rex, it's nice to meet you," India said.

"Have you been hiding this woman, Sherman?"

Rex took a hard look at India.

"Excuse me, but have we met before?"

"I'm afraid not," India said.

"Rex, India is a model," I said. "Maybe you've seen her work."

I was thinking to myself, damn, I can't catch a break! Everyone seemed to be having a good time. Tiny was always a crowd pleaser. He's really a gentle guy and the women love him. As for Carman, let's just say she had a field day questioning India about the two of us. It was a good thing that I'd warned India about her. I was pleasantly surprised at how well Angie and India got along. It was almost like they already knew each other. It kind of gave me a weird feeling. Here was a woman I once dreamed about, having a good time with the woman I was in love with. I found myself staring and wondering what they were talking about whenever I saw them together. I felt a slap on my back. It was Max.

"Hey, buddy, are you all right?"

"I'm fine."

"Look, man, you can't have them both!"

"You're a funny man, Max!"

"If it helps any, I don't blame you! I can't remember the last time I was around this many lovely women and it wasn't a vice raid!"

"Max, you're a great guy, and Angie is available, and Carman's not bad either. The only thing with her is that she may turn you into another Lopez! Come on, let's go inside and see if my dad has a couple beers."

We grabbed our beers and headed out to the patio, where we found my dad and Mr. Cartwright already eating.

"You guys look pretty happy," I said.

Mr. Cartwright was the first to respond.

"Why hell, Sherman, I think I'm gonna marry that ol boy!"

We decided that maybe we should get some food too. Finally Tiny found time to relax in a lawn chair. I was thinking we could use some music. Max grabbed a plate and joined Tiny, while I headed back inside in search of the stereo. Along the way, I saw India sitting alone in the garden, and I decided to join her first.

"So, Angie tells me you've saved her life a couple of times."

Oh boy, I knew where this is going.

"I was working and things got out of control. It just kind of happened. I don't feel like I saved her life. I was just doing my job."

"You know, you're quite a guy, Mr. Brothers!"

Just when I was starting to feel relieved, India, being all woman, dropped a bomb on me.

"You forgot to tell me about the Governor's Ball."

I had to think fast.

"So much has happened since then. I guess it just slipped my mind. So how do you like everyone?"

"That was pretty smooth, Mr. Brothers!"

I couldn't help but laugh myself.

"You can't blame a brother for trying!"

"When will I get to know everything about this brother?"

"Honey, you do know everything about me."

"I love what we have, Sherman. Let's not screw it up with poor communication. Neither one of us wants to get married, but I'll do whatever's necessary to keep us together."

"Look, I'm always going to make you crazy one way or another, but it's not by design. I don't always say and do the right thing at the right time. I guess in my mind I'm comfortable having you in my life and the details aren't important to me. I'm not hiding anything, but I do have one request."

"And what is that?"

"Don't let my past destroy what we have now."

"So you're saying I should be careful what I ask for?"

"No. I'm saying you should be prepared to live with it."

India stood and gave me a big hug.

"That's all I needed to hear. I do have one question of my own."

"Fire away."

"Are you crazy or something? How on earth is it that you wait for me when you had a woman like Angie right in front of you for years?"

"I admit she's very special, but she's not for me. You're everything she is and more."

"Well, she's missing out on a good man, because you're all mine now!"

India joined me on my second attempt to find the stereo. Inside, Angie and Carman were saying their goodbyes. It was their turn to take over the bar. India was having a great time. She thought Dad was quite the gentleman, and Mr. Cartwright was quite the character. The best part was that we were now out in the open, and everyone approved.

With a little jazz in the air, the atmosphere had changed. Everyone was relaxed and having a good time. Dad was right, this was a good idea. About an hour later, not only did Mai and Louie arrive, but so did Agent Calvin. It was really good to see him. He was a real company man, and I admired that, but there are times when everyone needs to let their hair down a little. After introducing him to everyone, I directed him toward the grill and told him he might run into Max on the grounds. Mai and Louie had set out already, and I told India to come with me to meet them. We found them out by the pool, talking to Carlton and Abigale.

"Mai and Louie, this is my girlfriend, India."

They both turned and gave me a funny look, and I stopped them right in their tracks.

"Please don't say it! I was waiting for the right time."

Louie gave India a hug and welcomed her to the family.

"It's a pleasure to meet you," Mai said. "You've got a great guy. Don't let him get away!"

"I've heard great things about Tiny's cooking, and we're starving," Louie said. They walked away, leaving India and me alone.

"They seem real nice," India said.

"Mai is a lovely young lady."

"You know, Sherman. In my field there's a big demand for exotic young Asian women, and you didn't tell me Louie is gay."

"He's not gay!"

"You're kidding me, right?"

"No, I'm not."

"Honey, I know he's a good friend and all, but…"

"I'm telling you, he's not gay!"

"Look, I've been in the modeling business for a long time, and trust me, I know what I'm talking about."

"Whatever! So now that you've met everyone, what do you think?"

"They're a great group of people, and the best part is that they all love you dearly. In fact, I'm a little jealous."

We headed back out to the garden, and it wasn't long before we saw Max and Mai coming around the corner.

"Oh, that's sweet!" India said.

"You don't even know what they're talking about!"

"Sherman, you're such a killjoy! I think they look nice together."

"This is coming from the same person who thinks Louie is gay."

"Well, I'm right about that too. I'll tell you what. Let's invite them back to your place for a nightcap, and if they agree, I get breakfast in bed. If they don't, you get to be right."

"That's all I'll get?"

India took the wheel as soon as Mai and Max made it over to us.

"You two seem to be getting along well!"

"India, please stop," I said.

"Sherman and I want to invite you two over for a nightcap."

I'd hardly moved my lips when India elbowed me before I could put in a disclaimer. Mai said sure, and India turned and stuck out her tongue at me.

"I want a pancake, two strips of bacon, and some fresh fruit!" India said.

"You see what you have to look forward to, Max?" I said.

"Hey," Mai said, "I'm standing right here!"

India took Mai by the arm.

"Come on, honey. Let's go see Tiny. He knows how to treat a lady!"

When the girls left, I told Max the whole nightcap thing was India's idea. He was cool with it, because he and Mai were really getting along well.

In the family room, Dad and Mr. Cartwright had everyone in stitches, telling old war stories about their days of being young practicing lawyers. Even

Agent Calvin was having a good time, but every fifteen minutes or so, he'd look at his watch. Through the window I could see Tiny coming toward the house carrying a container of leftovers. Max and I decided to go out to the grill and help him wrap things up. By the time the three of us were finished, Louie was saying goodbye.

Whatever Agent Calvin was waiting for must've come to light. He made a phone call, thanked Dad for his hospitality and took off. Max and I looked at each other. Something was definitely up.

"Sherman, I'm going to step outside and give my captain a call."

When Max stepped out, Mai came in from the patio.

"He's not leaving, is he?"

"No. He's just making a phone call."

I was thinking how she must really like the strong, silent type. The next to leave were Carlton and Abigale. Dad and Mr. Cartwright were looking pretty comfortable with a glass of scotch each, so there was no point in us sticking around. We all said our goodbyes and climbed into Max's unmarked squad car. The next stop was my place, and it was sure to be an interesting night. During the ride, I asked Max how things were going with his captain.

"Things are about the same. They still haven't found the one thing that's been missing."

I knew he was talking about the missing agent. India and Mai were in the back seat, and in the mirror I could see them whispering.

"What are you two up to?"

"Nothing," India said.

"We're just talking in code, like you two!"

They both started laughing, and then Mai tried talking in a deep male voice.

"Hey, India, did you find that thing?"

That's when we all started laughing. At my place we had a great time. We laughed and talked the night away. Finally Mai started blinking her eyes, and Max suggested that he take her home and allow us to get some sleep as well. The two of them took off, and we went straight to bed.

TWENTY-TWO

BAD NEWS

We took our time getting out of bed. India wanted to get as much rest as she could. Her photo shoot was the next day, and the makeup staff would get upset if she showed up with puffy eyes. I let her have the bedroom, and I entertained myself in the living room. I ended up stretched out on the sofa with my headset on and a magazine. A little past noon my cellphone vibrated. It was Max.

"What's up, buddy?"

"I've got bad news, Sherman. We've found the missing agent, or should I say Streets and Sanitation found him."

"Max, what happened?"

"The city was doing their routine trash pickup this morning, and there he was in a dumpster."

"Okay, now what?"

"All I know is there's a major shouting match going on right now in my captain's office. Agent Calvin is in there, and he's not taking this too well. At times like this I need to keep my nose clean and stay away from the captain. I'll keep you posted, buddy."

"All right, Max, I'll talk to you later."

CLICK.

❖❖❖

At the police station, anyone who had a desk within shouting range of the captain's office was trying to be quiet and hear what was being said. It appeared that Agent Calvin wanted to shake down every Hispanic punk he saw on the streets of the Pullman area. He still believed that one of them would give up Lopez.

The captain had put his foot down, refusing to authorize a sweep like that. He believed it would spark a protest from the Hispanic community, and the mayor would be all over his ass. Agent Calvin had all but threatened to go over the captain's head and use federal power. As the arguing continued, the captain got more and more pissed off, and now he was starting to take the agent's accusations personally. The argument ended with Agent Calvin telling the captain he'd better talk to someone and give him an answer by four o'clock, or he was going to do things his way. With that, he stormed out of the captain's office, the door slamming behind him.

Not ten minutes later, the captain himself stepped out of his office with a handheld radio. Trying to get out of his way, officers in the squad room parted like the Red Sea.

As time went on, I got impatient waiting to hear from Max. When my phone did ring, I answered it immediately. On the other end was Candee, not Max.

"Wow, Sherman, you must've been waiting for my call!"

"Not exactly, but what's up?"

"First of all, did you hear about the agent?"

"I did."

"Do you think he's tied to this whole mess?"

"I'm sure he is!"

"I think I've found something that's been right in front of our faces, but we overlooked it."

"And what's that?"

"Well, we know that years ago they built that new police station over east, but Sherman, the old police station is still standing, and it's abandoned!"

"What the hell! Why didn't we think of this? Where is it located?"

"It's on Indiana."

"Candee, you're the best!"

"Mr. Brothers, I've been telling you that for a few years now."

"Candee, can you please do me a favor? Can you hold on to this information for a while? I need to make some phone calls. I promise you'll be the first to know what we come up with."

"Okay, but don't let me down!"

"I won't, I promise."

I immediately called Max.

"I've got the building! It was right under our noses!"

"That's great news," Max said, "because Agent Calvin is about to shake down every Hispanic punk he sees in the Pullman community."

"He can't do that!"

"Right now, both he and my captain are off the radar. If we don't get word to one of them soon, all hell is going to break loose!"

Back at Lopez's makeshift prison and hideout, there was also some heavy conversation going on. It seemed his hired help was getting sick of doing his dirty work. Not only that, but they'd noticed he'd recently brought a suitcase with him, but hadn't mentioned going anywhere.

The leader of the punks was pissed off.

"What the hell is going on, Lopez? My boys are tired of this rat hole!"

"Look, dude, I'm paying you good money."

"What the hell are you going to do with those two dead gringos?"

"Don't worry about it. And they're not dead."

"Shit, man, they may as well be!"

"Well, I've got a question for your dumbass boys. Why the hell did they dump that homeless guy right in this freaking neighborhood? That was fucking stupid! There are going to be cops all over the damned place!"

"I guess that's why you have your freaking suitcase, isn't it, Lopez! That's right. I saw it, homeboy! You're not thinking about leaving me and my boys holding the bag, are you?"

"Look, everything is going according to plan," Lopez said.

"What fucking plan? You never had a plan! You're just another freaking loco cop!"

That's when Lopez drew his weapon, but he was outnumbered by four bangers that drew their pistols too.

"Let's all just calm down," Lopez said.

"Lopez, you have two more days, and then me and my boys are outta here!"

"Look, I've got to get back out on the streets and see what damage your boys did by dumping that body so close. I'll be back."

"Yeah, well, why don't you leave that suitcase here?"

"Whatever, dude!"

LOPEZ BUGS OUT

After going through a series of hallways, Lopez made his way to a door that opened to the alley. Halfway down the alley he had an old car parked. He got in and pulled around to the main street. Just about three blocks away he came across a black SUV and a couple of squad cars. They were in front of a small neighborhood bar with the doors open. Sitting on the curb were six or seven gangbangers, with their hands cuffed behind their backs. Lopez started thinking to himself:

SHIT, THIS HAS TO DO WITH THE DEAD BODY!

He kept on driving. Another six blocks away, another black SUV and two squad cars blew past him.

THAT'S IT! TIME TO DROP EVERYTHING AND GET THE HELL OUT OF TOWN!

He made a quick turn and headed south. At 115th Street he parked the old car and ran up the stairs to the Kensington Train Station. A train from there would take him downtown, where he could catch another one that would take him straight to O'Hare Airport.

Once he got onboard the second train he felt safe. Using his cellphone, he attempted to book a roundtrip flight to San Juan, Puerto Rico. He knew better than to buy a one-way ticket, which would draw attention. The airline representative told him the next flight was in three hours, and due to baggage and security, he might not make it in time. He told her he'd try his luck, and bought the ticket anyway. He hung up knowing the only baggage he had was the passport in his pocket and the pistol in his belt, which he intended to leave on the train.

When he got to the airport, everything was working in his favor. All he needed now was for his badge to get him through security quickly and without hassle. He did in fact go through security without a problem, and then he withdrew all the cash he could from a nearby ATM. Next he used his plastic to buy a carry-on bag, underwear, and toiletries. Knowing the Feds would eventually be on his tail, he wanted to look like everyone else who was traveling.

TWENTY-THREE

INDIA FACES FACTS

Over in the Pullman community, Agent Calvin's plan was in full swing. The scene was the same at every bar in the area. Max had exhausted all of his efforts at contacting Agent Calvin or his captain. At least they weren't answering their cellphones. With no other options, he called me.

"I'm not having any luck contacting the captain or Calvin. Why don't we hit the streets and try to dig 'em up?"

"That sounds good to me!"

"I've got a bad feeling about this, Sherman. I think you'd better suit up. I'll swing by in a little bit."

CLICK.

I took Max's advice and strapped my 380 to my ankle holster, put on my vest, and holstered my 9mm on my waist. Not thinking about how I looked, I went to the bedroom to tell India I was taking off. I should've put on a football jersey to cover my vest and pistol first. This was a first for her, and she immediately freaked out.

"Sherman, what on earth is going on? You're scaring me!"

"Look, honey, I know it's hard for you, but I'm going to be with Max and a whole bunch of federal agents. I'm going to be fine. You don't have to worry about me."

"How can you stand there and tell me I don't have to worry? You're wearing a bulletproof vest and carrying some kind of big-ass gun. Do you have any idea of how you look? Go ahead and go! I'll be here when you get back."

"India, please don't do this."

"There's nothing you can say that's going to make me feel better, Sherman!"

Before I could say another word, my cellphone rang. It was Max. I looked at India and walked away. He was waiting outside in his squad. When I got downstairs, I got in without saying a word.

"So what's eating you?"

"I screwed up."

"You're talking about India?"

"I went to the bedroom to tell her I was leaving and forgot to cover up my vest and pistol. Which of course freaked her out when she saw them."

"It looks like it's going to take time for her to adjust to your extracurricular activities. You have to remember that we hang out with the worst human beings in the world. If I wasn't the gun-packing moron that I am, I'd freak out too!"

"I agree with both of you, but she knows what I do."

"That may be, but it's still going to take time. Why don't we go and catch us some bad guys?"

"Let's do that!" I said.

"You know, Sherman, we may be walking into a hornets' nest. I'm sure Agent Calvin has put his plan into action by now."

"Then I guess that means we're headed for Pullman!"

"If we're going to find the captain or Calvin, that's where they're going to be."

"Damn, Max, don't you have a radio in this thing?"

"Yeah, but I figure they won't be using it because Lopez may be listening."

"Why don't we take Stony Island over to 95th Street, and make our way to

Cottage Grove."

"Works for me."

It didn't take us long to reach Cottage Grove, and just as we turned left, heading south, a black SUV with two squad cars behind it came up from the rear. They crossed the yellow lines and blew right past us.

"Damn, Sherman!" Max said. "It's started already! I'd better hit the lights and follow them."

TWENTY-FOUR

GROUND ZERO

At 103rd Street we hung a right, following the squads, and it seemed kind of strange to me.

"Hey, Max, this isn't Pullman yet."

"You're right. Maybe Calvin is getting a little desperate."

We blew past a couple of fast-food joints, a gas station, and a small grocery store. Up ahead on the right side of the street, the SUV and squads had stopped. Their doors flew open, and Max pulled around right in front of the SUV, trying to get their attention. It must've worked, because they all pointed their weapons at us. Max stuck his badge out the window, and they lowered their weapons. We then got out of the squad and went straight to the agent in charge.

"I'm Detective Maxwell Little, and before you storm into this place, I need to talk to Special Agent Calvin. I've got vital information that he needs immediately. Please get him on the horn right now. Time is running out!"

The agent told his men to stand down as he turned his back to us and got on his cellphone. After a few moments he handed his phone to Max.

"Agent Calvin, this is Max. I believe I have the building where Lopez is holed up! It's on Indiana near 111th Street. It's an abandoned police station. You need to round up your troops and meet us there. We may need EMTs as well as the Fire Department. I'm going to get them on the horn now and lead this team over there. There's one more thing, Calvin. You need to contact Captain Leonard."

Max gave the agent his phone back, and we took off with the bells and whistles blowing. It took us about five minutes to reach the abandoned police station. When we got there, the streets had already been cleared and the corners blocked off. In front of the building, Agent Calvin stood organizing his teams. With thirty to forty cops and agents, he'd have the building surrounded. There were sharpshooters on rooftops facing all four sides of the abandoned building. On the ground were men with automatic weapons, tear gas canisters, and battering rams.

As we all waited for Agent Calvin to give the command, I weighed the possibility of being wrong about this place. My reputation would be finished, and Max, he'd be lucky if he ended up being a beat cop. But it was too late to turn back now. Down at the corner I could see the EMTs waiting if they were needed. At the opposite corner were two fire engines. This was either going to be a huge success or a major screwup.

LOPEZ'S FANTASY

In San Juan, the seatbelt sign was activated as the jet prepared to land. Lopez was sporting his famous shit-eating grin as he fastened his seatbelt and returned his seatback to the upright position. He had no idea of what was about to happen back home, and he didn't care. For him it was time to take a load off, enjoy some good rum and the company of the local ladies. He was already preparing himself for the joys of his new life. He was satisfied with the amount of revenge he'd taken out on Governor Evans and D.A. White. The other suckers were just collateral damage. As for Mr. Cartwright, he had put the fear of God in him, and that was good enough.

IT'S TIME

I stepped off to the side unnoticed and sent Candee a text message.

WE'RE ABOUT TO STORM THIS PLACE. BE CAREFUL. I KEPT MY WORD.

I returned just in time to hear Agent Calvin give the command to tear the place apart. Every door of the building was rammed, and tear gas canisters were shot into every window. That was followed by cops and agents wearing masks and vests storming the building. Max and I went in with a secondary team. It was extremely dim inside, and we could hear rounds being fired and people coughing and gagging, and for a few moments, that included us. That's when we broke off from the team in search of the jail cells. Using flashlights, we prowled through the hallways and downstairs. The floors between us acted as a buffer, reducing the tear gas. We walked quietly and slowly with our weapons drawn.

I whispered to Max to listen closely. We could hear soft moans coming from down the hall. We had found the cells, but so far they were empty, so we continued to follow the sound of the moans. I was pointing my flashlight toward the cells on the left, Max to the right. He spotted them first.

"Sherman, there they are!"

Max got on his radio and requested the EMTs and blankets. Both the governor and D.A. White were handcuffed to cell bars. They were both nude and, at first sight, just inches from death. The cell door was unlocked, but Max had to use his cuff key to release them from the bars. Moments later Agent Calvin and Captain Leonard arrived with the EMTs. They brought blankets, oxygen and first-aid supplies.

One of the EMTs took one look at the captives and spoke right up.

"These people have one foot in the grave. We've got to get them out of here now, and we're going to need a Medivac!"

The captain said that no helicopter could land on these streets because of the power lines. That's when Max suggested nearby Gately Park. We had passed it on our way there.

"It's on 103rd and Cottage Grove."

The captain immediately ordered the Medivac. Agent Calvin asked the EMT where the governor and the D.A. would be taken to. His answer was the nearest trauma unit, but the captain immediately said no.

"That's not safe, plus it'll be a media circus. I'd like to take them to the safest place I know, but I have no pull there."

"Where's that?" Agent Calvin asked.

"I'm thinking of the Great Lakes Naval Base. They've got the best doctors in the world, and more than enough soldiers to hold off Lopez's punks and anyone else!"

Agent Calvin said, "I've got this," and got on his cellphone. The governor and D.A. White were transferred to a waiting ambulance outside. The captain, Agent Calvin, and two other agents climbed into a black SUV. Max and I followed in his squad. To avoid any possible media, we went through several alleys before heading north on Cottage Grove.

When we pulled into the parking lot of Gately Park, the Medivac had already landed. The transfer of the patients was made quickly. Captain Leonard and Agent Calvin climbed in behind them, and just like that they were in the air, headed for Great Lakes Naval Base.

We returned to the abandoned police station, and there were at least eight of Lopez's punks handcuffed and sitting on the curb. Inside the building there were three bodies on the floor covered with plastic tarps. The worst part was that Lopez was nowhere to be found. Outside, Candee and the WLOK News Crew had been allowed past the blocked-off corners, and she was reporting live. I stood across the street, right in front of her, and gave her the thumbs-up. I then called India and told her to turn on the TV.

It wasn't over yet. The governor and the D.A. weren't out of the woods by any means. It would be days before they could be any help to us, and even that would be with hope and a prayer. On the positive side, we saved two lives. A bulletin was put out on Ricardo Lopez, along with the warning that he might be armed and dangerous. At this stage of the game, all that Max and I could do was wait and let the wheels of justice turn. I personally had a good feeling about this, that it would just be a matter of time before we nailed Lopez.

Max and I agreed that we'd earned a cold beer. We stopped at my place and picked up India, and then headed for the Block. Fifteen minutes later, we were walking into the bar. We were shocked when the gang at the bar started cheering as soon as they saw us. At first we didn't know what was going on, but then Louie said they'd watched Candee's report on TV. Strangely, this had turned into a good day.

TWENTY-FIVE
THE PHOTO SHOOT

Today was India's big day. She'd be doing a photo shoot down at Union Station for a travel agency. When her day ended, she'd be staying at a hotel downtown. The plan was for me to try and have lunch with her before she headed back home. To start the day off right, I prepared breakfast and served it to her in bed. Afterward she took a shower. While she was in the bathroom, Candee called.

"Good morning, Sherman."

"Good morning to you, Candee."

"Wow, you sound awful chipper!"

"I always feel this way after catching a few bad guys!"

"Since you're in such a good mood, why don't you tell me where they are?"

"Why don't I tell you where who is?"

"Come on, Sherman, don't play dumb!"

"Candee, I can't. The Feds would hang me out to dry! They're really pissed off about losing one of their agents, and they're not in the mood."

"Well, what's your theory on Lopez?"

"I think he's holed up somewhere in town. With the bulletin that's out on him, I don't think he can get out of the state."

"Here's hoping! By the way, Captain Leonard is going to be holding a press conference this afternoon."

"That was quick!"

"I also wanted to say thanks for the story."

"Well, if you hadn't found that building, there wouldn't have been a story. I guess we make a pretty good team."

"Well, Sherman, real teams have very special celebrations sometimes."

"Candee, please, don't go there."

"You can't blame a girl for trying."

"I guess not, but I've got to get going."

"Don't forget to tune in later."

"I won't."

CLICK.

I sat on the bed and watched India get dressed.

"You know, Sherman, we should take a vacation."

"I've heard of those!"

"Really, honey, we should!"

"Where, when, and how much?"

"You know, there's a town car coming to pick me up in an hour, and you should be nice to me while I'm still here."

"We could do a lot of things in an hour."

"I can think of one thing we *won't* be doing, Mister!"

"You're no fun anymore."

"Honey, I'd love to jump your bones, but I've got to go to work."

"I have to admit, I do love to see a woman work."

"The next time I come to see you, I'm going to make you pay for this."

It wasn't long before India's ride arrived, and I called for Barney.

"We'll go downstairs with you, and then I think we'll go for a walk."

Downstairs Barney and I said our goodbyes to India and watched as the town car drove away. Barney and I looked at each other.

"You lead the way, little buddy!"

He started walking and I followed him. We headed south and ended up near the Museum of Science and Industry. A group of elementary school kids were getting off a bus, and they must've caught Barney's eye, because he led me down the sidewalk toward them. The kids loved him, and he loved them too, but they had to keep moving. As the kids disappeared into the entrance of the museum, Barney stood watching until they were out of sight. He looked at me as if to say, what now?

It wasn't even noon yet, too early for lunch.

"Well, buddy, I guess we'll just walk back home."

As we walked along, it dawned on me how nice it was to walk freely, without the aid of a federal agent. After cleaning the city of Lopez's hired help, the Feds felt there was no longer a need for tight security.

Twenty-Six

THE PRESS CONFERENCE

I took Candee's advice, and at noon I tuned in to the WLOK news broadcast. When the news began, they went straight to the coverage in front of the police station downtown. The scene was typical. There was a podium with about seven microphones on it, and I could see several uniformed police officers milling around. Candee stepped into the picture.

"Good afternoon. I'm Candee Harris with the WLOK News Crew. We're coming to you live from outside of the police station downtown. In just a few minutes, the chief of police, as well as the mayor, will be making statements regarding the rescue of Governor Phillip T. Evans and District Attorney Margret White."

Behind Candee, I could see the chief of police, Captain Leonard, Special Agent Calvin, and the mayor gathering at the podium. Candee spoke again.

"It appears they're just about ready to begin. Let's listen in."

The mayor was first to speak.

"Good afternoon. On behalf of the City of Chicago and the State of Illinois, I'd like to thank the Police Department and the FBI for the outstanding work they did that aided in the recovery of Governor Evans and D.A. White. In addition to that, I'd like to thank the lieutenant governor and the assistant D.A. for filling the shoes of two very vital individuals. It's people like them who add to the strength of this great city and state. At this time, I'm going to turn the microphone over to the chief of police."

The chief thanked the mayor before speaking.

"I'm going to briefly try to bring you all up to date about what took place yesterday afternoon. After we all speak, I'll try to answer your questions. At approximately 4:23 p.m. yesterday, a raid was made at an abandoned police station located on the South Side, on 111th Street and Indiana Avenue. That raid led to the discovery of the governor and the D.A. The two of them were airlifted to an undisclosed hospital for routine examinations. This is still an ongoing investigation. At this point I'm going to turn the podium over to Captain Leonard of the Chicago Police Department."

The two of them leaned in close and whispered before the captain spoke.

"Like the chief said, yesterday at 4:23 p.m., I, together with Special Agent Calvin, activated a raid. In addition to the discovery of the governor and the D.A., a total of eight arrests were made. Those arrested were known criminals related to this investigation. During the raid, gunfire was exchanged that resulted in the deaths of three known gang members hired from out of town. At this stage of the investigation, that's all I can say. For further details, I'd like to introduce Special Agent Calvin of the FBI."

Once again, whispering took place.

"Good afternoon. What I'm about to say is going to be shocking to you. Yesterday evening at six p.m. central time, an All-Points Bulletin was put into effect for the arrest of one Ricardo Lopez, a Chicago Police Department officer. Both the Chicago Police and the FBI believe he engineered the kidnapping of the governor and D.A. White, as well as being connected to several murders. Ladies and gentlemen, this is a scar on the face of men and women in law enforcement across the country, and all over the world. Working with us to track down Ricardo Lopez is every law enforcement agency across the country, plus Canada and Mexico. On a personal note, I promise that Ricardo Lopez will be apprehended and brought to justice. Thank you."

Lopez's face was then shown on one side of the TV screen, and the chief was taking questions on the other side. The sound of the live feed was reduced, and I could hear Candee continuing her report.

"Ladies and gentlemen, we're all happy to have our governor and D.A. back home and safe. That goes without saying, but it's also a very sad day for the men and women who so gallantly serve our communities every day. I'm sure that as the days go by, more details will be revealed. I'm Candee Harris with the WLOK News Crew."

I thought that was quite a conference and called Max to get his take on it.

"Hey, it's Sherman."

"I guess you saw it. You know, years ago I should've said or done something!"

"You had no idea he'd go this far. Don't blame yourself for this shit! He's the asshole, not you!"

"Well, I've got news for you! The governor was tortured and D.A. White was raped more than once. The public is never going to know this, but those two people are going to have to live with this the rest of their lives. Sherman, man, I'm sorry, but I really don't want to talk right now."

"I understand. Give me a call later."

CLICK.

I knew that leaving Max alone to dwell on this jerk was the wrong thing to do, but I also know that when a man wants his space, you should give it to him. All I could do now was wait it out. The truth was that this was a police investigation, and I was lucky to have been invited in. At that point the ball was in their hands.

I decided to order a pizza, stretch out on the sofa, and have a cold one. I got the feeling things were going to be quiet for a while. While waiting for my pizza to be delivered, I called Dad to see how he and Mr. Cartwright were doing. It turned out they had watched the press conference also, and Mr. Cartwright was already making reservations to go back home. I couldn't say I blamed him. There's nothing worse than being forced out of your own home.

My pizza finally came, and I did have that cold one, but I couldn't get Max off of my mind. I watched TV while Barney lay in the easy chair. I began to wonder how India's photo shoot was going. It was nearly six p.m. I guessed she'd call me when she could. Just like that, my phone rang, and it was her.

"Hey, honey, how was your day?" I asked.

"It was good until I checked my messages!"

"What's wrong? Are your parents all right?"

"They're fine, but I got a disturbing message from Mai. She was crying!"

"She was crying about what?"

"She seems to think that Max doesn't want to talk to her, that he's lost interest."

"She's got it all wrong! Max feels responsible for this nut we're looking for, and he's taking it personally. He doesn't even want to talk to *me* right now. She needs to just show up at his door. She's exactly what he needs right now! Did you call her back yet?"

"No. I wanted to talk to you first."

"Call her, and explain to her what's going on. It'll sound better coming from you. Call me back when you're done."

"Sherman, I'll give it a try."

CLICK.

I hung up and thought:

DAMN, MAX! GET IT TOGETHER. THIS LITTLE GIRL CAN'T TAKE MUCH MORE PAIN IN HER LIFE!

India did call me back, but it was too soon for her to know if she'd gotten through to Mai.

TWENTY-SEVEN

SAN JUAN, PUERTO RICO

Morning came, and the first thing that crossed my mind was my lunch date with India. After having breakfast, Barney and I went for a walk. Time passed quickly, and soon he and I were ready to head downtown to meet India for lunch.

Holding Barney in my arms, we waited for India to step out of an elevator into the hotel lobby. It was a beautiful day, and we took a leisurely walk in search of an outdoor café where Barney would be welcome. During the middle of our lunch, my cellphone vibrated. It was Max, and I told India that I thought I'd better answer.

"Hey, this is Sherman."

"We've got a real problem, Sherman!"

"I'm really sorry for interfering, Max."

"No, that was fine."

"So what's going on?"

"Lopez has left the country!"

"What! Where the hell did he go?"

"He flew to Puerto Rico."

"Puerto Rico!"

"How's your Spanish, buddy? Agent Calvin wants to meet with both of us in my captain's office today."

"So how is that going to work with me? I'm not a cop."

"I don't know, but it won't hurt to listen. By the way, was that India's idea?"

"What do you mean?"

"That's okay, buddy. Thanks!"

CLICK.

I looked at India and smiled.

"I'm a genius! I knew it would all work out!" India said. Then she gave me a funny look. "Please! What did he have to say?"

"He didn't give me any details, but you have to admit I was right in saying that Mai was just what he needed."

"Yeah, but don't go getting all big-headed!" she said.

"You're just a hater," I teased.

"So, what is this I hear about Puerto Rico?"

"Oh, that," I said.

"Yes, that."

"It seems Lopez has fled to Puerto Rico. Like what, he thinks it's a foreign country?"

"Can't the police hunt him down without you?"

"Sure, but I'm already in this mess up to my neck."

"Your neck is exactly what I'm worried about!"

"So far no decisions have been made. They just want to meet and discuss it."

"If you go, what are you going to do about Barney?"

"The ladies at the Block will keep him."

"Why can't I keep him?"

"You can't work and take him all across the country with you."

"Then I'll take some time off."

"Honey, let's just wait and see what happens."

"Well, okay."

Twenty-Eight

LOPEZ GETS SETTLED IN

Across the sand a man wearing shorts, sandals, and a floral shirt was sitting at a beachside bar, having a fruity drink in a hollowed-out pineapple. The beaches were packed with both tourists and locals. He smiled and thought to himself:

I CAN GET USED TO THIS!

Under a roof made of bamboo and covered with palm branches was a TV mounted up high. Currently CNN was broadcasting in Spanish. At that point, tourists were more interested in the view of the beach than the one on the TV. Lopez turned around to order another cocktail and saw two familiar faces on the screen, Governor Evans and D.A. White. That thought brought on another smile:

I KNEW THOSE PUNKS WOULD SCREW UP! I GOT OUT JUST IN TIME!

The feeling of being clever vanished when he saw the next face on the TV. It was a portrait of him in uniform. He asked the bartender to turn the volume up, and caught the tail-end of a reporter saying a bulletin had been put out for one Ricardo Lopez. He knew that meant all of his accounts would be frozen, so he finished his cocktail and found the nearest ATM. Sure as hell, his withdrawal request was denied. Not having money was going to be a problem.

Preoccupied, he turned away from the ATM so quickly that he collided with a hotel worker carrying a stack of folded towels. Not only did he knock her down, but the towels went flying everywhere. The woman sat frozen on the floor like she'd seen a ghost. He, on the other hand, made a beeline for the door. The hotel desk clerk ran to help the woman up.

"Are you all right, Señora?"

She didn't speak, but instead ran to the employees' locker room. It had been years since she'd seen the man who knocked her down, but this brought back the pain of his hand slapping her in the face. With trembling hands, she opened the combination lock on her locker and pulled her cellphone from her purse.

With all that had happened between her and a certain private investigator from Chicago, she had never stopped loving him, and she couldn't bring herself to erase his number from her phone.

❖❖❖

Back in Chicago, I was headed back to my place with Barney. India should have been in the air by now, and I was waiting to hear from Max about that meeting. My phone vibrated, and Barney barked. I looked at the screen thinking it was going to be Max, but it was a strange number that seemed disturbingly familiar. I pulled over to the curb right away and nervously answered

"This is Sherman."

The woman on the other end was so hysterical that I didn't realize at first that it was Maria.

"Maria, calm down! Calm down!"

"He's here! He's here!"

It didn't take me but a second to put two and two together. "You saw Lopez?"

"Si! He knocked me down in the lobby of my hotel!"

"Did he know it was you?"

"No. He looked like he was scared of something and ran away."

"Are you all right?"

"Sherman, I'm scared!"

"Can I call you back at this number?"

"Si."

"Be careful, and don't let him get a look at you if you see him again."

"Sherman?"

"Yes."

"I miss you!"

"I'll call you back, Maria."

CLICK.

On my way home, I stopped off at the Block. When I walked in, I got the usual greetings, which I cut short.

"Ladies, can I see you all in the office?"

The ladies and Barney followed me into the office.

"Close the door," I said.

Mai immediately asked what was wrong.

"I've got to leave the country for a while."

"Why?" she asked.

"We've got this bastard cornered, and we're going after him! I need you guys to look after Barney again."

Angie asked where I was going.

"Puerto Rico, and I need everyone's word that this conversation stays in this office. Other than the FBI and the chief of police, you guys are the only ones who know about my being tied up with this thing."

"What makes you think Lopez is there?" Angie asked.

"Someone I know spotted him, and they called me."

Carman immediately put two and two together. Her eyes got real big, and she raised her hands to her face.

That's when I lost my temper and yelled at her.

"Damn it, Carman, if you've ever cared about me at all, you'll keep your big mouth closed and your thoughts to yourself! I'm tired of going through women. Don't screw this up for me!"

I folded my arms and gave her a stern look. Angie asked what was going on, and with her eyes watering up, Carman told her nothing.

I picked up Barney and gave him a hug.

"I'm sorry, little buddy. Thanks, ladies."

I left the bar as suddenly as I'd entered. I got in my car and put it in gear. I yelled "Damn!" hit the steering wheel with my fist, and turned the car back off. I went back inside the bar and went straight to Carman. I wrapped my arms around her. She tried with all her might to push me away, but I wouldn't let go. She stopped resisting and looked me straight in the eye. It was then that I released her and left.

TWENTY-NINE

MY CONNECTION

I called Max on my way home and informed him of what was going on, and not surprisingly, he was blown away. I wasn't home for thirty minutes when my doorbell rang. Moments later I got a police-style pounding on my door. Max, Agent Calvin, and the captain marched right in.

Captain Leonard wasted no time in getting down to business.

"What's this connection you have, son?"

"Years ago Lopez used to make part of his weekly routine shaking me down and slapping me around. I got used to it, but two years ago, I started seeing this woman from Puerto Rico. To make a long story short, he began following her around until he finally pulled her over. He searched her, and just as he was about to leave, he turned around and gave her a backhand across her face. He told her it was a message for me. Earlier today I received a hysterical phone call from this woman. He was running scared for some reason, and knocked her down in the lobby of the hotel where she works. But he didn't realize who she was."

"Can you depend on this woman? Is she sure it was Lopez?"

"Captain, her hysterical behavior today was one hundred and ten percent identical to how she behaved two years ago!"

"What hotel does she work at?"

"All I know is that it's a big tourist trap. I guess it makes sense for Lopez to try and blend in with the tourists."

"But he really doesn't have to," the captain said. "He looks like a local and speaks their language. The big question is why did he panic? We don't have anyone down there looking for him, and I doubt these bangers would spend money to go after him. Get your friend on the horn and put her on speakerphone. Let's see if she noticed what he was doing just before their little incident."

I called Maria back.

"Sherman!"

"Maria, I've got you on speakerphone. The police are here too."

"But they're with him! How can you trust them? Do you remember what he did to me?"

"This time we can trust them."

That's when the captain broke into our conversation.

"I'm Captain Leonard with the Chicago Police Department, and Ricardo Lopez is no longer a police officer. At this time, he's a wanted felon. His picture is posted across the country, Canada, and Mexico. Is it all right if I call you Maria?"

At first there was a long pause.

"Si, it's all right."

"Look, Maria, we really need you to trust us. I know you trust Sherman, and he wouldn't risk your life. Can you remember what Lopez was doing when he ran into you?"

"I only saw him from behind at first, but it looked like he was trying to get money from an ATM machine."

"Did he have money in his hand?"

"That's what's so funny! He never reached for his pocket, and he should've dropped bills everywhere as hard as he hit me."

Max snapped his fingers.

"So he knows we're on to him! He also knows that if there's a bulletin out on him, his accounts are frozen. He went to that ATM, found out he had nothing, and panicked! That's why he didn't recognize Maria."

"Sherman?" Maria said.

"Yes?"

"What should I do?"

"Act normally, and if you see him again, stay away from him. Someone will be there in a day or two, and they'll contact you."

"Are you coming?"

"I don't know. Thank you, Maria. I'll call you. Be careful!"

CLICK.

"Well, gentlemen, what do you think about my friend?" I asked.

Agent Calvin was the first to speak up.

"I think we've screwed around with this guy long enough. Captain?"

"This is the closest we've been to this jerk in weeks. I think his financial loss may be our gain. Sure he bought a roundtrip ticket, but there's no way in hell he'll try going through airport security again!"

Agent Calvin rubbed his chin a bit before speaking.

"There's one problem. Desperate men make desperate decisions. He'll start committing petty crimes to generate cash flow. I'm sure the authorities there are willing to work with us, but they don't want our problems."

The captain turned to Max.

"I'm cutting this short. I need to discuss some things with Agent Calvin here. Mr. Brothers, I'm not sure what's going to happen, but I need you to dig up your Firearm Registration and Permit and your P.I. License by tomorrow. Gentlemen, stay near your phones. This is going to be touch and go. Let's go, Agent."

When they left, I turned to Max.

"Max, do you think we're spinning our wheels?"

"If we can sneak in without being noticed, it sure would give us an advantage! I've got a better question for you."

"What's that?"

"Have you told India about, how should I say, your friend?"

"No, and between you and me, I would've married this woman."

"Wow! What happened?"

"Candee Harris happened! Maria walked in on a meeting I was having with her, and took it the wrong way. She'd just been offered a job in her own country and well, Candee was the deciding vote. She left without giving me a chance to explain."

"Who else knows this?"

"Carman."

"Carman!"

"I asked her to keep it to herself, because it would only cost me another good woman."

"Sherman, I don't know how you're going to pull this one off."

"I'll call India in the morning. I may as well get a good night's sleep. Also Max, you may be hearing from Mai. She was at the Block when I dropped off Barney. By the way, what's the word on the governor and D.A. White?"

"He's doing better than she is, but not out of the woods yet. Rumor is he's been asking to make a statement on TV. The doctors, or anyone else for that matter, don't think he's ready. D.A White, that poor woman, I don't think she's ever going to recover mentally."

"I'd be shocked if she returned to her office. That son of a bitch screwed up her life, and no amount of punishment is good enough!"

"You know, the other day you were talking to me about hanging up my badge, and now you're about to be deputized. It's kind of funny."

"A wise woman once told me that sometimes God gives us experiences just for the education."

"Buddy, I don't know what you're about to learn, but it sure is going to be an experience!"

THIRTY

DROPPING THE BOMB ON INDIA

Max took off to talk to Mai, and I was trying to come up with a gentle way to tell India that I might be going to Puerto Rico after all. Who knew, maybe she'd take it better than I thought. I took a deep breath and called her.

"I'm at the baggage claim," she said. "Let me call you back?"

Twenty minutes later she was in a shuttle, heading home.

"So how was your flight?" I asked.

"I slept most of the way. How's your day been?"

"Interesting, to say the least."

"That doesn't sound good!"

"Earlier today I had that meeting I told you about."

"And how did that go?"

"They might want me to go with them to San Juan. Lopez has been spotted there."

"Why do you have to go?"

"My history with him is very valuable to them. Some very ugly things you don't want to hear about have happened between us."

"Honey, I know you're expecting me to give you a hard time, but for the sake of our relationship, I'm going to be a big girl. I don't like this one bit, Sherman, but I'll be praying for you every day. Is there anything else you want to tell me?"

"No, that's it."

"Don't sound so down! I know you wouldn't do it if you didn't have to. Will you call me before you leave?"

"Of course I will."

"Bye!"

CLICK.

LET THE GAMES BEGIN

At a San Juan nightclub in a resort hotel, Lopez was partying with a couple of young local women. They believed they'd cornered a horny old American tourist who was going to buy them cocktails all night. What they didn't know was that they were about to become the hunted, instead of the hunters. One of the ladies' favorite songs came on, and she grabbed her girlfriend's hand, and led her to the dance floor. She turned to Lopez and told him to watch their bags. He gave her a big smile and said sure. While they were on the dance floor, he didn't take their money, but he did lift a credit card.

He smiled again as the ladies waved at him from the dance floor. When they came back, he ordered another round and then excused himself to go to the restroom. While in the john, he took out his cellphone and booked himself a suite with the credit card. After returning to the bar, he slipped the card back into the purse without being noticed. He then flashed a big smile and said goodnight.

Sitting back on the sofa, with his feet on the cocktail table, Lopez sipped complimentary champagne from a crystal flute. On the other end of the table sat a dish filled with fresh fruit. Looking out the balcony doors of his suite, he could see young lovers strolling along the beach in the moonlight, and he started thinking to himself:

NOT BAD FOR AN EASY NIGHT'S WORK! THAT SHOULD TEACH THOSE LITTLE TRAMPS! I CAN BE THE PUERTO RICAN ROMEO

FOR ALL THOSE SINGLE FEMALES LOOKING FOR A LITTLE ROMANCE. I'LL GIVE THEM THE TROPICAL VACATION THEY'RE LOOKING FOR, ALL RIGHT. IT'LL BE LIKE TAKING CANDY FROM A BABY!

Thirty-One

THE CLOCK IS TICKING

When morning came, I gathered the things the captain requested. After packing a bag, I relaxed and waited for my phone to ring. When it did, I was surprised to see Carman's name on my screen.

"Good morning, Carman."

"I just called to tell you to be careful."

"Thank you. I will."

"By the way, I'm not going to say a thing about Maria. Just remember that she's the one who walked out on you. I know how much you love India, and I wouldn't interfere with that."

"Thanks, Carman. I'm sorry for coming on so strong the other day."

"That's okay. It showed me how much you care for India. I'm going to say goodbye for now, and remember to be careful."

CLICK.

I felt much better after talking to Carman, and at 10:30 a.m. I got a call from Max.

"Hey, buddy," I said.

"It looks like we've got the green light! Do you have a bag packed?"

"I'm all set."

"I'll swing by and get you, and then we're headed to the captain's office for a briefing."

"All right. See you in a bit."

CLICK.

While waiting for Max, I started to worry about being somewhere where I didn't speak the language. I wasn't afraid, but it would make it hard to be one hundred percent in control. Even the thought of being law enforcement was playing with my head. Max wasn't kidding when he said this would be an experience.

I wanted to get one last look at India, so I went to my computer with the web cam she'd sent. I started with a simple good morning, hoping she'd be near her computer. At first there was no response, but just as I was about to give up, I heard her voice call my name. I turned around, and there was her lovely face.

"Good morning!"

"So, you're all packed up and ready to go?"

"Max is on his way to pick me up."

"You be good! I'm going to miss you!"

"I'll miss you too."

My cellphone vibrated, and I saw Max's name.

"I'm sorry, honey, but I've got to go. I love you."

"I love you too, Sherman."

Just like that, my monitor screen went black.

THE BRIEFING

When we arrived at the captain's office, Agent Calvin was already there with a new agent, and he did the introductions.

"Good morning, gentlemen. This is Special Agent Juan Rodriquez. He's going to be our interpreter, but he's every bit the real McCoy! Max, you and Sherman know the city doesn't have the budget for this little excursion, so you guys can thank the American taxpayers."

The captain then reached into his desk and took out a bible. He looked at me.

"Son, put your left hand on this bible and raise your right hand. Now, we don't have time to go through the B.S.! State your full name."

"My name is Sherman Brothers."

"Okay, you've been deputized! Little."

"Yes, sir."

"Sign and date this form as a witness. Son," the captain asked me, "did you bring the paperwork I asked for?"

"Yes, sir, I did."

"Good. I need to run copies of it."

The captain reached into his desk again and took out a black billfold. Inside was a badge, which he handed to me. I looked at the badge. I'd never given it any thought before. Not only was it well crafted, but the gold finish appeared to be real. I was impressed.

"Now, just for the record," the captain said, "Agent Calvin and I went through hell and high water with both the state and the federal brass to pull this off. Listen to me good, son! If you come back here without that badge, don't bother coming back!"

"Yes, sir!"

"Little."

"Yes, sir!"

"If you screw this up, you'll be walking a beat so much, you'll need a new pair of shoes every week! Do I make myself clear, gentlemen?"

In unison, we both said, "Yes, sir!"

"There's one more thing. I wouldn't put it past Lopez to start a gunfight in a public place. Don't let him sucker you into that! Remember, law enforcement over there is working with us. That means we can't shoot up their citizens! Throw ideas at each other, and think before you make a move. Now, from this point on, you'll be under the command of Special Agent Calvin. Good luck!"

"Gentlemen, there are boarding passes waiting for us at O'Hare," Agent Calvin said. "Be ready to leave in twenty minutes."

I took advantage of the time and called my dad. I told him what was going on. He was concerned, but wished me luck.

Thirty-Two

Up, Up and Away

In one of the Feds' black SUVs, the four of us plus the driver were on the Kennedy Expressway headed for the airport. The downtown skyline was fading, and we were approaching open highway. Everyone was quiet. I guess we were all in our own thoughts about the task ahead of us. As for me, I was thinking about the break-in at Mr. Cartwright's place, the shootout at Dad's, and the kidnappings. It still blew my mind that one man was responsible for all of it. I wondered if maybe he thought he'd gotten away with it. The funny part about justice is that when we brought him back, he'd still get his day in court. What a huge waste of taxpayers' money!

When we arrived at the airport, a TSA manager greeted us. He handled our bags and hardware, making our transition smooth. As we walked through the airport, it felt strange being there, but not for pleasure. I also felt that everyone here knew who we were. It seemed you could put lipstick on these two agents and they'd still look like Feds!

Waiting made me restless, so I decided to go for a walk. As busy as the airport was, I could still focus on things around me, like an advertisement featuring India. I wondered what she was doing right then. Finally I heard an announcement that was clearly not a boarding call.

ATTENTION ALL PASSENGERS, FLIGHT NUMBER 317 EN ROUTE TO SAN JUAN, PUERTO RICO, WILL BEGIN BOARDING IN TWENTY-FIVE MINUTES.

You would've thought the building was on fire! Everyone jumped out of their seats, only to look like idiots when they realized it wasn't the boarding call and had to sit down again.

After the twenty-five minutes had passed, boarding began. The plane was a jumbo jet, and it was nearly one-third full by the time we boarded. We took two rows of double seating along the windows. I couldn't wait for the seatbelt sign to go off so I could recline my seat. We had a long flight ahead of us, and I wanted to get some sleep if I could. We were scheduled for a layover in Miami. We wouldn't have to change planes, but we would have to step off so the plane could be cleaned. Finally, I was able to recline and put plugs in my ears. I closed my eyes and let sleep settle in.

The flight was relatively smooth. When we landed in Miami, we had lunch at the airport. The four of us took seats and made phone calls. Max gave the captain a call and found out a pistol registered to Lopez had been found on a Metra Electric Train. That was good news. At least he didn't have a gun on him, not that finding one on the street would be hard. Agent Calvin's sources had verified that the security cameras at the San Juan airport had indeed captured Lopez in the terminal.

I took the opportunity to call India. She was glad to hear from me, but her mood hadn't changed much. After lunch, the four of us headed back to our terminal. This time when we boarded, I took a seat next to Max.

"Sherman, I talked to Mai for a little bit."

"What did she have to say?"

"Among other things, she said the media is blowing up about the raid at that abandoned police station."

"That's no surprise!"

"Also, there have protests at City Hall by the Hispanic community. Agent Calvin's bar shakedowns didn't go over very well. Hopefully things will have calmed down by the time we get back."

"Max, what do you think Calvin has in mind?"

"You know, he's a hard guy to read. One thing's for sure, he's taking it all personal. I would think he'd have a big meeting with the La Uniformada, at the Cuartel General."

"You lost me there, buddy! I don't have a clue what you just said."

"I'm talking about the local police. The Cuartel General is the station house."

"Well, it looks like you've been doing your homework. I'm impressed!"

"I spent a little time on the internet last night."

"Since you're on a roll, tell me something. What's their version of the FBI?"

"The FBI has offices there. But Puerto Rico also has Tactical Operations. They are known locally as Fuerza De Choque."

"Meaning?"

"Strike, Shock, and Crash Force."

"So basically they're S.W.A.T.," I said.

"I guess so. Hopefully we won't need them."

"Mostly what we're going to need is eyes."

"Speaking of eyes," Max said, "I'm going to try and close mine. I've got the feeling Agent Calvin is going to want to hit the ground running."

"Good point!"

I tried sleeping, but I couldn't get Maria off of my mind. I knew if I was strong enough to resist Angie, I could resist her as well. India was my world now, and I wasn't going to screw that up. I wasn't surprised that Maria missed me, because I missed her too, but the only satisfaction I could give her was to put Lopez in prison for life. I wore myself out just thinking about my situation, and finally fell asleep.

The next thing I knew, Max was elbowing me and pointing at the seatbelt sign. We dropped below the clouds, and just as I had imagined, the view of Puerto Rico from the air was spectacular! The white, sandy beaches and aquamarine water were picture perfect for a travel advertisement. As we prepared for landing, I had to snap out of my dreamy tourist mood.

After we had landed and were walking through the mobile tunnel, we could see two uniformed officers standing in the terminal looking our way. They wore light blue shirts and navy pants with a black stripe running down the leg. On the shoulder of one of the officers were two stars. The other officer had one star on his shoulder. To find out the difference, I turned to Max for his vast internet knowledge. It turned out that two stars ranked Commander, and one star was Inspector. The two of them greeted us in both Spanish and English.

"Welcome to San Juan. Please come with us."

We were escorted from the airport with no problem. We were then given key cards for the rooms we'd be staying in at the hotel. So we'd blend in with other tourists, they'd booked us at a place called the Casa De Sands Resort. Now that was what I called good use of taxpayer dollars! Outside the airport, two taxis waited. Showing up in policía cars would have drawn too much attention.

Even though we had our keys, we were still greeted by the resort manager. He was the only staff member who knew we were cops. I couldn't believe I was thinking the words *we* and *cops* in the same sentence. Special Agent Rodriquez did all the talking, his fluent Spanish easing the tension a little for those of us who didn't speak the language. We were told our bags would be delivered to our rooms. Max and I paired up, and the agents shared a room. As we rode up in the elevator, Agent Calvin told us our vests and hardware would be delivered the following morning. It was late afternoon right then, and the plan was to meet in the lobby in one hour.

During my one hour, I went down to the gift shop and made a purchase I wasn't crazy about. I needed a couple of loose-fitting, button-front shirts. The kind with some loud-ass tropical print on it or surfers on the beach. They'd make me look like a tourist, plus hide my vest and hardware. On impulse, I bought a new pair of sandals and some sunscreen.

I went back to the room to find Max relaxing on the balcony, drinking lemonade, and checking out the view down on the beach.

"You seem to be enjoying yourself," I said.

"When you're in Rome, do as the Romans do."

"Well, don't let your eyes get your ass in trouble, young man."

"It seems to me that you're the one who has a meeting with trouble."

"Don't remind me."

"Is she really that hot?"

"She really is."

When we all met in the lobby, Agent Calvin told us that our first stop would be the Cuartel General. We were scheduled to meet with a Colonel Cortez. We all squeezed into a taxi and headed for the station house. The ride was incredible. The road we took ran parallel with the beach and had nothing but four- and five-star resorts on it, all with breathtaking views of the ocean. There were small boats taxiing tourists back and forth to cruise ships out on the water. I even saw people sunbathing on the decks of expensive sailboats.

THE CUARTEL GENERAL

After clearing the resort area, we finally made it into town. The driver let us out right in front of the station house. At the main counter, Agent Calvin showed his ID and told the officer we had an appointment with Colonel Cortez. We sat and waited a few minutes for the colonel. Aside from his uniform, he was the Puerto Rican version of Captain Leonard. He was tall and slightly overweight, with salt and pepper hair thinning on top. He shook all of our hands and then led us to a small briefing room. With a strong Spanish accent, he opened the meeting speaking in English.

"First of all, I want to welcome you to my homeland. I can only imagine what it must feel like to track down one of your own. You have my sympathy! My men and I are at your disposal. Hopefully we can capture this felon without any bloodshed. Here we take extra caution when using our firearms. This city operates on tourist dollars, and so far we have a pretty good record for tourists not being injured during policía activity. Bad press would have a direct impact on our economy."

As he removed a file folder from his briefcase, Agent Calvin assured the colonel that we understood.

The colonel continued, "When my superiors informed me of your plans to come here, I took the liberty of reviewing your case."

He removed a small notepad from his pocket.

"I see that this gentleman, Ricardo Lopez, is a very nasty man. I can assure you that if he's on this island, my men will find him! I've communicated with your Captain Leonard of the Chicago Police Department, and I agree that Ricardo Lopez has shamed us all."

Agent Calvin opened his file so that Colonel Cortez could get the complete profile on Lopez. After reviewing the file, he got a strange look on his face and rubbed his chin.

"What is it, Colonel?" Calvin asked.

"Uno momento," he answered.

He picked up a nearby phone, spoke in Spanish, and then hung up.

"Agent Calvin, I think you may want to speak to one of my men. We've been investigating a rash of petty thefts and credit card fraud. It appears that some of our female guests have been getting lured to a gentleman's hotel room, and in the morning they're finding that their credit cards and cash have been stolen. Each of these women has given the same description of the predator. I have reason to believe that our man and your man are one and the same."

Agent Calvin looked at us, and then at the colonel.

"I'm sorry to hear that! We were thinking he might stoop to this kind of crime to support himself. Back in the States, we put a freeze on all of his accounts so he wouldn't have cash flow. It's good that your men are already after him. Can you tell if these thefts all took place in the same area?"

The colonel paced a bit.

"Right now they've all taken place in the more populated tourist areas.

Perhaps this is a good thing. He may feel he's having good luck there. His own greed may be what helps us!"

That's when Calvin started doing a little pacing of his own.

"There's one other detail, Colonel. We have a contact here that's already seen Mr. Lopez. She's a massage therapist at one of your resorts. A couple of years ago she was a Chicago resident. During that time she had a nasty run-in with Lopez, and he became physical with her. Two days ago he was in a hurry and knocked her down, not realizing who she was. A couple of my men are going to meet with her this afternoon."

The colonel expressed concern for Maria's safety, and offered security for her. Calvin told him that at this point it wasn't necessary.

"Agent Calvin, if you need anything, please let me know. And, oh yes, please keep the lines of communication open."

At that point I excused myself to give Maria a call. On the second ring she answered.

"Sherman! I'm going loco waiting to hear from you!"

"I'm sorry, but I'm here now. When and where can we meet?"

"I get off in thirty minutes. Write this down."

"Okay, one hour, I got it. Be careful, Maria!"

CLICK.

I rejoined the others.

"Excuse me, gentlemen. I've just arranged to meet with our contact. She wants to meet me in one hour at a place called Munoz Rivera Park."

"Ah, yes" the Colonel said.

"It's an oceanside flower garden full of tourists. It's out in the open, and fairly safe."

"Can I make it there in one hour?"

"Yes, you can, my friend."

MARIA

Agent Calvin suggested that I take Agent Rodriquez along, in case I ran into any language issues. We took off immediately. The well-manicured park was beautiful, with its large trees and flowers in what seemed like every color of the rainbow. The cherry on top was that it was oceanside.

As we walked through the garden, there was plenty of room for tourists. We passed by an older woman sitting on a bench with a toddler. He appeared to be learning how to stand on his own. We smiled and kept walking. At a break in the path, I saw a young woman carrying her shoes, with her pants rolled up. She walked along the ocean shore, and it appeared she was letting the water cool her feet.

I tried not to stare at her, but I couldn't help myself. For some reason she stopped walking and turned around. For a moment we both froze without making a move, but taking a long, hard look at each other. She then broke into a run, dropping her shoes along the way. She yelled out my name and got Agent Rodriquez's attention as well.

She ran into my arms, holding me so tight that for a moment I thought she'd never let go. When she finally did, it seemed the old passion was still there. We looked at each other in the same way we used to look at each other after making love. The moment was interrupted by the old woman with the little boy. Maria then reached out and took the child from the woman's arms.

"Sherman, this is my son, Javier."

My eyes must have gotten real big on that bit of news.

"Relax, Sherman! He's only a year old."

I was trying to be cool, but obviously she knew me well. Pointing toward the old lady, she said, this is my mother. She then spoke in Spanish, and whatever she said, both her mom and Agent Rodriquez got a kick out of it. The old woman gave me a hug, and said something I didn't understand. Maria gave the boy back to her and led me over to a nearby bench.

I tried to get down to business.

"Maria, tell me about your encounter with Lopez. Have you seen him again?"

She ignored my question.

"How are you, Sherman? You look good! I miss you. I haven't seen you look this good before. You're happy, aren't you? Is it that same woman?"

Finally, I broke in.

"You were wrong, Maria, but you never let me explain. The woman you saw me with was a reporter. She was giving me inside information on some murders that were going on."

Maria's eyes got big, then she covered her face with her hands and lowered her head. After a few moments she raised her head and put one of her hands on my cheek.

"Oh, Sherman, honey, I'm so very sorry. I didn't know. I truly am sorry."

There was a long period of silence, and then she spoke again.

"So, this woman, is she good to you?"

"Yes, she is. We're currently in learning mode. What about you?"

I pointed at the little boy.

"I see you've started a new life."

"I love Javier more than anything in the world! He's what keeps me going. His father, he's a different story! He's a little boy that can't keep his pants on, and yes, this time I'm sure. The last time that I saw him was about a week after Javier was born."

"Maria, you deserve so much better! I feel bad for you. If I could, I'd…"

She put her fingers across my lips so I wouldn't speak.

"To answer your question, no, I haven't seen Lopez again. I've heard rumors that someone that sounds like him has been ripping off female tourists."

"Is it happening in the neighborhoods, or just the tourist areas?" I asked.

"It's in the tourist areas, all right!"

"What makes you think that?"

"The people who work at these big resorts are like family. Everyone knows everyone else. They say he uses these poor women's credit cards to book a first-class suite the following day."

"Has he stayed at your hotel?"

"I don't think so, but it's not like he uses his own name."

"Can you write down your address for me?"

Maria got excited.

"You're going to come and see me?"

"I'm sorry, but no. I don't trust either one of us. I didn't come over here to hurt you, or to get hurt myself. We've both had enough of that. I only asked for your address so we can keep an eye on you. By the way, if you should see me in public, remember that I'm undercover."

"So you really have moved on!"

"Maria, the truth is that I never stopped loving you, but I have a new life now, and I can't screw it up. Do you really want someone else to feel the pain that you once felt?"

"That doesn't mean we can't have dinner while you're here."

"I really don't know. I have to think about that. I should be going now."

"Can I have a hug?" she asked.

"I'm just going to say goodbye for now, and walk away. I'll be in touch."

I was touched by Maria's situation. She was the one who had walked away from me. I was such a good man that she wouldn't give me a chance, and her life was what she made it. Why she chose this loser and allowed herself to get pregnant beat the hell out of me. I knew that little boy would give her a lot of love, but he couldn't ever give her what I would have.

Now I had two challenges. One was Lopez, the other not letting Maria get under my skin. Seeing her was too much for me. I'd just have to avoid her as much as I could. As Agent Rodriquez and I waited for a taxi, he could see I was a bit shaken.

"Why do I feel like there's more to this woman than just being a contact? Do you two have a history?"

"Is it that obvious?"

"It's either that or some serious love at first sight! Can I give you a word of advice?"

"Sure."

"Keep it in check, and stay focused! Don't take this the wrong way, but now isn't the time to get caught with your pants down."

"You're telling me!"

"Hey, here's our taxi."

Thirty-Three

THE NIGHT LIFE

B ack at the General Station House, Max and Agent Calvin were making plans to hit the tourist areas. It was about to get dark out, which meant the nightlife was about to go into full swing. Max felt that he and I could take it on with our limited Spanish skills. We were given maps of the city streets. Colonel Cortez suggested we start off on Sebastian Street, with lots of bars that draw the kind of tourist who likes to go pub-clubbing. In the States we call it barhopping. It would be the ideal place for Lopez to find his victims.

The four of us agreed to check in with each other every couple of hours or so. While Max and I would work the club scene, the agents would be going to a place called Plaza de San Jose. Known for a bronze statue of Ponce de Leon, it was supposed to be a meeting place for all kinds of people, the young and the old, you name it. We split up, and it was game on.

Riding in the taxi, Max and I agreed that we were nervous without our hardware. At that point, if we spotted Lopez, we'd have to depend on the colonel's men to take him down. We had our driver drop us off right in the middle of all the excitement. I immediately flashed back to Bourbon Street in New Orleans. But instead of jazz, blues, and rock and roll, there were serious Latin rhythms rocking the cobblestone streets.

The sound was so loud that we had to yell at each other. The streets were full of people, and there were crowds at the entrance of every joint on the block. The first club we went in reminded me of the seventies. The floor was lit from underneath, and there were squad car type lights flashing. Topping it all off was a big mirrored ball hanging from the ceiling. The place was packed, and everyone was dancing the salsa. Mojitos and rumbas seemed to be the drink of choice. The band was jamming, and the place was simply off the hook.

Did I mention the women? Somewhere in the world there's a shortage of stilettos, because that was the shoe that all of the women were wearing. Along with those, they wore the tightest outfits their bodies could squeeze into. Due to the noise, Max and I couldn't communicate, so we decided to split up. All we could do was keep an eye on each other.

There was one thing I'd learned about the men and women in every city I'd been to. They all seem to pounce on tourists. I don't know if we're fresh meat, or we just look easy. In any case, tonight was no different. I made my way through the crowd, and then on to the bar.

Along the way, I got several "come and get me" looks from the ladies. I ordered a beer and turned to leave the bar, but got stopped in my tracks. Standing just inches away from me was a super-tight skirt with a bikini top supporting an ample pair of breasts. With a big smile, the young lady yelled in my ear.

"You look like you're looking for a friend tonight!"

It seemed as good a place as any to start. I told her yes, you're right, which turned out to be the wrong words to say. She immediately put her arms around my waist.

"My name is Rosa. Do you salsa? Come on!"

"Wait a minute, Rosa. I'm looking for a friend."

"I knew it! What's her name?"

"It's not a she."

She got the strangest look on her face, and then rattled off something in Spanish.

"Don't tell me you're gay!"

"No, it's not like that, but I really need to find this guy!"

"So what's this guy's name?"

"His name is Rick, and he's Latin, bald, and muscular."

She turned around and looked out into the crowd.

"Yeah, I've seen him!"

She started pointing.

"Right there, right there, and over there!"

Damn, she was right! There were a number of guys in the club that looked like Lopez. Apparently being bald was in now. I thought Rosa was going to take off, but she didn't.

"So, are we going to dance or not?"

"No, but I'll treat you to a mojito."

"I'll take it!"

MAX MEETS HIS MATCH

Out on the dance floor, I saw that Max had been taken hostage by two lovely bandits, and he was being bounced between them like a tennis ball. I made eye contact with him, and he gave me a look that said he didn't know how he got there. All I could do was smile at him. Finally he broke loose and made it over to me. Without saying a word, he grabbed my beer and drank it all.

"Can you believe this place, Sherman?"

"You should've seen the one who just walked away!"

"Was she any help?"

"That's a matter of opinion! Take a look out into the crowd, and tell me how many guys you see that look like Lopez."

Max turned and took a look.

"This isn't going to be easy, my friend!" he said.

"Did you have any luck with your new friends?"

"I never got a chance to speak!"

"Well, don't look now, but your chance is on the way over here!" I said.

Max turned around to find his new friends right in his face. To avoid going back out on the dance floor, he told them we were looking for Lopez. After he gave them his description, the ladies freaked out. They stepped back, holding each other with scared looks on their faces.

That was followed by one of them yelling at Max.

"What the hell, man! Are you guys working with that fucking scumbag?"

That's when I jumped in.

"Wait a minute. Have you ladies seen this asshole? Look, we're trying to stop him before he hurts someone!"

"Well, you're too damned late!"

"Tell us what happened to you," I said.

"It wasn't us. It was our girlfriend! They partied one night, and then that son of a bitch stole her cash and credit cards! The bastard ran up a tab at some damned resort. If you guys catch him, kick his ass!"

"Trust me, ladies, we will!" I said.

The two left, and Max turned toward me.

"You know, Sherman. The hair on the back of my neck is standing up. That son of a bitch is near!"

"Yeah, he's close. I do know one thing. If he keeps this up, the locals are going to kill his ass and turn him into shark food!"

"I hope you're wrong. If that happens, he'll be getting off way too easy. Why don't we get some fresh air?"

"I'm behind you, buddy."

Outside, Max took out his cellphone and checked in with Agent Calvin.

They hadn't gotten very far either, although they too found out that word of Lopez was getting around to the local women. That was a good thing, but it didn't help the female tourists at risk. Max told Calvin that we were going to stick around a couple more hours, and then head back to the hotel.

Before we hit the next club, I checked in on Maria.

"Sherman, I didn't think I'd hear from you so soon! Did you catch him?"

"Not yet, but it seems the local women all know he's here and what he's doing."

"So what are your plans for tomorrow?"

"We're going to get back out on the streets."

"Why don't you stop in at the hotel and get a free massage?"

"I can't, Maria. The truth is that I couldn't handle it."

"You mean I still make you feel that way?"

"Look, I'm trying to focus on Lopez."

"I'm sorry. Thanks for checking in on me."

CLICK.

WE'VE BEEN SPOTTED

Sitting at a table in a bar across the street was Ricardo Lopez. He was staring out into the street as he downed a cold beer. He saw Max and me standing in the middle of the street, spinning our mental wheels. With a nasty grin, he made a gun with his hand and fingers and fired two rounds out into the street, one for me, one for Max. Lopez got up and ordered another beer, blended in with the crowd, and thought:

POOR SUCKERS! I CAN TAKE 'EM OUT ANYTIME I WANT!

Not knowing that Lopez had spotted us, we headed for our next club. After an hour or so, we came up with nothing and decided to call it a night. We hailed a taxi and took off.

Thirty-Four

SEX SELLS

Max and I went back to the hotel, both of us with a creepy feeling. It was the kind of feeling that only someone in our field would get. It's when you know you're close, but not close enough to touch. Knowing that we had given it a good shot that night, we decided to get a good night's sleep. In the morning we'd meet with the others to plot our next move.

I wanted to talk to India, but I didn't want to keep Max awake, so I grabbed my cellphone and headed down to the hotel bar. To keep up my tourist appearance, I ordered a mojito. I couldn't help but notice the single women lounging around. The bar would be closing in a couple of hours or so, and they'd be prime targets for someone like Lopez. I took a seat at a table for two and called India. She answered on the first ring.

"Sherman! Are you all right?"

"I'm fine, honey. I just wanted to hear your voice."

"Are you and Max getting any closer to catching that guy?"

"We think so, because he's been picking up women and stealing their cash and credit cards, and word is spreading among the locals."

"So he has no money, and he's sleeping with women to support himself?"

"It seems so."

"What a bastard!"

"I hate to say it, but if this guy is careful, he can make a career out of this."

"What are you guys doing to catch him?"

"We've been splitting into teams and hitting the tourist areas."

"Can I offer my opinion?"

"Sure."

"Do you know why the cosmetics and fashion industries make millions of dollars every day?"

"Not really."

"They use young, pretty girls to advertise their products."

"What does that have to do with our investigation?"

"Honey, I think that tropical air is getting to you! You men are absolutely incredible. You bend over backward trying to get laid, but if the subject isn't about sex, you forget that women even exist."

"I still don't get it."

"Stop thinking like a cop. Now tell me, how many men has your guy gotten into bed?"

"Damn it! Why didn't we think of that? You can catch more flies with honey!"

"Finally! And here I thought I loved you for your brain."

"I love you, India, but I've got to go and wake up Max."

"Wait, don't wake him up! Can't it wait until morning?"

"I guess it can."

"Good night, Sherman. I love you."

CLICK.

India definitely took my mind off of Maria. In fact, I was so excited about this new approach that I forgot all about her. I went back to the room and was surprised when I didn't see Max in bed. The breeze off the ocean led me to him sitting out on the balcony.

"Where did you go?" he asked.

"I wanted to call India but didn't want to keep you awake, so I went down to the bar."

"How's she doing?"

"She's doing great. Not only that, she had serious input regarding our case."

"You're kidding me. So what did Sherlock have to say?"

"She said we've been using the wrong bait to catch Lopez. Let's face it. Lopez can spot a cop from a mile away, and he has no interest in men."

"Are you suggesting we can catch more flies with honey?"

"Exactly what I said!"

"Well, what's the plan now?"

"I don't know, but it's going to involve some of Colonel Cortez's female officers. I'm going to sleep on it, and in the morning I'm going to run it by Agent Calvin."

Around nine in the morning we met with Agents Calvin and Rodriquez. During breakfast, there was random chitchat. After eating, we sat around drinking coffee, and that's when business started.

Agent Calvin opened things up.

"I think today we should take advantage of the beaches and leave the nightclubs for nighttime. Any comments or ideas?"

That was my cue.

"I have something I'd like to run by you guys. I had a conversation with my girlfriend last night, and to make a long story short, she told me that the cosmetics and fashion industries sell so much because they use pretty, young models in their advertising. That's when things clicked. If we want to catch Lopez, let's offer him what he wants."

"And where do we get these pretty girls?" Agent Calvin asked.

"For starters, maybe we can turn to Colonel Cortez's female officers. He did say he'd be here for us," I said.

"But what if he doesn't want to put them at risk?"

"Well, they are police officers, but if he feels that way, I guess we're back at square one. Could we do it without jeopardizing their safety?"

"With Lopez's history, I doubt it."

"You mentioned hitting the beaches today. Out of the four of us, Rodriquez is the only one Lopez doesn't recognize. He can pose as a bartender while the female officers do their thing. If Lopez goes for one of them, she can take him up to one of our rooms. We can watch from across the hall. The public will be safe, and we'll have him cornered."

"I don't know, Sherman. I think Lopez is too smart for that."

Calvin looked at Max.

"What do you think, Max?"

"I think the success of this plan depends on if Lopez has become overconfident."

That's when Rodriquez spoke up.

"Why don't we let Cortez decide? Sometimes a simple plan is the best plan. As for me, I'm in."

Calvin still wasn't crazy about my idea, but he did step out to the lobby to call Colonel Cortez.

"Good morning, Colonel. This is Special Agent Calvin."

"Good morning, my friend. How can I be of service to you today?"

"My men and I have tracked down a few leads, but we're considering changing our strategy. The plan we've come up with requires your help."

"I see. Perhaps we should discuss your plan here at the General Station House."

"Would an hour from now be okay?"

"That will be fine, my friend."

CLICK.

Over Calvin's shoulder I could see one of the colonel's men standing at the entrance of the hotel's restaurant. He was holding a large suitcase. I motioned to Calvin, and he turned around.

The officer approached us.

"Good morning. I'm looking for a Special Agent Calvin."

Calvin stepped behind him and identified himself.

"Forgive me, but may I see your credentials?"

Agent Calvin then presented his federal identification.

"Perhaps we can continue our conversation in private."

Calvin agreed.

"Why don't we all go up to my room?"

In Calvin's room there were papers for him to sign, and the suitcase was opened, revealing our vests and hardware. We all thanked the officer, and he was on his way. It wasn't long before we were climbing into a taxi and heading to see the colonel. After the typical greetings, he led us to the same briefing room we'd used before. In the center of the conference table were glasses and a pitcher of water. We took a seat, but the colonel remained standing. He wasted no time in getting down to business.

"So tell me, Agent Calvin. What is it I can do for you today?"

"Colonel, Mr. Brothers here actually came up with the plan. Perhaps I should let him present it to you."

"I see. Mr. Brothers?"

"So far our investigation has led us to the local women here, and it appears that word of Lopez's game is being spread around the community."

"This is good, is it not?"

"Yes, but it doesn't protect your tourists."

"So what is your suggestion?"

"Lopez is focusing on women. I think that instead of trying to track him down, we should offer him what he's looking for."

"So this is why you need my help. Are you suggesting that I provide my female officers to lure Mr. Lopez?"

I looked at Calvin and then back at the colonel.

"Yes sir, I am."

"This would be an undercover investigation, would it not?"

"Yes sir, it would."

"I'd like to hear more, but I must tell you. I can give the order to my officers, but I can't guarantee that they'll be willing to parade up and down the beach in bikinis. But if they do agree, what's your plan?"

I gave the colonel the details of my plan as I'd done with the guys following breakfast. He paced a little and gave it some thought before replying.

"It sounds like a simple plan. Are you sure this Lopez gentleman will fall for it?"

"We believe he's become overconfident due to his success. I guess it would depend on how comfortable your officers make him feel."

Again, the colonel did some pacing.

"I'm going to work with you, gentlemen, but if your plan doesn't work, I'm going to do things my way."

Agent Calvin went to stand up, but Max touched his wrist. It was enough to make him harness his emotions.

"I'll need time to contact the beach bar management, and to brief my officers. In the meantime, maybe you gentlemen should get back out on the street and wait to hear from me. Is there anything else?"

Agent Calvin took a deep breath and said, "That will be all, Colonel."

THIRTY-FIVE

BACK ON THE HUNT

We left the General Station House and split up. The agents decided to hit the beaches most popular with the tourists. Max and I headed for a cheap beer bar called El Café Seda. The joint looked like it hadn't changed since the sixties. It was early afternoon, but already the place was busy. Not seeing any immediate sign of Lopez, we just relaxed. Max stepped outside to call the captain and give him an update. It appeared that Governor Evans had gotten what he wanted, the chance to make a statement from his hospital room. He was dressed and sitting in a chair, but there had been no media present. Only a video was made that aired on WLOK.

LOPEZ TARGETS THE WRONG WOMAN

After about two hours, Max contacted Agent Calvin. They hadn't gotten anywhere either, but they'd seen plenty of possible victims.

❖❖❖

At another bar more popular with the neighbors than with tourists, things were heating up. Five young locals were sitting at a table. They'd been there awhile, enjoying the party atmosphere. There were two ladies, one accompanied by her three brothers. While the good times were rolling, Lopez walked in. He took a seat at the bar and ordered a rumba. After his second cocktail, he began to check out the local talent. That's when he caught the eye of one of the ladies at the table. He smiled and tipped his glass. He then turned his back to let the prey approach him. Just as his ego had told him, she appeared beside him.

"Hi, my name is Lilly. You must be new around here. Are you a tourist?"

"Not anymore," Lopez said. "I'm here to stay. Are you a tourist?"

She laughed. "This is my home. My family has been here for generations."

"It's a pleasure to meet you, Lilly. Can I buy a drink?"

Before saying yes, she turned and gave her girlfriend the eye. She then took a seat on a stool next to Lopez. They shared a few cocktails and seemed to hit it off. At one point she excused herself to check in with her girlfriend. Back at the table, her friend's brothers had mixed in with the crowd. While the two ladies were talking, they were interrupted by a waitress.

"Excuse me, ladies. Do you guys know that man over there?"

She turned to point at Lopez, but he was no longer sitting there. That's when Lilly realized she had left her purse on the bar. She freaked out, and her friend yelled to her brothers. The waitress put her arm around Lilly.

"Honey, I saw him reach into your purse and then head for the restroom!"

The three young men ran toward the restroom. Inside Lopez stood in front of a urinal, counting Lilly's cash. In the meantime the waitress was calling the General Station House. Facing the wall, Lopez never saw the brothers coming. One of them pushed his face into the wall, breaking his nose. Another brother then punched him in the kidneys. From that point he was thrown to the floor, where he dropped the cash, and that's when the real beating started. The three men kicked him in the head, torso, and knees. When they felt he'd had enough, one of them picked up the scattered bills, and they walked out. They then grabbed the girls and took off.

Lopez knew he couldn't be found there. In agonizing pain, he slowly picked himself up, washed the blood off his face, and staggered out holding his ribs. About ten minutes later, the colonel's men came rushing into the bar. The only thing they found was a bloody mess on the restroom floor and in the sink. After interviewing the waitress, they knew they had missed Lopez by minutes. They didn't bother asking further about the party of five. As far as they were concerned, Lopez had gotten a beating he deserved.

❖❖❖

Back at El Café Seda, Max and I had given up on the place and were about to take off when his cellphone rang. It was Agent Calvin.

"Hey, Lopez was spotted! It's a place called Basilliko. Get over there now! I'll meet you there."

CLICK.

We jumped in a taxi and were there in ten minutes. When we got there, the place was crawling with policía. Obviously we were too late. The agents arrived shortly after we did. After interviewing the people in the bar, we still had nothing. The good thing was that Lopez had taken a well-deserved ass kicking. Judging by the amount of blood in the restroom, we figured he'd be lying low for a while.

Colonel Cortez had gotten wind of the incident, and was indeed hot under the collar!

Meanwhile, on a secluded beach, Lopez staggered toward a group of trees, where he collapsed. The beating had been too much for him, and he finally passed out.

It's a Small World

There wasn't much we could do the rest of the day, so the agents set out in search of dinner, while Max and I went to check out the beach at night. The sun was just beginning to set. There were couples walking along the waves, people partying around campfires, and the sound of music in the air. We stopped at one of those grass hut bars for a drink. Max had a beer, and I had something fruity served in a hollowed-out coconut. I didn't know what the fruit mix was, but it had plenty of rum in it.

"You know, Sherman," Max said. "I really like this place!"

"It sure is easy to get comfortable here. The beaches, the women, the slow pace of life. It's great, but I'd have to live here a long time before I could call it home. You know what they say. The grass is always greener!"

"I'll drink to that!"

As we were toasting, a couple of lovely tourists joined us. One of them was African American, and the other one was White, dark-haired and maybe of Italian descent. I had the feeling they were career women. It was a certain air they had, like they weren't there for a week of tropical romance.

I decided to break the ice.

"Hi, my name is Sherman, and this is my friend Max."

The ladies extended their hands. Their names were Jessi and Valerie.

"It's nice to meet you ladies. Are you enjoying your stay?"

"Are you kidding? This place is great!" said Jessi, the one I believed to be of Italian descent. "The sunset and the nightlife alone are worth coming here."

Her friend Valerie spoke up.

"Plus we needed to get the heck out of town!"

"You ladies aren't on the run, are you?" I said.

"No, but the city we're from has gone crazy! We both had time saved up at work, so we decided to take off."

Max then stepped into the conversation.

"What kind of work do you two do?"

"I'm a court reporter, and Valerie here is a court secretary," Jessi said.

"So, how has the legal system been treating you?" Max asked.

"It's been crazy, and I won't get into details, but if you've been watching CNN, you can put two and two together," Valerie said.

"If you don't mind me asking," Max said, "what city are you ladies from?"

"Chicago," Valerie said. "What about you guys?"

"We're just a couple of guys trying something new," Max said.

"Sure you are!" Jessi said. "I've been in the legal world for a long time, and I don't know about your buddy here, but you quack like a duck!"

I almost spit out my drink laughing, and Max looked at me like I was Benedict Arnold.

"You're a cop, aren't you? Tell me the truth, where are you guys from?" Jessi asked.

"My buddy here is from Hyde Park, and I'm from the Near North Side."

"I knew it!" Valerie said. "You guys are Windy City boys! I can't believe we came all this way to meet neighborhood guys!"

"I guess it's a small world after all!" I said.

That's when I decided we'd better get going.

"Hey, ladies," I said. "It's been a blast meeting you, but we'd better get going. Have fun, but be careful."

"Bye, guys!"

THIRTY-SIX

IT'S A NEW DAY

When morning came, Max and I woke up talking about the two ladies we'd met. I told him I'd backed off because, if those two had connections back home, this whole thing could blow up in our faces. I was ready to climb out of bed, shower, and give India a call. Just as I was sitting up in bed, my cellphone rang.

"This is Sherman."

"Hi, Sherman, I'm sorry for bothering you, especially this early in the morning."

"Maria, what's going on?"

"I thought you'd want to know that there's a new rumor going around this morning."

"And what's that?"

"It looks like Lopez ran into a little bad luck yesterday. It seems he screwed around with the wrong lady and got beat up."

"Great! Chalk one up for the good guys!"

"I just thought you'd want to know."

"Hey, Maria, I don't hate you, and thanks."

"Thanks for what?"

"Thanks for the most exciting months of my life!"

"Thank you too. I've got to go now. Take care of yourself, Sherman."

CLICK.

"Wow!"

"Wow, what?" Max asked.

"I think it's finally over."

"Let me guess? That was that Maria woman."

"You've got it, buddy."

PLAN B

After I came out of the shower, Max went in, and forty minutes later we were dressed and having coffee in the hotel's café. It wasn't long before the agents joined us. We had our ceremonial breakfast and then headed for the General Station House. During the ride over, I was thinking about how interesting the day was going to be, most of all because Lopez had thrown a monkey wrench into our plan. Depending on how bad the beating was that he took, he might be lying low today. If so, our day would be nothing but a dress rehearsal.

At the station house, the colonel and his officers were already waiting for us. Everyone was introduced, including the manager of the beachside bars. The colonel's officers consisted of two females and two males. The males were to pose as locals and work the perimeter. The female officers were to take turns sunbathing on the beach, and occasionally going to the bar for a cocktail. Agent Rodriquez would be posing as a bartender trainee, as I suggested. Agent Calvin, Max, and I would be working the resort where we were staying.

Colonel Cortez suggested that the three of us take a ride out to where the operation would be taking place. He also provided us with a small statue of Ponce De Leon that had a small camera mounted inside of it. Along with the statue, he supplied a laptop computer. The statue was to be placed in Agent Calvin's room, the room to which the female officers would attempt to lure Lopez. The operation was scheduled to go into action at one p.m. that afternoon.

Agent Calvin, Max, and I headed for the beach, while the others remained at the station house to go over some details. The beach was just coming to life when we arrived. The bars were opening, cabana boys were setting up their stations, and lifeguards were taking their posts. A few sun worshipers were trying to get an early start, but that was about it. So there wasn't much to see, although we did take note of the beach staff and a small marina that docked boats that looked to be twenty-four feet or smaller in size. After a little while, we took off.

Back at the resort, we decided to rotate three details. One of us would man the surveillance room, across the hall from Agent Calvin's room. One of us would work the hotel's lobby, while another worked the grounds. To keep from getting bored, we'd switch positions every hour and a half. We set up the camera and laptop, and waited for one p.m. to roll around.

In the meantime, Max called Captain Leonard on speakerphone so we could have a conference call.

"Captain, Max here with Agent Calvin and Sherman. I've got you on speakerphone."

"Hold on, let me close my office door," the captain said. He came back on the line.

"Good morning gentlemen. Give me some good news."

"Well, Captain, we have semi-good news," Max said.

"At this point I'll take anything!"

"Yesterday Lopez screwed around with the wrong woman. It appears she was in a party of five with three men. As soon as the lady realized she'd been ripped off, the men found Lopez in the restroom and beat the hell out of him!"

"So this is semi-good news because he got away, right?"

"That's about the size of it. We were a few minutes late."

"Well, I don't feel one bit sorry for his ass! What's your next move?"

"Colonel Cortez is providing female officers to set up Lopez. We figure if he wants women, that's what we're going to give him."

"Good luck, gentlemen!"

"How are things going back there?" Max asked.

"Let's just say you guys are having better luck than I am. The mayor wants results now. Even worse, a spokesperson from the D.A.'s office announced that D.A. White would not be returning to work. There's also a public group petitioning to have the old Pullman police station torn down. As you can imagine, the media is having a field day!"

While we were still on the phone with the captain, Agent Calvin's phone rang. It was Colonel Cortez telling him the operation had been activated.

THIRTY-SEVEN

BAMBOOZLED

It wasn't like we had to jump up and run to our stations, so we finished our conversation with the captain. Following our call, Calvin went to his room and returned with lapel pins and ear bugs for listening. Max took the first watch in our room. Calvin took the lobby, and I headed for the grounds.

I started out near the pool. Why not? My time there wouldn't last long, so I stretched out on a lounge chair. There were couples and families enjoying the pool. After settling in, I focused on the job at hand. I'd keep my eyes on the single women, and wait for Lopez to show up. After about twenty-five minutes, I moved to an area where people were registering for different activities. Some were booking midday lunch cruises, and some were booking guided hikes up to the falls, but none of the women I saw were being escorted by Lopez. There was no point in sticking around, so I moved on.

This time my stroll around the grounds was different. I guess it was apparent I was alone, because I was approached by a woman who was somewhat older than me. She was very well kept, and very attractive, I might add, but just the same, older than me. She had a touch of class that I rarely see in younger women, so I gave her a bit of my time. She politely asked if she could join me at my table. After taking a seat, she motioned to a waiter and ordered lemonade for the two of us. I knew I was on duty, but the lapel pin and ear bug made me think I was all right.

I went out of my way not to mislead her, but I did let her know that I was enjoying her company. She took it quite well, revealing even more class. We laughed and talked for about another twenty minutes. It turned out that she was a writer doing research for her upcoming novel. I told her that it had been a pleasure, but it was time for me to go. We both stood and shook hands, and I headed for the lobby.

When I got there, Max and Agent Calvin were waiting for me. Max was more than happy to work the grounds, while I took over the lobby. Calvin had no problem with working the surveillance room. It gave him the privacy he needed to make some phone calls. The air conditioning in the lobby felt great, but the view didn't compare to the pool area. The first thirty minutes in the lobby was quite busy, but then things slowed down. It was the time of day where people were heading outdoors.

After a while, I started getting a funny feeling whenever the resort staff members walked by. They were all very nice, but not one of them suggested any activities to me or questioned why I was just hanging around. I wondered if maybe the manager had let the cat out of the bag. I stuck to the plan, though, because I believed Lopez would stick to his.

While Calvin was working the surveillance room, his cellphone rang.

"Calvin, this is Captain Leonard. We may have a problem!"

"Hold on a minute, Captain."

Calvin took out a small suction cup device from his pocket and stuck it to his phone. He then spoke to Max and me through his lapel pin.

"Listen up, guys! I've got the captain on the phone! Okay, Captain, go ahead."

"Gentlemen, I don't know if this is a problem, or if I'm just paranoid. Yesterday a woman by the name of Cheryl Lennox came into the station asking my desk sergeant questions about Lopez. She pushed him pretty hard, but wouldn't say what her interest in him was. After she left, the sergeant ran a background check on her."

"What did he find?" Calvin asked.

"I hope you guys are ready for this! For the past year she's been working as a TSA agent out at the airport. Their records show that prior to being hired, she was a freelance writer who worked with reporters, but was down on her luck."

As soon as the captain said that, I interrupted him.

"Excuse me, Captain, but what does this woman look like?"

"She's a tall brunette, attractive, maybe about fifty-two years old, and the problem is that she purchased an airline ticket to San Juan."

"Shit!" I yelled. "Max, she's out by the pool!"

Outside Max jumped up out of his seat, looking in every direction. By the time I made it outside, he was standing in one spot, turning in circles, but she was nowhere to be seen. Damn it, not only did we have to nail this lunatic Lopez, but now we had a freelance nut trying to make it to the big time!

After Max and I had exhausted all of our efforts, we headed back to the lobby, where we found Calvin looking at a photo of our freelance writer. The captain had faxed it to him.

I took one look at it.

"That's her all right!"

"So tell me, Sherman," Calvin said. "What did you and this woman talk about?"

"She did tell me that she was a freelance writer working on some novel, but it was mostly just tourist chitchat."

"Well, with all of the stories on the air covering Lopez, and the fact that she works at the airport, I'd say it's safe to say she knows who we are. Please tell me you didn't give her your name."

"We never exchanged names."

I was thinking to myself that was the only thing I'd done right. At that point I felt like a king-sized sucker. Maybe our meeting had been a chance encounter, but I still couldn't believe I'd fallen for her charm. With nothing else to do, we returned to our details.

THIRTY-EIGHT

A SNAIL'S PACE

The rest of the day dragged on. At five p.m. Colonel Cortez replaced his officers with four fresh officers. Agent Rodriquez remained posing as a bartender trainee, but now with a new supervisor. After a while the sun began to set, and the temperature was nearly perfect. So far this had been one of the longest days of my life, and it wasn't over yet. I yearned to be driving my car down Lake Shore Drive with Barney in the passenger's seat.

The hours rolled on, and at 10:30 p.m. we decided to call it a day. The following day we returned to our routine. At around two p.m., Agent Calvin said the hell with this!

"We're spinning our wheels hanging around this place. Why don't we grab our hats and shades, and head for the beach? I think we'll do better there, but try to look like a tourist."

GAME ON

We all put on our best tourist look and headed for the set-up area of the beach. The other officers were surprised to see us, but they didn't let on that they knew who we were. We immediately split up and started our surveillance. Max took a seat at the bar and ordered a cocktail from Rodriquez. I stretched out on the sand, and Calvin went for a stroll. The scene was pretty normal. To my right were a couple of ladies playing with a Frisbee. In front of me there was a volleyball game going on. The one thing I saw that I didn't like was that there were several bald guys who reminded me of Lopez. It would only make spotting him harder.

Down at the far end of the beach, I saw a man and a woman sitting on a blanket. There were a small cooler and an oversized handbag beside them. The woman was wearing a one-piece black bathing suit and a straw hat with a huge brim on it. In fact, it was so big that it covered the guy's face. Off in the distance, around fifty yards from them, was the small marina I'd seen before. I noticed that walking between the couple and the marina was one of the colonel's officers. That's when I spoke into my lapel microphone.

"Hey, Max, there's one of the colonel's men approaching the couple to my left."

"I see them. Hey, Calvin, heads up!"

At the other end of the beach, Agent Calvin broke into a full sprint, running in our direction. Rodriquez and Max left the bar in a fast-paced walk. At that point, the guy sitting on the blanket noticed the officer walking toward him. He then jumped up, pulling the woman up by her wrist as well. That's when the officer broke into a full run toward the couple. By now every cop working the detail was running in their direction. During all of the excitement, the woman's hat fell off. Lo and behold, it was that freelancer!

While I was running, Max was yelling in my ear.

"Did you guys see that?"

To my horror, I then made eye contact with Ricardo Lopez! When he saw me, he started running toward the small marina, but holding on to his ribs at the same time. The beating he'd taken had weakened him considerably, but he wasn't about to give up easily. He was dragging the freelance writer right along with him. While focusing on me, he must've forgotten about the officer running right toward him, and when the three of them collided, the strangest damned thing happened.

The ground started shaking, and the tide came rushing in on the beach! I'd never experienced one before, but I knew for sure it was a freaking EARTHQUAKE! We all lost our footing and fell to the sand. The beach turned into a complete panic zone, with families and beach employees running in every direction. Out on the water, boats were being tossed around like toys.

We got back up and the chase was on! By now Lopez had gotten back up also, but he now had a pistol in his hand. The officer tried to get up, but he'd turned his ankle during his fall. Lopez took advantage of that and the fact that we couldn't fire our weapons because of tourists running in every direction.

At the marina, there were two guys in a small fishing boat trying to regain their balance following the earthquake. With the pistol in one hand and the woman in his other, Lopez was running right toward them. When he got within twenty feet, he pointed the pistol at them. The two men wasted no time in diving off the boat into the water, leaving the engine running. Lopez literally threw the woman into the boat and climbed in behind her. Still focusing on us, he didn't realize that she had hit her head on the aluminum bench seat of the boat and passed out.

By now Max and I were running down the pier toward the boat. Lopez then pulled the throttle all the way back, pulling out of the marina at full speed. To make matters worse, he turned around and gave us his famous shit-eating grin! We couldn't shoot at him, because we feared hitting the gas tank, killing the writer as well as him. One of the colonel's female officers, Max, and I watched as Lopez headed out across the waves.

The officer then yelled out.

"He's headed for Ponce!"

She took a small cellphone from her bikini top and called Colonel Cortez. At the time, the colonel already had his hands full with panicked tourists and locals crowding the streets. Resorts were in full evacuation mode. He contacted the General Station House in Ponce. They hadn't been hit as hard as we'd been in Yauco, but they did have pandemonium on their streets. The colonel told the Ponce policía that Lopez was headed their way with a hostage. He was assured that the Ponce policía would fill the streets and line the harbor, waiting for Lopez to arrive.

THIRTY-NINE
THE STREETS OF PONCE

Special Agent Calvin and Rodriquez had joined us on the pier. The colonel's officer was now on the phone. When she got off, she told us that a policía boat was en route to pick us up. During the wait, my own cellphone rang. I was wondering who in the hell it could be. I looked at the screen and saw Maria's name. Damn, Maria, not now! I pressed the talk button and told her I couldn't talk right now.

"Don't blow me off, Sherman! What the hell is going on? I can't even get to my casa!"

"Calm down! It was an earthquake."

"Don't give me that shit, Sherman! There's policía all over the freaking streets! What's going on?"

"Calm down, Maria!"

"Oh my God, he's here! He's here, isn't he?"

"Maria. Get off the streets right now! Go home!"

CLICK.

MARIA'S ON THE RUN

Fifteen minutes later we were in a boat, bouncing across the waves. The town of Ponce was just twenty miles away. Maria had gotten off the phone, hysterical once again.

Holding her son tightly, she tried to make her way home. The streets were congested with people running in all directions. Some of them were running because of the policía presence and some because they'd never experienced an earthquake before. The old folks used to tell tales of an earthquake that occurred back in 1918, years before most of these people were even born. The harder that Maria tried to move, the more she got pushed back. Her *madre* was home alone, and she worried about her. To make matters worse, the policía were now going door to door, and Maria figured they must be searching for Lopez.

At a wooded area along the shore, Lopez drove the small boat right up on land, grounding it. He then grabbed his female passenger by her wrist.

"COME ON, BITCH!"

Her body was limp, and that's when he realized she'd been injured and passed out.

"FINE, I'LL JUST LEAVE YOUR ASS HERE!"

He made his way through the woods and ended up on the edge of town. He saw that the policía and crowds of people had filled the cobblestone streets. On the back porch of a broken-down shack of a house, he spotted a New York Yankees baseball cap lying on a rocking chair. He grabbed it to cover his bald head. He took his time and blended in with the crowds on the streets. After a while he gained confidence as the policía ran right by him. He had to find a place where he could lie low and get some rest.

❖❖❖

As we approached Ponce, shore patrol radioed that they'd found the stolen fishing boat, as well as the hostage. With a head injury and a broken wrist, she'd been taken to the hospital, where a guard was posted outside her door. When we finally reached shore, we paired up and hit the streets in search of Lopez. We had to move quickly, because soon it would be dark, when it would be easier for Lopez to move around.

The only good thing was that the town of Ponce is far smaller than Chicago, so the policía could go door to door. Unknowingly, Lopez had drawn the attention of a policía officer who believed he was a possible looter. He had dropped back twenty yards behind Lopez, who had now become the prey himself. When Lopez stopped and stood in the shadows, so did the officer. It was a game of cat and mouse that the officer was enjoying, far more fun than going door to door on a manhunt. After a while it occurred to him that Lopez's movements were odd. He had more than enough opportunities to steal from earthquake-damaged properties but didn't touch a thing. The officer began to take notice of the people in front of Lopez.

He saw a woman with a little boy who was always in the path that Lopez was taking. Not only that, but the woman seemed to have a different look of fear on her face than other people. They all seemed to be looking forward, but she made frequent stops, and kept looking back. The officer figured out that something was going on between this woman and Lopez. He continued to follow the man in the baseball cap as that man followed the woman and little boy.

As they all moved along, there was suddenly an aftershock from the earlier earthquake. As the officer reached for a lamp post to support himself, the people on the streets became even more panicked. At the same time, he lost track of the mysterious man in the baseball cap. After things calmed down a bit, the officer took off running. He turned the corner of a building, and that's when he felt the hard steel of Lopez's pistol hit him in the side of the head. His vision instantly went dark, and he fell to the ground, passing out cold. Lopez then stood over the officer, looking down at him.

"FREAKING ROOKIE!"

Lopez had taken care of one problem but created another one. His assault on the officer had been witnessed by Maria. He couldn't believe who he was looking at, and he was pissed off. The two of them made eye contact, and he headed her way. She knew that if he got his hands on her, he'd kill her. With the phone still to her ear, she put one arm around her son and took off running. Luckily for her, the people in the street were constantly interrupting Lopez's progress.

Ten minutes away in another part of town, I reluctantly answered my phone.

"Please tell me you're at home, Maria!"

In the background I could hear the screaming voices of the people on the street, and Maria yelling at the top of her lungs.

"Sherman, he's here! He's chasing me!"

"Where the hell are you?"

With that I got the attention of Agent Calvin and Max.

"She's spotted him, and he's chasing her! Where are you, Maria?"

"I can't stay here, Sherman! He's coming right at me! Please hurry!"

I told Maria to go home, and that we were sending a team of officers to her house. We then headed for the area she'd called me from.

❖❖❖

While Lopez was making his way through the crowd, he made one bad move. He came in contact with a speeding motor scooter, and both he and the rider fell to the ground. Considering the condition he was already in following the beating, he got flashbacks like it just happened again. He managed to get up limping, to continue his pursuit of Maria. Suddenly he stopped, realizing that he'd lost sight of her.

❖❖❖

Just about then, we were making our way through the people in a policía car. Both Max and I spotted him at the same time. When Lopez saw us, he froze for a moment, as if he was inviting us to a showdown. We drew our weapons and headed his way. When the people in the street saw our weapons, they scattered, terrified. Lopez then took out his weapon and turned around, returning to where he'd come. By now the area had cleared of all people, and when Max and I turned the corner, Lopez fired a couple of rounds at us, breaking out the window of a nearby business. He then took off running again. That's when we fired back at him, but missed.

We continued firing back and forth as we moved along the street, and around another corner. We thought we had him cornered, but we were in for a big surprise. The son of a bitch came around the corner speeding on a wrecked motor scooter! We were so surprised that he damned near knocked us on our ass. He headed straight into the crowd, leaving behind a trail of screaming people. At some point he must've laid the scooter down, because he suddenly faded into the crowd. We'd lost him again!

Things weren't sitting well with Agent Calvin. Lopez had made fools of us one too many times. Calvin didn't let Colonel Cortez or Captain Leonard in on it, but he had changed the rules of the game. We were no longer looking to apprehend a wanted fugitive. The new mission was to take Lopez out if we got the chance, and there would be no questions asked. I saw a hatred in Agent Calvin's eyes that I hadn't seen before, and for the first time in my career, I witnessed law enforcement plan the assassination of a known criminal. We'd unofficially taken an oath that the conversation never took place. Through radio contact we were informed that there was now a female officer in Maria's house.

It was nighttime by now, and Lopez was holed up in a rundown store that was damaged during the earthquake. The motor scooter he'd been riding was found, and officers were going through that area with a fine-toothed comb. The streets were much less frantic as people tried to restore their damaged homes. There had since been three more aftershocks.

❖❖❖

For his own safety, Lopez had been forced to move from one abandoned building to another. He had moved into his third residence of the night. But he wasn't alone. It seemed every rat in town had chosen that place for shelter. They didn't bother him, and he didn't bother them. In fact, the place reminded him of the old Pullman Police Station.

As the night rolled on, he looked out now and then between broken boards at the streets. He saw his pursuers slowly patrolling the area in their policía cars. Their 1960s style flashing lights rotated on the roofs of their vehicles, and spotlights were pointed at every nook and cranny. For the moment he needed to stay put. He was still suffering from the beating he'd taken at the bar, and the accident he'd had with the scooter wasn't helping. He cleared a space on an old countertop and stretched out on it. It was the first time he'd gotten any real rest since the day he slept on the secluded beach. He slowly closed his eyes and went to sleep.

The four of us were holed up at the local station house. The tension there was so thick you could cut it with a knife. No one was talking, and it was impossible to sleep. We were in constant communication with the officer at Maria's place, as well as officers patrolling the streets. At around four a.m., we couldn't take it anymore. We borrowed vests from the station house and hit the streets of Ponce.

We shined our flashlights in every abandoned or damaged building that we came across. It was painstaking but better than not being in the game. On two separate occasions we ambushed a bald guy, thinking he was Lopez. Cornering these guys with our guns drawn only resulted in scaring them shitless. Unfortunately, being bald right then in that town was a curse. Other officers were doing the same thing. We were pumped up and continued working the streets. Every movement or sound we heard made us jump with our guns drawn. On one occasion I damned near shot a dog.

Dawn was approaching, and it wouldn't be long before sunrise. We decided to make our way toward Maria's house. When we had left the station house earlier, Agent Calvin had stayed behind, and now we needed to check in with him.

❖❖❖

Morning came, and a ray of sunlight passed through a crack in a board and into Lopez's face. He rubbed his eyes and sat up on his makeshift bed. The events of yesterday were all coming back to him. Between two boards, he checked out his latest surroundings. To his amazement and joy, he saw a police officer across the street, walking with a cellphone to his ear. As he watched, it got even better, because the officer was being followed by Lopez's old partner, Maxwell Little, and his favorite whipping post, me! Lopez was so excited that his mind started racing.

WELL NOW, HOW SHOULD I DO THIS? I'M TIRED OF BEING THE FREAKING PREY! THAT PUNK SHERMAN IS STILL IN

LOVE WITH THIS BITCH! I THINK I'LL JUST LET THESE MORONS LEAD ME TO HER CASA!

Lopez left the building through a back door, snaking his way behind us, but keeping a block away. So far the baseball cap had worked for him, but he knew that soon that too would have to change. Not only did he have to worry about us, but he knew that the locals saw him as a stranger. About mid-morning, we started seeing small groups of seven to eight men who appeared to be searching for something. At first we didn't think much of it, but then Rodriquez got a call from Agent Calvin.

"Heads up, we've got a problem! The General Station House has been getting bombarded by citizens that are pissed off and threatening to find Lopez themselves. Apparently some guy on a scooter saw him, and knows him from ripping off women that he knows."

"I hate to tell you, Calvin," Rodriquez said, "but we've already seen some of these search parties. The truth is that these people are entitled to protect themselves."

"Well, I hope you guys find him before *they* do!"

CLICK.

Now the question was, would we take Lopez out, or would we let the people do it? Things could get ugly real fast. All we could do was keep our eyes peeled. We continued our routine, and for the moment things were fairly quiet. Shop owners were making repairs and cleaning up. We were able to catch our breath for a change, but of course, all good things come to an end. Lopez was so caught up in following us that he didn't realize what was going on right in front of him. As he stood behind an old, broken-down truck, he heard a voice yell out in Spanish.

THERE HE IS!

Run For Your Life

Still not aware of what was going on, Lopez hesitated for a moment. When he finally turned toward the sound of the voice, he saw seven to eight men carrying sticks and bats. He knew there was no question they wanted his ass, and he disappeared into a wooded area behind the old truck. The mob then split up. Half of them followed him, and the other half ran down the street, as if they knew where the trail ended. We jumped when we heard the running footsteps of the mob coming up behind us.

They circled around us like we were a parked car. The three of us looked at each other and said what the hell? We followed them. By now they were more than a half block ahead of us, and moving fast. Up at the end of the block, some guy wearing a baseball cap came running into the intersection. It was then that one of the guys in the mob threw his bat at him. When the guy ducked, trying to avoid the bat, his cap fell off, and the bat hit the windshield of an approaching policía car. That's when we drew our weapons, because the baseball cap-wearing runner was none other than Ricardo Lopez.

The officer driving the policía car stopped, got out and fired at Lopez, hitting him in the arm. Lopez returned fire, striking the officer in the upper body. With the officer down, Lopez had a clear path to his squad car, which was still running. He jumped in, put the car in gear and took off.

Rodriquez called Calvin and brought him up to speed. He told him that Lopez, as well as the mob, was headed toward Maria's place. All of this was taking place as we were following the patrol car on foot. I couldn't believe all of our investigating and hard work had been reduced to a freaking mob running down the street trying to do *our* job.

I had to say one thing for these people. When they come together, they come together. I mean every rock, bottle, and stick that could be picked up was thrown at the policía car Lopez was driving. Before he got into the car, I got a good look at his face, and I can honestly say those people put the fear of God in his ass!

❖❖❖

At that point Lopez had no plan. He was stopping and going, repeatedly changing his mind. Whenever the mob got close, he'd speed up again. It was then that my worst fear was realized. Lopez made a left turn onto Maria's street. That's when Rodriquez fired two rounds into the sky to get the attention of the mob. The three of us then took out our badges and held them up in the air. Rodriquez yelled at the crowd to clear the path for us. When they did, we took off running again. We made it around the corner just in time to see the female officer come running out of Maria's house, leaving Maria standing in the doorway. The officer stood in the middle of street, pointing her weapon right at the windshield of the oncoming policía car. Behind her at the end of the block, three patrol cars were approaching with their sirens on.

Lopez had no way out, but he kept on moving. The officer ran up to the squad car with her pistol pointed at his face. That's when he opened his door and knocked her to the ground. He quickly got out, yanked her up off the ground, put his pistol to her head, and slowly backed his way into Maria's house.

I was horrified. That little boy and the old woman were in there, as well as Maria.

The patrol cars all stopped in front of the house, and the officers jumped out with shotguns and pistols drawn. In moments they had the house surrounded. I knew then it was going to be a long ordeal. Max, Rodriquez, and I stood on the opposite side of the patrol cars. We were soon joined by Agent Calvin. Despite all that had happened, he had a pleased look on his face. Maybe it was because we could finally see the light. My only prayer was that we wouldn't end up with a mass murder and suicide on our hands.

The four of us had a little pow-wow. It was time to go back to the book. We needed to set up a command post. Not only that, but before this was over, we might need the support of Tactical Operations. Agent Calvin immediately got on the horn with Colonel Cortez.

FORTY

THE STANDOFF

I'd never trained for any kind of hostage situation, or, for that matter, *any* kind of law enforcement operation. With Lopez being so desperate and unpredictable, I doubt it would have mattered even if I had. The clock was running, and we needed to set up a line of communication. Most of all, we needed to know that everyone inside the house was alive. I took my cellphone out, and Agent Calvin gave me another one of his looks. To my surprise, he said go for it. I took a deep breath and pressed the talk button. On the first ring, Maria's phone was answered.

"What do you want, punk?" Lopez asked. "I'm busy!"

"Give it up, Lopez! There's no way out!"

"What are you doing, reading some negotiation manual? Save your breath. I'm calling the shots from here on out, just like always!"

"This ain't Chicago, Lopez!"

"Shut up, and get me a first-aid kit!"

"Now why would I do that?"

"Fine, have it your way!"

"Wait, let's make a deal!"

"So now I'm a contestant on a freaking game show?"

"Just hear me out! Trade me the little boy for the first-aid kit."

"Forget it, he's too valuable."

"Okay, how about the officer? That way you won't have to worry about her trying something."

"Let me think about that. Nope, I don't think so!"

"Look, Lopez, I know you took a slug. We've got all the time in the world to let you bleed out. It's your call."

Lopez hung up on me. I tried calling him back two times, but he didn't answer. Calvin suggested calling the officer he was holding. Her phone rang twice, and he answered it.

"She's tied up and can't talk right now!"

The next thing we knew, the phone came crashing through the window and landed on the front lawn. I was about to try him again on Maria's phone when the front door slowly opened.

Agent Calvin yelled out.

"HOLD YOUR FIRE! STAND DOWN!"

To our surprise, the little boy came crawling out of the house, and a female officer ran up and grabbed him. I tried Lopez again, and he answered.

"Where's my first aid?"

"It's coming. See how easy that was?"

"Don't play with me, punk!"

"I've got a question for you, Lopez."

"Get my first-aid kit, and then we can talk."

CLICK.

We had one of the officers take the first-aid kit from his trunk. After leaving his weapon on the hood of his squad, he walked up and placed the first-aid kit on the front porch. Moments later, Maria stepped out to retrieve it. For a moment we made eye contact, and I could see tears running down her cheeks. I couldn't help but think that if I hadn't gone into that piano bar years ago and met her, she wouldn't be in this mess.

Inside the house, Lopez had the officer sitting crosslegged on the floor, and handcuffed to a cast iron radiator pipe. With her out of the way, he held Maria at gunpoint and forced her mother to nurse his wound. The old woman was terrified, and was shaking like a leaf as she cleaned his wound and sterilized it with antiseptic. Lopez screamed so loud that we heard him outside. She then ripped an old shirt apart and wrapped the wound. Afterwards he gave the old woman his shit-eating grin.

"Nice work, Grandma. Now sit down!"

With that he gave her a little shove, which pissed Maria off. She was ready to risk her own life and go after him, but Lopez looked her straight in the eye.

"Don't try it, bitch!"

I called Lopez again.

"Yeah, punk, what do you want?"

"You've got your kit. Now answer my question."

"What?"

"Why did you do the D.A.'s driver?"

"That sucker? Wrong place at the wrong time. Any other questions?"

"I'm sure I'll come up with something."

"Don't push your luck!"

In the meantime, Agent Calvin was having a heated phone conversation with Colonel Cortez and the head of Tactical Operations. It seemed the colonel wanted to wait it out for the sake of the hostages. Tactical Operations wanted to storm the house right now and get it over with. Agent Calvin wanted to sneak in on his own and try a surprise attack. I was in favor of that. I pulled Calvin aside.

"How do you feel about a little inside help?"

"That's too risky, Sherman. Besides, how is she going to help us?"

"I don't know. First I've got to get Lopez to let me talk to her. Can I try?"

"What the hell. Go for it!"

I pressed the talk button.

"What do you want this time, punk?"

"Work with us, man. Let the old woman out."

I knew he wouldn't do it, but I wanted to mislead him.

"Look, I'm not going to send everyone out so you guys can rush me. I'm not freaking stupid!"

"At least let me talk to Maria."

"Oh, you miss the little tramp? Isn't that sweet? Sure, but mind your manners!"

In the background I could hear him telling Maria that the phone was for her, and to watch her mouth. The next voice I heard was hers.

"Sherman, I'm sorry!"

"Don't be. It's not your fault. How are you guys doing in there?"

"We're doing all right."

"I'm going to ask you a question. If the answer is yes, don't say anything."

"Okay."

"Do you guys have a gun in the house?"

She didn't answer.

"Good. Don't try anything. Now I have another question."

"Okay."

"Is the back door unlocked?"

Again she didn't answer.

"Good. Try to relax, and don't piss him off. We're trying to get your mom out first."

I heard Lopez telling her that her time was up. He then hung up, and I looked at Calvin.

"Well, they do have a gun in the house, and the back door is unlocked."

"Sherman, I don't think he's going to let her near a gun, but that back door may come in handy."

Just about then, we were interrupted by Max and Rodriquez.

"Have you taken a good look around us lately?" Max asked.

We both turned and looked at opposite ends of the street. To our amazement, the mob had gotten huge and was closing in from each corner of the street. We had to do something soon.

"This is going to sound crazy," Max said. "But why don't we punt?"

His idea did sound crazy.

"Just hear me out," he said. "Why not pull back all of the cops, the patrol cars, and everything? We can push this mob back at least a block in each direction. We'll make Lopez think the safety of this residence is now priority. Just leave the guy alone for a while, and screw with his head at the same time."

Agent Calvin commented on his idea.

"For starters, Max, I don't think the colonel is going to go for that. But you know Lopez better than any of us. How do you think he'll respond?"

"That's a tough question. I don't even know what I'd do in his shoes. I do know it'll definitely change any plans he may have. Why don't you run it by the colonel while I check in with the captain?"

Max called the captain right away, who wasn't in a very good mood at all. In fact, he started talking before Max could get a word in edgewise.

"Captain, this is Maxwell."

"Well now, Detective, you know, a funny thing happened this morning. The chief paid me a surprise visit to have coffee, only he forgot to bring the coffee! Do you know what he did bring?"

Max knew he was about to get his ass ripped.

"No, sir."

"He brought a damned newspaper! On the front page was a picture of two of my officers sitting at a bar having cocktails near the freaking beach! Damn it, Little, you'd better have something awful freaking good for me!"

From where I was standing, I couldn't hear what Max was saying, but his face didn't look good. Something must have gone wrong back home. I saw him end the conversation and take a deep breath. He walked over, but before I could say anything, he let loose.

"What a bitch! Are you ready for this shit? The other day when we had the cocktails at the little hut, we made the front page back home! To make matters worse, the captain had to hear about it from the chief."

"Wait a minute. Let me guess? This is due to my friend the writer."

"I can't think of anyone else."

"I'll be damned. We've got to finish this shit now. If Candee gets hold of this, she'll have her ass over here next!"

FORTY-ONE

THE NEW PLAN

Ten minutes later, Agent Calvin rejoined us. "Okay, guys, here's the deal. Seeing that the colonel is so big on public safety, he's all for it."

"Great. Let's do it," Max said.

"Slow down," Calvin said. "I said the colonel is up for it, but Tactical Operations sees it as a window of opportunity."

"So what do we do now?" Max asked.

"We've got to put our heads together and come up with a plan before they do," the agent replied.

While we were talking, the colonel had already put his men into action. At each end of the street, the mob was being pushed back by a line of officers. It took nearly thirty minutes to push them all back far enough to where they couldn't be seen from Maria's house. Next up were the officers and their patrol cars.

Tactical Operations was only willing to cooperate if they could place their sharpshooters within firing range. We all agreed that might not be a bad idea. With the street now cleared, the four of us moved to where we could see Maria's place but Lopez couldn't see us.

I didn't know about Lopez, but my nerves were on edge. It had been nearly an hour without communication with him, and we were waiting for him to make a move. While waiting, Max ordered a laptop and a video cam. He then contacted Captain Leonard and set up a live video feed to his computer.

We pictured the captain sweating bullets while watching the view of Maria's front door.

As it turned out, Lopez was so focused on what was going on inside the house that he had no idea of what was going on outside the house. Finally we saw him peep out the window and see nothing. He must've gone straight into panic mode, because my phone rang right away. Agent Rodriquez immediately grabbed my hand.

"No, wait, let him sweat a little bit! He'll call back, trust me!"

That's when the four of us did something we hadn't done in days. We all looked at each other and smiled. It was a small victory, but a victory just the same. Just as Rodriquez predicted, Lopez did call me back. This time it was easy not to answer. I was expecting another group cheer, but that's when I noticed that one of our little group was missing. We looked around, but Agent Calvin was nowhere to be seen. I remembered his earlier interest in the back door to Maria's place being unlocked. All I could do was hope he didn't get anyone killed. I had no choice but to tell the others about our conversation.

The third time Lopez called me, I answered, but I decided to give him a taste of his own medicine.

"Yeah, Lopez, what do you want?"

"Don't play with me, punk! What the hell's going on out there?"

"We're tired, Lopez, so we're calling it a day!"

"That's bullshit, and you know it!"

I was taking a risk, but I was also thinking about Agent Calvin, so I hung up on Lopez. I could picture him in the house, throwing a fit just like he did at the Governor's Ball. Only this time he wouldn't have the support of his gangbanging buddies.

Max gave me a strange look.

"I don't know, Sherman. Maybe you shouldn't have done that."

Agent Rodriquez got a big smile on his face.

"I love it! The hell with this punk! Why make it easy for him?"

We tried reaching Calvin through his ear bug, but he didn't answer, and the Tactical Operations guys were getting nervous, so I decided to call Lopez again. He answered but didn't speak.

"Hey, Lopez, how are you doing in there?"

"Maybe I have something for you," he said.

"Now why would I make a deal with a lowlife like you?"

"You'll make the deal because you get off on being the hero, punk. Remember your little girlfriend, the murderer?"

"That should tell you I don't make deals."

CLICK.

Fifteen minutes later, the front door of Maria's house slowly opened, and the sharpshooters took aim. We all held our breaths, and I'm sure that back home the captain was doing the same. When the door was fully open, the colonel's officer was standing there with her hands cuffed behind her back. Lopez shoved her out the door, and she staggered and fell to the ground. When she got up on her knees, she looked around with a surprised look on her face, because she didn't see anyone. She managed to get up on her feet and start walking. That's when she saw us waiting in the shadows. Moments later my phone rang again.

"Okay, punk, are you happy now?"

"That was cute, but I still want the old woman."

CLICK.

At point, I had no problem pushing Lopez to the limit.

❖❖❖

Inside the house, Maria had already made her peace with God, and she was slowly building up courage. She and her mom were communicating through eye signals, and she was trying to get her mom to focus on the broom closet that was right off the living room. As Maria gazed into the kitchen, she remembered that the back door was unlocked. She knew that if she made a run for it, Lopez would surely kill her mom, if not her. What she didn't know was that Agent Calvin was right outside the door, waiting to make his move.

Another ten minutes went by, and Maria finally got the message to her mom that she'd been trying to send with her eyes. With a surprised look on her face, her mom remembered that her beloved, departed husband always kept his shotgun in the broom closet. With that she gave Maria a wink.

❖❖❖

It was then that we were all surprised by Agent Calvin breaking his silence as he whispered in our ears.

"I need a diversion."

We looked at each other and agreed it was time for a bold move. I told the others that I was going in, and Max told me I was nuts.

"Don't worry, Max. I won't make it."

"That's what I'm worried about!"

"Let's have a little faith in Calvin. Besides, I'm wearing a vest."

Max threw his hands in the air, and that's when I called Lopez again.

"What do you want now, punk?"

"I'm coming in, Lopez."

"Great! The more the merrier!"

CLICK.

I'd distracted Lopez enough that he didn't realize that Maria's mom had been inching her way toward the broom closet. He was so happy that I'd soon be joining him that he'd stopped watching the old woman. As I slowly walked up to the house, Max's cellphone rang. It was Captain Leonard.

"What the hell is he doing, Little?"

"We've run out of options, Captain."

"That may be, but when I said that I wanted my badge back, I meant that I wanted him to hand it to me! Damn it, Little!"

Max held his breath as he watched his career flash before his eyes. With my 9mm in my belt, behind my back, I stopped walking just ten feet short of the front door and put my hands in the air. Moments later the front door slowly opened. I saw Maria, but Lopez and her mom weren't in view. I knew Lopez would be standing to the side, trying to stay out of the sights of our sharpshooters. As I slowly started to enter, Agent Calvin must've taken a wrong step. I'd find out later that he kicked over a flowerpot and broke it.

Lopez quickly turned around, and Calvin came rolling in firing rounds. I drew my pistol, and just as I got Lopez in my sights, a loud blast rang out that drowned out the sound of our pistols firing. There stood Maria's mom like a statue with an old-ass shotgun still pointed at Lopez. Half of his face and one side of his head were completely missing, but his body was still trying to function like a chicken with its head cut off. Behind him on the wall was a bloody mess of brains and bone fragments. Finally, his body fell to the floor. IT WAS OVER.

I'd find out later that both Calvin and I had double-tapped him twice in the back, and twice in the front. Maria ran straight into my arms, and her mom remained frozen, holding the shotgun as everyone else came running inside with their weapons drawn. While holding Maria in one arm, I raised my other hand in the air and Max gave me a high-five.

FORTY-TWO

THE LIVE FEED

During all of the excitement, Max had forgotten about the captain. When it dawned on him, he ran outside, cut off the live feed, and called the captain.

"Captain, this is Max. It's all over! He's gone, and this time for good! Believe it or not, Maria's mom blew half of Lopez's head off with an old-ass shotgun!"

"I'd rather he did life, but that's satisfactory. Now wrap it up and get that body back here! This thing is costing a lot of damned money! Tell Mr. Brothers I want my badge back!"

Max came back in the house.

"Well, what did he say?"

"He said to tell you he wants his badge back."

"What? No thank you?"

"If I were you, I wouldn't say that to him!"

Maria and her mom were taken to the General Station House while the investigation was wrapping up. Agent Calvin told me he planned on offering Maria and her mom temporary housing while the damage to her place was being repaired.

"You know, Calvin," I said, "if I know Maria, she's not ever going to set foot in that place again. Seeing Lopez's brains all over the wall is too much for her."

"Well, I'm sure the U.S. Government can compensate her."

For the moment, the house was crawling with law enforcement, and once the coroner arrived, the body could be removed. Then a hazmat team would come out to clean the mess up. Both Calvin and I had to surrender our weapons, as well as the old shotgun. We'd spend the next morning filing our reports, another reason I never wanted to be a cop.

Colonel Cortez cleared the four of us to leave the scene. He requested that we all stay at the resort until we hear from him. When we stepped outside the house, there was a complete Spanish-speaking media circus going on. We were hustled past them by the colonel's men. The scene was crazy. The mob that we had pushed back had returned, and as of right then, they completely surrounded the media.

As we were escorted away in a patrol car, there was no doubt I'd lost all illusions about the place being a paradise. The beaches, the flowers, and the breathtaking scenery meant nothing to me anymore. I could never imagine myself being a tourist here. I couldn't wait to get home. I even missed arguing with Carman!

Our friend the freelance writer had been treated but kept in custody until she could be escorted back to the States by us. It was an attempt on Captain Leonard's part to control what would be released to the media.

Back at the hotel I took a well-deserved shower, and then I enjoyed a well-deserved cocktail. Best of all, I was able to take off that stupid shirt. I put on a tank top and a Bears cap. It kind of made me feel like I was at home. By the time I calmed down and relaxed, it was nearly midnight. I grabbed my cellphone and my cocktail, and headed out to the balcony. I stretched out on a lounge chair and called India. She answered on the second ring. I'd forgotten how soft and sweet her voice sounded.

"Hey, honey, it's all over," I said.

"Thank heavens! Are you all right?"

"I'm fine, honey."

"What about Max? Is he okay?"

"He's good too."

"Are you guys bringing that man back with you?"

"We are, but he's dead."

For a few moments India didn't say anything.

"How do you guys feel about that?"

"We aren't sad, but we aren't disappointed, either."

"Well, just hurry home!"

CLICK.

FORTY-THREE

THE GENERAL STATION HOUSE

Morning came, and we were all up bright and early, eager to get back home. Agent Calvin suggested that we pack and bring our bags along to the General Station House. His hopes were that we'd be able to leave from there and go straight to the airport.

When we arrived, Colonel Cortez had arranged a continental breakfast in the conference room. We were accompanied by all of the officers who took part in the operation. After breakfast, we were all given file folders and pens. Each of us had to give our account of what had taken place the day before, as well as how things had led up to those events. Thirty minutes later we were all done. Colonel Cortez told us we'd receive our hardware back once we cleared airport security in the States.

We had a little time to kill, so we spent it getting to know the other officers a little better. Two of them had only been on the force for a couple of years, and this was the first time they'd been involved in an operation like this. They were especially happy to have worked with officers from a big city with a reputation like Chicago's. I didn't bother to tell them I wasn't the real McCoy.

It would've been nice to say goodbye to Maria, but it would be best left as it was. I only hoped she could forgive me for bringing all of this down on her. In any case, she and her family would end up with a new home to start a new life in.

There was a knock on the conference room door, and another officer stepped in.

"She's here, Colonel."

The colonel thanked the officer.

"Well, gentlemen," he said, "the time has come. Your traveling companion is out in the lobby."

The colonel shook all of our hands and then saluted us.

"Maybe next time we can work stateside," he said. "And yes, Mr. Brothers, not bad work for, how do you say, for a gumshoe!"

Agent Calvin pointed at me, and we all started laughing. I didn't ask how the colonel knew, but through it all he'd been a good sport. When we stepped into the lobby, my friend the writer took one look at me and dropped her head in shame. One side of her face was bruised. Her left arm was in a cast, held by a sling.

For her sake, I was pretty sure she didn't know that her beachside date was a wanted murderer. It was obvious she knew who I was when she first saw me. What she didn't know was the damage she could've done by releasing my photo to the press. With that said, she'd paid a hefty price for sticking her nose where it didn't belong.

At the airport we checked in our bags and waited for the boarding call. Once we were onboard and had our seatbelts fastened, I started to feel relieved. Even though my idea of the island being a paradise had been crushed, I couldn't help but admire the view from the air. Maybe someday my feelings would change, and I'd go back for the proper reason. Right then, though, I just wanted to close my eyes and not open them until I could see the Chicago skyline.

WELCOME HOME

This time we had a direct flight, and for that I was grateful. During the flight I lost all track of time while I slept, and once again, Max elbowed me and pointed out the window. There it was, the Chicago skyline in full view. I looked at him and smiled.

After landing and departing the jet, we found a surprise waiting for us in the terminal. There standing side by side were India and Mai. They worked their way through the crowd and greeted us with hugs and kisses. Yes indeed, we were back home! I looked at India.

"You see, honey. I told you Max wouldn't let anything happen to me!"

That's when India released me and gave Max a big hug and a kiss. Agent Calvin then said, "Come on you lovebirds," and that reminded Mai of something.

"Oh, I almost forgot. I have a message for you, Agent Calvin."

She handed him a small envelope. He opened it and pulled out a notecard. He read it and then gave it to me, so I read it out loud.

THERE'S GOING TO BE A WELCOME HOME PARTY AT THE CITY BLOCK, AND I EXPECT YOU TO BE THERE!

The card was signed by Carman, and we all started laughing.

"That's my girl!" I said.

The ladies followed us downstairs to get our bags. With all the laughing and talking, the ride home didn't take long. When we arrived at the City Block, the parking lot was full, and we had to park across the street. As we stepped out of our cars, we could see Carman standing in the front doorway holding Barney.

"There's your daddy!" she said to Barney.

Barney saw me, barked, and jumped out of her arms. Just as he did, there was a city bus coming along, and I immediately put my hands up flat, yelling at him to stop, but he was too excited. The driver of the bus tried to stop and went into a skid before coming to a rest. He jumped right off the bus, and he and Carman ran to one side of the bus, while the rest of us ran to the other side. On our knees now, we all expected the worst. To our surprise, there was Barney sitting and looking around. As it turned out, there was more than enough clearance between the ground and the bus to miss Barney. Thank God he's a small dog! He ran to me, and I couldn't help but be angry with him. I thanked the driver for his efforts, and then talked to Barney like he was a little kid.

"Don't you ever run out in the street like that again, do you hear me?"

He barked like he understood, and then licked my face. We were all laughing so much as we were crossing the street that we forgot about the party. When we got inside, we were truly surprised, no acting.

FORTY-FOUR

GOOD TIMES

Inside the Block, a banner hung that said "Welcome Home." There were lots of hugs and kisses going around. Carlton, Abigale, Rex, my dad, and to my very delighted surprise, Mr. Cartwright himself was there. Of course he had a girl half his age on each arm.

"Why hell, son," he said, "this ol tinhorn is startin' to like this ol City Street!"

Good old Mr. Cartwright, always the life of the party, even if he didn't know the name of the bar.

The Silver Fox stepped over and gave me a hug.

"Good work, son. I'm proud of you!"

"I love you for saying that, Dad, but I couldn't have done it without the other guys."

I reached into my pocket and took out my badge.

"Hey, Dad, check this out!"

Dad took one look at the badge, and his eyes got big.

"What the hell! You're kidding me, right?"

"It was just temporary."

Those guys had pulled out the stops, and the party was in full swing. There was food, music, and champagne flowing, guaranteeing that a good time was being had by all.

At one point Rex pulled me aside.

"So tell me, buddy, how was it?"

"It was pretty ugly, man."

"That's not what I meant."

"What?"

"The Puerto Rican women, dude! Did they all look like Maria?"

I didn't want to burst his bubble, so I said "even better," and his eyes got real big.

"Man, I knew it!"

I walked away laughing. It was good to be home, and I finally got a chance to get Carman alone. We gave each other a hug that was long overdue. Over her shoulder I saw that Agent Rodriquez and Louie were getting along really well, and I mentioned it. Carman turned around to see what I was looking at, then looked at me.

"What?" I said.

"Man, you're slow."

Then she walked away, with me following her and asking what? The party went on until Angie stopped the music and got everyone's attention. She pointed at the TV mounted on the wall. On the screen was Captain Leonard standing behind a podium, about to hold a press conference. He was accompanied by the mayor and the chief of police. The usual media personalities were there as well, including Miss Candee Harris herself.

"Good evening. I come to you today with a heavy heart and the message of a secure and safe future for the citizens of this city. As you know, it has saddened me to have to take part in the investigation of one of my own. I now stand here with mixed emotions, because yesterday evening, one Ricardo Lopez was fatally wounded while trying to avoid being apprehended."

Before the captain could say another word, there were cheers from the media present, as well as the gang at the bar. He put his hands up to silence the crowd.

"Before I turn the podium over to the chief, I'd like to give a special thanks to Special Agents Calvin and Rodriquez of the FBI. Along with them was one of Chicago's own. Before I say his name, I want to establish the fact that this officer has endured more than I can say during this investigation. Not only did he tolerate my own wrath, but he showed outstanding courage, and carried himself like a true Chicago police officer. I have no doubt that someday he'll be wearing my shoes! Ladies and gentlemen of the media, let's raise our glasses to Detective Maxwell Little!"

At that, the gang at the City Block went wild. Mai was the first to give Max a big hug and a kiss. I looked at him and shook his hand.

"It's about damned time!" I said. "I guess you won't be hanging up that badge after all."

The music came back on, and I stepped out of the way so others could congratulate Max. The press conference had given our party an added boost. It wasn't that things were calming down, but it was now obvious that we'd be partying for hours to come.

Out of the corner of my eye, I saw Angie staring at me. I looked across the room and smiled at her. She smiled back, but this time her smile looked kind of wicked. I couldn't put my finger on it. I wondered what she was thinking, but whatever it was, it was definitely personal. Maybe she was feeling completely free now that Lopez was dead. I personally felt like we were winners, but little did I know that she had a deadly secret she'd take to her grave.

As the party went on, Max and I got another surprise when Captain Leonard himself walked in the door. Mai was the first to greet him.

"Thanks for coming, Captain."

Max looked at the two of them with a surprised look on his face. Mai had arranged it all. When the others realized who the newcomer was, the cheers started all over again. After things calmed down a bit, he made his way over to me.

"Captain Leonard, what a surprise!"

"Good work, son."

"Thank you, Captain."

"Now give me my badge!"

I laughed and reached into my pocket.

"Here you are, Captain."

"Now son, can you get me a GT?"

"What's a GT?"

"You kids! Can you please get me a gin and tonic?"

"Yes sir, coming right up!"

After serving the captain, I took a seat and looked around the room, appreciating what I had. Lopez was dead, Barney was alive, and India was here to stay.

EPILOGUE

So ends the tale of Lt. Ricardo Lopez. The fact that he's out of my life forever does make a difference in my future, but it doesn't mean that another nutcase just like him won't step up to the plate. Maria's mom did a world of good by taking Lopez out. As for my pal Angie Cruz, if you haven't figured it out yet, she'll be spending her days in denial, because she believes that she's satisfied her thirst for revenge. As she displayed her wicked smile, she was pleased for obvious reasons to hear the news about Lopez's death. However, if she's a normal red-blooded human being, she'll be spending plenty of nights staring into darkness, and seeing the faces of the frat brothers. The saddest part of her life is that she fooled us all, yet loves us all.

As for my loving brother Carlton and his best friend Rex, they too will be spending plenty of sleepless nights. I love them both dearly, but what they did was despicable, and I don't care what age they were when they did it!

Now let's talk about my dad, a.k.a. the Silver Fox. What can I say? He proved just how sly he could be when he checked himself into that hospital on behalf of Angie two years ago. Don't get me wrong, he's a stand-up guy, but due to Angie's illness, the skeletons in his closet walked right up and bit him in the ass! Just like the frat brothers, he never saw it coming. Will he take his secret to the grave, or will he shock the world and devastate both Angie and me by revealing the truth? Only the future holds the answer to that question.

As for the rest of the gang at the City Block, there's no doubt in my mind that Carman won't continue being the fireball that she is. As for my man Louie, I still don't get why everyone keeps saying he's gay.

Me myself, I'm well overdue for a major vacation, but at the same time I can't wait to hit the streets again. Working with Detective Maxwell Little was a real blast, but not enough to make me want to be a cop. However, he's touched all of our lives, especially Mai's, and I'm sure he'll be around for years to come. Thanks to India and Barney, I now have my own little family.

A WORD FROM THE AUTHOR:

The novel titled *City Block* was intended to be a onetime thing, but when I began creating the supporting characters around my main character, Sherman Brothers, I knew I was onto something good. It was then that I decided to create a series featuring Sherman Brothers. The character Lt. Ricardo Lopez as well as Sherman's first love, Maria, moved me to write the novel titled *Dark Cells*. I put myself in the place of my readers and found that two major questions would arise at the conclusion of reading the *City Block* novel.

For starters, Lt. Lopez had disgraced the law enforcement community, as well as ruining the state's case against Angie Cruz, and for that reason alone, I knew that readers wanted to know what he'd do following the Lipstick Murders trial. Bringing Maria back into the picture was easy. Readers loved the spicy relationship that she and Sherman had. I took advantage of these two facts by bringing her and Lopez together again. I made this decision at the very beginning of the novel titled *Dark Cells*. Despite India being Sherman's current love interest, I believed that readers wanted to hear from Maria again. Along with that, Lopez needed somewhere to run to, and the fact that he's Hispanic made going to Puerto Rico a slam dunk. Maria would be there, and my three characters would be reunited once again.

The good news is that I've now created a series featuring Private Investigator Sherman Brothers. If you enjoyed reading the *City Block* and *Dark Cells*, rest assured, because more novels in this series are in the works.

About the Publisher

LIFE TO LEGACY, LLC

Let us bring your story to life! Life to Legacy offers the following publishing services: manuscript development, editing, transcription services, ghost writing, cover design, copyright services, ISBN assignment, worldwide distribution, and eBooks.

Throughout the entire production process, you maintain control over your project. Even if you have no manuscript, we can ghost-write your story for you from audio recordings or legible handwritten documents. Whether print-on-demand or trade publishing, we have publishing packages to meet your needs. We make the production and publishing processes easy.

We also specialize in family history books, so you can leave a written legacy for your children, grandchildren, and others. You put your story in our hands, and we'll bring it to literary life!

Please visit our website:
www.Life2Legacy.com

Or call us at:
877-267-7477

You can also email us at:
Life2Legacybooks@att.net